"Will you not tell me your guardian's name?"

Lord Dake spoke gravely as he looked down into Melody's distressed face.

"I'm sorry," she said stoically. "I know you mean well. If you take me back to London, I suppose I must go, but I will not help you by telling you my guardian's name."

Lord Dake stared down at her in silence. For the first time a new thought occurred to him. What if Melody, despite her youth and inexperience, knew better than he how oppressive the life her guardian wished to arrange for her would be?

He glanced at Melody who was regarding him intently. He began to shake his head in mock despair.

"I fear I shall regret what I am about say," Lord Dake finally began. "But I know when I am defeated. Tell me where you want to go in Yorkshire, child, and I shall take you there."

Melody cried out in delight, only to sober a few seconds later.

"Are you certain, my lord?" she enquired cautiously.

"Yes, I am," he assured her with a smile. "That is the worst of it; I'm afraid I'm very certain."

THE SUITABLE SUITOR

ALICIA FARRADAY

Harlequin Books

TORONTO • NEW YORK • LONDON
AMSTERDAM • PARIS • SYDNEY • HAMBURG
STOCKHOLM • ATHENS • TOKYO • MILAN
MADRID • WARSAW • BUDAPEST • AUCKLAND

To Susan who would have laughed

Published March 1992

ISBN 0-373-31169-9

THE SUITABLE SUITOR

CHAPTER ONE

"THERE'S A GENTLEMAN to see you, sir. He is waiting in the library."

The ninth Baron of Dake paused in the act of divesting himself of his greatcoat and looked down at his butler with one eyebrow raised enquiringly. Conscious of having given offence, Jennings failed to meet his master's eyes.

"And why has this gentleman not been advised that since it is well past two o'clock of the morning he had better go away and call again at a more reasonable hour?" Lord Dake asked with deceptive mildness.

Jennings knew himself to be on shaky ground. Lord Dake was not a harsh master—far from it—but he did not suffer fools gladly, and he expected his orders to be obeyed. Jennings was more than capable of dealing with unwelcome and untimely visitors. But the present situation was different: it concerned Family. He tried to convey both his sympathy with Lord Dake's disgust at finding an unwelcome visitor ensconced in his library at this hour and his own dilemma in considering what was due to familial obligation. He gave a discreet cough and carefully addressed the air some inches above Lord Dake's lofty form.

"It is Mr. Steele who wishes to see you, my lord. I told him you were engaged for the evening, but he insisted upon awaiting your return."

"Mr. Steele!" Dake had shrugged himself out of his coat and tossed it carelessly to a waiting lackey, who smoothed its sumptuous folds reverently before bearing it away. "What does he want with me?"

"He did not say, sir. But as he is your cousin..."

"I know he's my cousin, man," Lord Dake said, cutting off his butler's excuses impatiently. "I suppose his mother's sent him here on some damned errand. I don't know why that woman thinks that it is my business to rescue every member of my family from whatever domestic crisis he or she may be undergoing."

Jennings declined to speculate, merely indicating, by the sudden extreme stiffness of his expression, what he thought of a master's discussing his family with his servant. A glint of amusement lit the baron's fine grey eyes. Jennings's notions of propriety, and his inability to express them without himself transgressing the rules of conduct he considered proper between servant and master, were a continual source of amusement to Lord Dake. His annoyance disappeared, and he found himself in a far better mood to deal with whatever Elliot, or more probably Elliot's mama, wanted from him. Pausing only long enough to be sure that Jennings had caused refreshments to be served to his caller, the baron went to join him in the library.

The room was an opulent one, but comfortable, too, with an obvious air of being much used. The collection of books, a collection to which the present Lord Dake had contributed perhaps more than his share, filled the tall oak shelves which lined all four walls. The sofa and chairs, and the heavy velvet curtains which Jennings had prudently drawn against the night, were of a deep crimson hue, and the occasional tables and the desk were made of oak which a succession of parlour-maids over the years had polished to a rich patina. In the centre of the far wall was a huge fireplace in which a fire burned brightly, providing the only illumination in the room. Dake's cousin Elliot was sitting appreciatively before the fire, his legs stretched towards its warmth. The side-table by his chair held a silver salver; the crystal decanter and glasses upon it shined luxuriously in the firelight. He was staring into the fire, apparently deep in thought, and gave a small, startled jump when his cousin hailed him.

"Bredon, thank God you're back at last. Where have you been?" he cried.

Lord Dake have him a quelling look. "Hardly your concern, Elliot," he pointed out. "Surely I may go out if I wish. And, I had thought I might come home without finding my relatives camped in my library demanding my attention!"

"No, that's not fair, Bredon," Mr. Steele said plaintively. "It ain't as if the whole brood were here!"

"I should hope not," his stern cousin replied. "I should not have entered if they had been. I'd have heeded Jennings's warning and slipped off to the country till the coast was clear."

Mr. Steele laughed, apparently reassured by this threat. "Lord, yes. And no one would blame you. But it's only me, Bredon," he added ungrammatically. "And I pray you won't slip off, for I need your advice."

Lord Dake went to join his cousin, moving his own chair back slightly from the fire's heat. "I wonder you haven't burned up while you've been waiting," he said. "Apparently the servants were under the misapprehension that I wished to roast a whole ox in this fireplace tonight."

"It feels good," Mr. Steele said wistfully. "I can never get a decent fire at home. You'd think the fuel was paid for out of the servants' pockets, judging from the miserly little fires they build."

"Perhaps if you told them what you wanted they would oblige you," his cousin pointed out unsympathetically.

"Oh, no one ever listens to what I want. And Mama would just tell me I was wasting money if they did; she's always complaining about the tradesmen's bills."

"Forgive me; I was under the impression we were speaking of your household, Elliot, and not my Aunt Clarice's."

Mr. Steele knew he was being deliberately provoked, but as usual he declined to enter the lists against his older relation. "No, no," he said instead, "you know what Mama is like, Bredon. She'll have the running of the place, and I'm sure she does a better job than I could. I've no head for things like that. If the servants started coming to me with questions I'd have no notion what to say to them."

"If you employed competent servants they wouldn't have to bother you with questions about the running of the household," the baron pointed out.

"But you know how that would be, Bredon. If my servants ran my home as efficiently as yours do, Mama would be at loggerheads with them. She likes to feel responsible for our comfort, you know."

Since Lord Dake knew that what Mr. Steele could not bring himself to say was that his mother was a domestic tyrant who bullied incompetent servants and drove competent ones away in disgust, he forbore to pursue the question further, simply recommending that his cousin tell him the purpose of his visit. Thus reminded, Mr. Steele resumed his harried expression.

"Lord, yes, Bredon. I can't think why we are nattering on about my domestic arrangements. It don't signify about the house; I'm never there anyway. I spend all my time in Town. I know you don't like us all running to you whenever anything goes wrong, Bredon, but I'm in a quandary now and I don't know what else to do."

Since of all his troublesome relatives, Elliot was by far the least troublesome and the only one for whom he felt any real

iking, Lord Dake relented and gave his companion a warm
mile.

"Don't be a looby, cousin. Just tell me what it is you
need."

Mr. Steele smiled gratefully in return. "It's this dratted
girl, Bredon. Or young lady, I suppose, though what a
young lady should be doing in my stables, brother or no
brother, is beyond me."

His lordship, perceiving that the matter was bound to be
somewhat complicated, replenished his cousin's glass and
poured himself a drink. "The whole matter is beyond me,
Elliot, and believe me, if you think that you have explained
anything so far, you are sadly mistaken. What dratted girl,
and why is she in your stables?"

"That's the point precisely, Bredon. I don't know. Harkness found her. You remember Harkness, don't you? My
head groom?"

"Thank you, I remember Harkness perfectly well. What
I am still confused about is the identity of this girl."

"But I don't know her identity. That's what I'm trying to
tell you. Harkness found her in the stables along with a boy
he claims is her brother. He was about to throw them out,
but she asked to speak to the master. Harkness was apparently impressed by her manner, and he sent one of the boys
for me. Well, the long and the short of it is that she claims
she and her brother are travelling together and have been
robbed of all their funds. She wanted my permission to sleep
in the stables for the night before they continued on their
way in the morning."

"And why do you feel it is necessary to consult me before you give leave to two vagabonds to spend the night in
our stables or throw them out as the mood takes you?"
Lord Dake asked impatiently.

"It's difficult to explain, Bredon, but something is wrong about them. The girl's no vagabond. She's Quality, I'm quite sure of that. But the boy don't seem to match. And I think she's in some sort of trouble. If she *is* a gently bred female I can't just give her leave to sleep in my stables and dismiss her without a second thought. But she won't tell me anything more. So I thought of you. I was sure you'd be able to advise me what to do."

"Without having seen this girl or her supposed brother, I don't know what you expect me to say."

"Exactly!" Mr. Steele cried winningly. "Which is why I want you to come see them, Bredon. You'll be able to make her tell you what is really going on, I'm sure of that."

"Your confidence is touching, Elliot," Dake replied, "but I fail to see why you think this girl, whoever she is, will tell me more than she has told you."

"Because you'll look at her over your nose with that devilish glint in your eyes, and she'll find herself babbling out everything to you just the way I used to do when I was younger and in a scrape. I never could keep anything from you when you got up on your ropes, Bredon, no matter how badly I wanted to. And I did want to—you can give a person a blistering set-down, you know."

Lord Dake laughed at the plaintive note in his cousin's voice. "Poor Elliot," he teased. "May I pay you the compliment of saying that you were the only one of my relatives who ever paid the least attention to any of my setdowns, and the only one to actually listen to any of my advice?"

"Not much of a compliment, Bredon," Mr. Steele protested laughingly. "Mama never listens to anything anyone says, and as for Aunt Adelia, she's been deaf as a post these past ten years. That leaves only my sisters and our cousin

Rawleigh, and they were too much in awe of you to come up against your tongue.''

"Too much in awe of my fortune, you mean," Dake corrected him drily, "and too conscious of how they must never antagonize their rich cousin."

Mr. Steele squirmed uncomfortably in his seat. "Now, it isn't as bad as that, Bredon," he protested placatingly. "It's very natural that Mama and Aunt Adelia should look to you for assistance, with both of them losing their husbands. It ain't easy for a widow to raise a family or for a woman to understand financial matters."

"Both of my aunts are quite comfortably situated as you know, Elliot," Dake said quietly. "I would never have seen your family or Aunt Adelia's in need, and indeed I am sure it seems quite natural to them to apply to me with whatever desires take their fancy, since, as your mama says, I have entirely more money than is good for me. I have never begrudged them a groat. But why they must turn to me in every minor crisis is beyond me. I was not left their guardian nor the guardian of their children, you know."

"No, no, of course not, Bredon," Mr. Steele said soothingly. "No question of that. I know you were only a boy when your parents died and not yet seventeen yourself when my father died. And as for Uncle Leigh, we were both still in short pants when he went to his reward—no question of your being appointed guardian to Rawleigh then or since."

"A circumstance for which I am appropriately grateful. You are bad enough, Elliot, but our cousin Rawleigh is more than any man should have to endure. I don't remember Uncle Leigh very well myself, but whenever Aunt Adelia starts in about his 'going to his reward,' I cannot help but reflect that escaping from her and from our sapskull cousin Rawleigh must have been reward enough for him," Lord Dake said with a gleam of humour in his eye.

"No, no," Elliot protested. "A very worthy man from what my mother has always said, and I'm sure that was not his only reward. That is, Aunt Adelia is very trying, I know, but she's a good woman. I'm sure Uncle Leigh was sorry to be parted from her."

"More sorry than she was to see him die, apparently," murmured the irrepressible baron.

"Now, Bredon, don't try to pull caps with me," his cousin pleaded. "All I mean is that even though you were far too young when my father and Uncle Leigh died to be a guardian for anyone, it is natural that my mother and Aunt Adelia should turn to you. Even I do it, Bredon, though I suppose I shouldn't. For all that you're only five years older than I, you've always been so level-headed you seem older than your years. And you are the head of the family, after all."

Lord Dake relented and smiled again. "Yes, I am sure you are right, Elliot, though why both of my aunts continue to solicit advice which we all know they will ignore has always been a puzzle to me. However, we were not speaking of them or of their problems. We were considering your present problem."

"Yes, and I know how tiresome it is for you that I should be plaguing you in this way, Bredon, and I promise you I would not if I only knew what to do instead."

"Yes," Lord Dake retorted. "Now you've made me feel a bully, and no doubt think that that will prod me to grant your request with no further protest. So you wish me to come along and speak to this girl and her brother myself?"

"Yes, please, Bredon. I would be very grateful."

"No doubt," his cousin replied dryly. "I, on the other hand, would be greatly inconvenienced. And I still do not see the necessity for my involvement. Surely you can determine for yourself whether this is a gently bred girl in distress or the shameless hoyden I suspect her to be.''

"But I can't, Bredon, I promise you. She sounds well-bred to me, but even I can tell there's something rum goin' on. And as for the brother, I don't know what to think. He don't seem to be in the girl's class, but it's hard to say. You know I'm no good with people. If only she were a horse. No one is a better judge of horseflesh than I, Bredon; even you will grant me that. But it's not so easy with people. I wish it were. I wish one could just look at the mouth and check the withers and judge people's quality that way."

"I wonder what Miss Otterleigh would think if she knew you were judging another young lady's withers," the baron said mischievously.

At this reminder of his fiancée, Mr. Steele blushed rosily. A faintly haunted look came into his eyes. The baron, who knew that his cousin had been bullied into the match with the very correct and very overbearing Miss Amelia Otterleigh by his mama, felt a pang of guilt.

"Very well, Elliot," he said. "If it will make you happy, I shall come and take a look at this enterprising pair."

Mr. Steele shot him a look of pure gratitude. "I knew I could rely on you, Bredon," he said, shaking his cousin's hand.

"Mind you, I think it will do little good. It sounds to me as if this girl is a shameless romp, and this boy no more her brother than I am. No doubt they're a mismatched pair of runaway lovers if what you tell me about his manner is true."

"Well, you may be right, Bredon," Mr. Steele admitted, "but he may be her brother, too. You can't tell anything by how the fellow talks. Look at me. My sisters always know just what to say, but let anyone ask me a question about anything except horses and before I know it I'm stammering and babbling like an idiot. No one who heard me would ever dream I was Allison's or Lucinda's brother. More likely to think I was their stable-boy.''

"You're not half as foolish as you pretend to be, Elliot," Dake replied. "Your problem is that your sisters take after their mother, and between their sharp tongues you're never allowed to get a word in edgewise. And if, by chance, you do manage to say anything, none of them pays the least attention. Which is a shame, since I have always thought since your father died, that you are the only one in the family with any sense."

"No, no, you're wrong, Bredon, I promise you," Mr. Steele protested loyally. "Lucinda and Allison are sharp as tacks, and Mama don't lack understanding. I daresay you think I make sense, but that's because I'm more at ease with you than with most people."

"Quite surprising, too, when you consider how frightened you've always been of my blistering set-downs," his cousin teased. "But never mind; I know it is not the slightest use to expect you to say anything critical of your mama or your sisters. Nor of anyone else, for that matter. You are too kind-hearted, Elliot, and you let people take advantage of you. All I am saying is don't let this precious pair of vagabonds do the same."

"They could not take advantage of me if you were there," Mr. Steele pointed out slyly.

His cousin gave a shout of laughter. "Yes, I shall look them over for you and I shall even give you some of my precious advice. But not until I've had some sleep! Go home, Elliot, and wait for me to call at a more decent hour."

"Thank you, Bredon. I knew I could rely on you. But are you sure you will not come tonight and get it over with? They will no doubt want to be leaving early in the morning, you know."

"No," Dake said firmly. "I will not come tonight. Surely you can manage till morning."

With this Mr. Steele had to be satisfied, and after clutching his cousin's hand once more and wringing it gratefully, he took his leave.

CHAPTER TWO

MELODY MAITLAND sat composedly in an empty stall in Mr. Steele's stables, considering her situation. The morning sun poured in through the unshuttered windows, setting alight the golden straw and the rich blue horse blanket on which she sat, and warming the burnished copper coat of the dark-eyed chestnut gelding who surveyed her calmly over the top of the adjoining stall. She could hear Tom crooning to one of the horses several stalls away. Melody stretched and began brushing stray bits of straw from her gown. On the whole, she thought, things were going well: she was having an Adventure, and a rather splendid one at that.

When Melody and Tom had found themselves stranded with no money and nowhere to sleep the night before, it was Tom, a stable-boy all his life, who had discovered Mr. Steele's stables and proposed they take shelter there. As the stables were roomy and airy, scrupulously clean and set just off a pleasant mews, Melody thought it an excellent solution. True, there had been that brief but unpleasant encounter with the fiery head groom when he'd discovered them and threatened to evict them from the premises, and then the much more pleasant encounter with Mr. Steele, who rented the stables along with his rooms. Mr. Steele had proved less inclined than the groom to throw the vagabonds out. He was, however, much more curious as to how they came to be there. Melody frowned a little as she recalled that she had been less than truthful with Mr. Steele. Honest by nature, she regretted the necessity of deceiving him. But she was shrewd enough to suspect that the truth could only serve to make a complicated situation even more so. And she consoled herself with the knowledge that although she had dissembled in claiming that she and Tom were brother and sister, her story in other respects was at least a version, if a rather partial version, of the truth. She had merely left out a great deal of the confusing detail.

Tom's voice interrupted her reflections. "Lord, Miss Melody, this Mr. Steele must be rich as a nabob. I've never seen such prime bits of blood as he has in his stables."

Melody agreed cordially that the horses were quite lovely, an expression which Tom obviously found inadequate to describe such cattle. She was about to discuss the next stage in their journey with him, but one of a pair of matched greys across from them tossed his head and neighed impatiently, and Tom went to feed him a handful of oats from the bin. Watching his rapt absorption with the horse, Melody sighed and tried not to envy Tom his apparent unconcern over what the future might hold. Tom was a kind companion and a biddable one, but he was in many ways unsatisfactory as a fellow adventurer. For one thing, he left all the planning to her. For another, he seemed to know far less than she had imagined a young man would know about the practical aspects of getting on in the world. But, she reminded herself firmly, that was unfair. Tom had not asked to go on an adventure with her, and it was only fitting that she should assume the greater responsibility in planning a journey which had been all of her own seeking. And besides, though Tom might not show as much initiative as Melody would have liked, it was undisputably true that without him she would never have made her escape from Mrs. Beehan's Academy for Young Ladies.

It was difficult for Melody to believe that she had left Mrs. Beehan's just one day earlier. That single day had been far more eventful than her entire stay at the Academy. Here she was, thrust in the midst of an adventure more interesting than any she had imagined in day-dreams with which she'd whiled away the tedious hours at Mrs. Beehan's. True, making her escape had been almost disappointingly easy; she had simply slipped out the unattended front door on Sunday afternoon during those hours which were set aside for the girls to pursue solitary meditations in their rooms. But events after that quiet beginning had more than made up for its tameness. And Melody was almost giddy with excitement now at the prospect of freedom which that prosaic leave-taking had placed before her. And to think that it would never have happened if Mr. Stanhope had not decided she was old enough to come out of the schoolroom and make a match soon, and if Tom Baxter had not appeared in Green Park that day.

Mr. Stanhope was Melody's guardian, appointed nine years ago when Melody's parents had died in a coaching accident. Melody had been eight years old at the time, and an heiress. Her half-sister, Lily, who was then twelve, had gone to live with her Aunt Augusta, the oldest sister of Lily's long-dead father, who had been Melody's mother's first husband. But Melody was left under the care of her father's friend, Mr. Stanhope. At first she had lived in Mr. Stanhope's house, with a nanny and a new governess and other servants who were almost her sole companions. When she was older she was sent to board-school. She supposed she had been happy enough there. The other girls were quite nice and the mistresses kind. And Melody actually had rather a flair for learning. She especially enjoyed learning languages, and had surprised the French mistress with the ease with which she had mastered that language. She knew

Italian, too, and would have liked to learn German, but Mrs. Beehan's Academy for Young Ladies did not offer lessons in German, which Mrs. Beehan considered to be an unattractive and vulgar tongue. Since Melody quickly acquired all the learning that Mrs. Beehan's Academy considered suitable for young gentlewomen, she found herself more and more bored as time went on, and chafed under the endless lessons in comportment and etiquette. And yet, Melody would no doubt have gone on there dutifully until Mr. Stanhope decided she was ready to make her debut into Society, had it not been for certain events which took place during the Christmas holidays last year.

Melody did not enjoy the holidays, during which she left Mrs. Beehan's for her guardian's house and spent far more time than usual with him. Mr. Stanhope was a pompous man, rather inclined, Melody thought, to take his position as her late father's most trusted advisor and guardian of his heiress rather too seriously. Melody did not in general find fault with people, but she found Mr. Stanhope's complete absence of humour very difficult to endure. His attempts at wise counsel seemed prosy and old-fashioned to her, and though she tried to be a dutiful ward, she was in general much happier at Mrs. Beehan's establishment than during the periods she spent with Mr. Stanhope.

But last Christmas the situation had become far worse than usual. Mr. Stanhope had invited several friends to dine with them every evening, something he had never done before. At first Melody enjoyed the novelty of such "grown-up" diversions; only gradually did she realize that unattached gentlemen predominated among their guests. And then came the evening when Mr. Stanhope scolded her after their visitors had left for neglecting the elderly, deaf nobleman he had seated next to her at dinner. She had, her guardian told her, reached the age where he must set about finding her a suitable husband. The dinner parties were his attempt to introduce her to some gentlemen he believed might make her a good match, and he let her know that she was expected to make the effort to get to know them.

It was not that Melody was opposed to making a good match; she had always assumed that she would be married one day. But until last Christmas she had been able to sustain the romantic if somewhat vague notion that the "suitable husband" would be someone of her own choosing, someone she loved, or at least someone she felt she could grow to love.

This romantic notion had collided with the reality of the men Mr. Stanhope had invited to dine with them, and Melody had soon realized that her notion of a suitable husband did not in any way match her guardian's. But Melody had little doubt that when it came time to make a decision, it would be Mr. Stanhope who would prevail. She was just a green girl, as Mr. Stanhope had sternly pointed out, and an heiress to boot. She could not have the slightest notion of what qualifications were necessary in a good husband.

Melody had returned to Mrs. Beehan's after the holidays with the knowledge that after the winter term, Mr. Stanhope would have her removed from board-school in order that she might come out for her first Season. Coming out had long been a dream of hers. She had looked forward to the almost painful excitement of the Court Presentation; the possibility (or even probability, for Melody's connections were excellent and Mr. Stanhope's own sister had once been a bosom bow of Lady Sefton) of obtaining a voucher for Almack's; the balls, routs, assemblies, evenings at Vauxhall or Drury Lane. All these promised glories had formed the subject of many conversations among the girls at Mrs. Beehan's Academy, and naturally Melody had anticipated with great pleasure the prospect of taking her place among the *haut ton*.

But Mr. Stanhope's plans, as he outlined them for her, did not include such giddy pleasures. A Court Presentation, yes; that was essential. And even, perhaps, a few sedate Wednesday evenings at Almack's, if he could persuade his sister to leave her large and vigorous family in the Cotswolds to serve as chaperon. But Mr. Stanhope did not approve of heiresses going to balls and routs and other places where, he was convinced, they were bound to be exposed to the worst sort of coxcombs, fops, fribbles, bucks and rakeshames. No, Mr. Stanhope would select a handful of suitable suitors from whom, he told her sternly, Melody would be expected to make her choice by the end of her first Season, for he did not intend to be put to the bother of a second. Melody was optimistic by nature, but she found this prospect unappealing.

Still, she might not have run away from Mrs. Beehan's and, indirectly, from Mr. Stanhope, if Tom had not come back into her life. Tom's father, Alf Baxter, had been a worker on her father's estate, and Tom himself a stable-boy. He was a kind boy, somewhat younger than Lily, and Melody and her half-sister used to steal away to the stables and play with Tom and the horses and the stable cats and their kittens. When her father's estate had been broken up, Alf Baxter and Tom had gone into service with Lily's Aunt Augusta in Yorkshire.

When Tom decided to leave Yorkshire nine years later and travel to London, he had resolved to pay a visit to Melody, the only person in the metropolis with whom he was acquainted. Melody and Lily had exchanged letters over the years, which meant that Melody's address in London was known to the footman who delivered the mail and, therefore, to everyone in Augusta Napier's household. Tom had

been too shy to seek Melody out directly at Mrs. Beehan's
very superior academy, but he had been clever enough to
wait for her next outing and to approach her in the park.
Melody had been delighted to see her childhood companion and had arranged another, private meeting later that
evening. When Melody learned that Tom had rebelled
against his abusive father and struck out on his own, she was
inspired by his bravery and initiative. And very soon she had
decided that it would be wonderful if she were to do the
same.

Tom, of course, did not share her enthusiasm for such a
plan, but Melody found her childhood friend was now curiously susceptible to her wishes. She still thought of him as
the boy who had been kind to her and her sister, and though
he was now a young man of some twenty years, the idea that
he had straight away fallen in love with her had never occurred to her. She treated him as a friend, warmly and af-
fectionately, and never suspected that his feelings might run
deeper. But despite his infatuation, Tom did not entirely lose
sight of reason. He would not consent to Melody's first
plan, that she should set off with him to become an adventurer and roam the world. But the compromise they eventually reached, that Tom would escort her back to Yorkshire
where she could put her case before Aunt Augusta, was acceptable to both of them. Melody was sure that Aunt Augusta would permit her to join her household without
forcing her into marriage with some elderly and thoroughly
boring gentleman, and Tom was secretly pleased that duty
had made a necessity of his almost unadmitted desire to return to the security of Yorkshire. London had proved far
more awesome than he had imagined.

In fact, Melody had to admit to herself, neither she nor
Tom was quite up to snuff when it came to making their way
in Town. Scarcely had they left Mrs. Beehan's than they had

encountered their first difficulty. Neither of them knew how to book passage on a coach, nor where the nearest coaching inn was to be found, nor whether passage to Yorkshire was to be had on a Sunday evening. Nor did they have any idea where would be the best place to bespeak two rooms for the night. Melody knew of several respectable hotels where a young lady might safely spend the night, but precisely because they were so respectable, they did not seem suitable in the present situation. Alone, with no baggage and no proper chaperon, Melody realized she did not seem precisely the sort of client to which Stanton's catered, nor did the shabbily dressed Tom fulfil that role any better. They were deep in discussion, attempting to decide upon a course of action, when a kind-looking gentleman approached and introduced himself.

He had, he said, overheard their conversation and he had a solution to recommend. He would be happy to take care of the matter of booking passage for them. But apparently he had not been the fine gentleman he seemed, for after Tom had entrusted him with their little store of funds, he had disappeared, failing to keep his promised rendezvous with them. Tom had been bitter with self-blame after the incident, but Melody had remained philosophical. After all, one could either choose to trust people or distrust them. If one trusted everyone who seemed trustworthy, one might meet with the occasional disappointment. But to distrust everyone seemed a far more unpleasant alternative, and was foreign to Melody's nature. Nor was she one to waste much time in regret over past errors. She was far too preoccupied with deciding what to do next. Perhaps they might set off for Yorkshire on foot and rely upon being taken up for some distance in passing carts. Tom had apparently travelled from Yorkshire to London that way, and Melody saw no reason why they should not reverse the process. Or perhaps Mr.

Steele might have some other ideas which might prove useful. Melody had found him a very pleasant-seeming man during the short discussion they had had. He had allowed them to sleep in the stables despite the protests of his groom, and had promised to consult his cousin, who was a peer of the realm and a man of superior intelligence and considerable experience, for advice concerning their plight. Melody was not sure that she approved of this last notion. Something about the troubled look on Mr. Steele's face as he'd spoken of his cousin had made her apprehensive about that gentleman. But, she reflected, though he might not help them, Mr. Steele's cousin could hardly hinder them in their journey. If they did not like what he had to say, they could simply thank him and be on their way.

Melody was therefore able to bear quite cheerfully the news, brought by the surly groom, that Mr. Steele wished them to join him in the mews to await the imminent arrival of Lord Dake. As the groom had also brought them a simple breakfast of bread and cider to eat before joining Mr. Steele, even Tom was able to overcome his reluctance towards their momentary encounter with a peer of the realm. He was almost cheerful as he ate, though Melody noticed that he grew much more quiet as they went to join Mr. Steele. She found herself wondering what Mr. Steele's noble cousin was like. She had not long to wait to find out, for she and Tom had scarcely exchanged more than a few sentences with Mr. Steele when they were joined by a tall, broad-shouldered man in an elegant riding cloak. He did not speak as he joined them, but any doubt as to his identity was dispelled by his cousin, who grabbed his hand and pumped it heartily.

"Bredon! Thank God you're here at last!" he cried.

Lord Dake raised a quelling brow. "I apologize if I have inconvenienced you by taking a few hours of sleep, Elliot," he murmured with deceptive sweetness. His cousin was suitably abashed, but Melody found her own hackles rising. She could not help but compare Mr. Steele and his noble cousin, and in her opinion Lord Dake did not benefit from the comparison. True, Lord Dake was a much more imposing figure, taller by some five or six inches than his younger cousin, trimly built but powerful, his broad shoulders emphasized by the cape he wore. Even without the cape Lord Dake's figure would have made Mr. Steele appear awkward, loose-limbed, and almost gaunt. He was darker than his cousin; his complexion was brown where Mr. Steele's face was fair and prone to blushes. Lord Dake's dark and crisply curling hair contrasted with his cousin's rather wispy, straight blond locks. And where Mr. Steele had a pleasant, slightly foolish expression, with mild blue eyes and a rather high-pitched, diffident speaking voice, Lord Dake's handsome face was alive with intelligence, his voice firm and deep in tone. His best features, though, were his well-formed, generous mouth and his expressive grey eyes. There was no doubt, Melody admitted a little grudgingly, that Lord Dake was by far the more handsome of the two men. But she did not like the irony in his words, nor the coolly analytical light in his eyes as he gave her a quick, appraising glance.

For his part, Lord Dake had little fault to find with Melody's appearance. He noticed her eyes first; she had the most lovely pair of brown eyes which it had ever been his pleasure to see. Very soon he noticed that the owner of these eyes was a young lady, scarcely more than a schoolgirl, with an elegant, slender figure, soft, dusky curls, and a lovely, serene face rescued from too much gravity by the mischievous tilt of her mouth. Even the decidedly disapproving gaze she'd fixed upon him could not obscure the sweetness of her expression. She was wearing a neat suit of deep maroon

merino, cinched in tightly at her little waist with a black kid
belt, and trimmed in the currently fashionable military style
with black piping upon the bodice and up the sleeves. Her
elegant little boots were also of soft black kid, as were the
gloves she held in one hand. Her skirts were a trifle wrinkled and there were other traces of her travels, including a
tiny bit of straw which clung to one shoulder, but both her
manner and her clothes, which were of excellent cut and just
fashionable enough without being in any way dashing, pro-
claimed her a young lady of Quality. He had expected a sad
romp or even a barque of frailty attempting to take advantage of his kind-hearted cousin. But now that he had seen
her, he was able to acquit her of all such charges. Much of
the scorn and cynicism which he'd first affected vanished,
leaving him torn between disapproval and amusement.

"Ah, Bredon, this is the young lady I was telling you
about," Mr. Steele explained unnecessarily.

"I had gathered that much, Elliot. And does the young
lady have a name?"

"I do, but I won't tell you," Melody replied firmly.

"Indeed," he said. "That makes our meeting somewhat
awkward, does it not?"

"Why, yes, it does," Melody admitted. "But that is
hardly my fault. I don't know why we had to meet at all. I
was just explaining to Mr. Steele that he need not trouble
himself further on our behalf, but he insisted we stay till you
arrived. I believe he would have had us forcibly detained if
necessary."

"Like to see him try!"

Lord Dake was somewhat surprised at these truculent
words from Melody's companion, whom he had already
come to regard as a sort of silent watchdog. The sullen,
gangly youth seemed recently to have grown more rapidly
than his clothes could accommodate, for his thin wrists

stuck out from his sleeves and his trousers were several inches too short. His ragged clothing was a far cry from the young lady's expensive wardrobe, and his accent suffered even more deplorably from comparison. Lord Dake dismissed the possibility of their being brother and sister immediately.

"And do you also refuse to tell me your name?" he asked.

Tom stared back at him in angry confusion, but made no reply. Lord Dake turned from him to Melody.

"May we not at least have the pleasure of first names?" he enquired. "They do not have to be true, but they would be a convenience in conversation."

To his surprise she blushed rosily. "I wouldn't give a false name. That would be lying."

"How commendable. And yet I believe you have told my cousin that you and your companion are brother and sister."

Her flush deepened. There was a mixture of distress and anger in her eyes which made Lord Dake regret goading her, but she replied with a great deal of dignity. "I'm sorry for that, but it could not be helped. People are very suspicious, and I thought they would accept our travelling together more readily if we claimed to be related. But you are quite right; we are not. Tom told me people would not believe us, but I thought we had better try. This is Tom and my name is Melody. Those are our real names," she added with a defiant tilt of her chin.

"Thank you, that makes things much easier," Lord Dake replied. "And now may I ask where you are going, Tom and Melody, and why you have been reduced to sleeping in my cousin's stables?"

"We are going to Yorkshire, as I have already explained to Mr. Steele, in order to visit my aunt. At least, I am going to visit my aunt. Tom is simply escorting me."

"I see. And if your aunt anticipates a visit from you, why did she not arrange transport for you and a more suitable companion than a tongue-tied halfwitted boy?"

"Tom does not lack wit!" Melody protested passionately. "He's been taking very good care of me, which is kind of him, especially since he did not wish to come along at all and only relented in the end because he saw that he could not dissuade me from leaving."

"From leaving where?" Lord Dake enquired blandly, but despite her anger Melody was not one to fall into so obvious a trap.

"I shan't tell you," she said firmly. "And neither will Tom, so don't bother badgering him. You won't, will you, Tom?" she added anxiously. "He can't make us tell if we refuse. Just say nothing at all, that's all you must do."

Tom, who had been gazing at her with a look which reminded Lord Dake even more forcibly of a devoted dog, nodded his head and assured his companion fervently if somewhat ungrammatically that saying nothing at all was within his powers. Melody turned back to his lordship with the mulish expression to which that gentleman was becoming accustomed.

"I don't wish to be impolite," she said firmly, "but it really is none of your business where we are coming from—or going to, for that matter. We simply asked permission to sleep here for the night. If I had known that you would try to become involved in our affairs as a result, I would have left without saying a word when that horrid groom found us."

"Here, now!" protested Mr. Steele, surprised into speech by hearing the best groom he had ever employed so described. "Harkness was simply doing his job. Can't have every Tom, Dick and Harry sleeping in one's stables, you know. The horses wouldn't like it."

"My dear child, the point is that we have now, whether we like it or not, become involved in your affairs," interrupted Lord Dake, ruthlessly declining to enter into a consideration of the likes and dislikes of his cousin's cattle. "You are obviously a young lady of Quality and breeding, and you are just as obviously a runaway. Whether this young man has persuaded you to accompany him in an extremely unsuitable romantic escapade, or whether he is looking after you against his better judgement, as you claim, the fact remains that he is no fit chaperon for a schoolgirl, and that neither of you is fit to be out in the world on your own. Your presence here in my cousin's stables proves that, if proof were needed. You must tell us the names of your parents, who are no doubt very anxious about your whereabouts, so that we can see you safely returned to them."

"I have no parents!" Melody replied, and despite himself his lordship had to bite back a smile at the triumphant air with which she refuted him.

"I stand corrected," he said gravely. "But you must, then, have a guardian, who will be equally concerned."

"No, he will not," Melody said firmly. "He does not care about me at all. He will be glad to learn that I have gone away so he will not have to be bothered with me any more."

"I am sure that you are mistaken," Lord Dake said. "I do not believe your guardian, whoever he may be, could be so indifferent to your safety and your good name."

"Well, you are probably right about that," Melody admitted fair-mindedly. "I'm sure he hopes that nothing bad has happened to me, because I am his responsibility, and he takes his responsibilities very seriously. And I know he is concerned with my reputation, because he is forever forbidding me to do things which he thinks might damage it. But he doesn't care about what I want, or whether I'm happy. So I am going to live with my aunt; she can be my guardian, and the burden will be removed from him."

"And have you discussed this plan with your guardian?" Lord Dake demanded suspiciously. "If he is as concerned with his responsibilities as you claim, surely he would never have let you set off alone like this. He must be frantic with worry about you."

"Well, he isn't," Melody retorted. "Because he is travelling on the Continent right now, and no one will be able to reach him with the news that I've gone. And by the time he gets back, I shall be at my aunt's, and I shall have her write him a letter explaining that she will take care of me from now on."

"And is this plan as unknown to your aunt as it is to your guardian?" his lordship asked.

Her frank eyes shifted to avoid his, and he knew he had scored a hit. "She will be glad to have me with her," Melody said stoutly. "Especially when she understands how very unhappy I was where I was."

"Forgive me, but you do not look particularly ill-used," his lordship pointed out gently.

She flushed, then raised her dark eyes to his. "There's more than one sort of ill use. You don't know what it's like, to be placed into the guardianship of someone who scarcely knows you, and who doesn't care to learn to know you, and who plans your life for you without taking the slightest consideration for what you are like or what you want or what will be bound to make you miserably unhappy."

"But I do, you know," Lord Dake said softly. "My own situation was not so very different. But it doesn't last. You grow up at last, and the petty restrictions cease to chafe.

Once you are of age, and free to do as you wish, you may even see the reasons behind some of them."

Something in his tone caused Melody to warm to him for the first time. It was almost as if he did understand. But he could not realize how different it was for her. For some reason it was important to her to make him understand, and she spoke very earnestly in reply. "For you, perhaps that is true. But not for me. I'll be wed to some suitable man, who understands me as little as my guardian does, and then what will become of my freedom? I cannot wait for time to free me; I must do it myself."

Lord Dake was not an unsympathetic man, but he was growing tired of this conversation in the mews, with his cousin and Tom as more or less silent witnesses and several curious stable-boys at some greater remove obviously straining to hear what was going on. He believed Melody was sincerely unhappy, but he thought he knew how impetuous, and how transient, such emotional storms were at her age. He believed that her piteous depiction of servitude, first to her guardian and then to an unknown future husband, was missish melodrama bordering almost on hysteria. He was, therefore, incensed when Mr. Steele chose to rush to Melody's aid.

"Bredon, the girl's right. She deserves the chance to be happy, too," Mr. Steele said. "You mustn't stop her from going to her aunt, if that's what she wishes."

Lord Dake gave his cousin a look so cold that that gentleman paled visibly. "Thank you, Elliot," he said icily. "But may I point out that I do not appreciate your attempts to cast me as the villain in this melodrama? I have no interest in keeping the young lady from whatever happiness she believes she will find in the company of her aunt—if, indeed, she *has* an aunt, and this is not all another Canterbury tale she is making up for our amusement. However, I cannot see a gently bred, apparently penniless young woman wandering about London accompanied only by a young clod who obviously hasn't got the sense of a superior sheepdog, and make no attempt to detain her or to inform her family of her plight. I cannot reconcile it with my notions of what is expected of a gentleman, and I am surprised that you can.''

"That's not fair," Melody broke in. "Mr. Steele is a perfect gentleman, and he hasn't let me wander about anywhere. He insisted that we remain here until you came, though I wish he had not, as you are so disagreeable. And you mustn't speak so about Tom. He is very kind to escort me to my aunt, who does exist, no matter what you think. He is not forever making objections and sneering at my lack of propriety and insulting everyone the way you do. Tom is doing something to help me, and I think that is by far more gentlemanly than *your* behaviour!''

"Tell me the name of your aunt, and I shall be glad to help you," Lord Dake said.

"No, you won't! You'll use my aunt's name to find out who I am, and who my guardian is, and you'll pack me right back to him, against my wishes!''

Since this was, indeed, exactly what his lordship had planned, Melody's accusation left him momentarily at a loss for words. His slower-minded cousin, who had been mulling over Melody's words, chose the moment to break into the conversation again.

"Do you know, Bredon, I believe she's right. Young Tom here has acted the gentleman after all. Aiding a young lady in distress—that's very chivalrous of him.''

"If you believe that assisting a hysterical schoolgirl to run away from her proper guardian is more gentlemanly than seeing that she returns to her home, where she belongs, Elliot, I can only say that you must be as addlepated as you have always claimed to be," replied Lord Dake, goaded beyond endurance. "I had thought that you underestimated your own mental powers, but now I see I was mistaken. You *are* a fool! You were a fool to believe that these two could possibly be brother and sister, you were a fool to run to me for help, and you are the biggest fool imaginable if you seriously propose to assist this girl to run away from home simply because you imagine her guardian—whose identity you don't even know—misunderstands her. I suppose next you'll be proposing to escort the chit to Yorkshire and her problematical aunt yourself."

Mr. Steele had not intended to propose any such thing, but at these words Melody turned a gaze full of such hope and admiration upon him that he found himself befuddled. Young ladies did not generally await Mr. Steele's utterances with breathless anticipation; the young ladies of his acquaintance, mostly his sisters and his strong-minded fiancée, were far more likely to tell him fondly that he was talking nonsense and should hold his tongue. This was a new experience for him, and a heady one.

"*Were* you proposing to escort me?" Melody asked shyly. Mr. Steele swallowed and gazed back into her shining dark eyes.

"Yes," he heard himself say. "Yes, that is exactly what I propose. No doubt it would be the best thing all round."

"I'm escorting her already!" Tom protested loudly, but Melody turned to him and laid her small hand on his arm.

"To be sure you are, Tom, and very splendidly, too. Only think how much more comfortable we'll be if Mr. Steele joins us. He can afford to pay for our travel and accommodations, you see, and my aunt will reimburse him once we arrive. And Mr. Steele is a man of the world—he'll know all the details of how to arrange for travel, and what sorts of inns are respectable, and everything else we'll need to know.

People will listen to him, and when we're with him they won't call us nasty runaways and chase us off. And no horrid man will dare pretend to help us and then steal all of our money with Mr. Steele about. Won't that be better?''

Tom nodded sullenly and allowed that Mr. Steel's contributions would be of some use, and Melody awarded both of her knights errant with the serenely sunny smile of a successful peacemaker. Lord Dake, who had been struck dumb by his meek cousin's declaration, shook his head grimly as if coming out of a bad dream.

"Elliot, think what you are doing," he advised. "You can't be such a fool as to involve yourself with this ramshackle scheme!"

But Mr. Steele, who had just heard himself described for the first time ever as an omniscient man of the world, replied with dignity that he thought it best.

"All right, then!" his lordship snapped. "Run mad, if you must. Do whatever you please. I wash my hands of the whole affair!" He turned on his heel and strode off, and the rest of the company felt themselves much more comfortable for his leaving.

CHAPTER THREE

SKIMMING ALONG the Great North Road to Yorkshire in Mr. Steele's stylish landau, Melody surveyed her surroundings approvingly. Mr. Steele's elegant team of greys were as fine a pair of steppers as they were lookers, and the countryside seemed to melt away behind them as they flew along the road. A great wave of happiness and freedom buoyed Melody up; things were going splendidly. She caught Tom's eye and he grinned at her, almost as excited as she.

Tom's reluctance to share his role of protector with Mr. Steele had persisted during the preparations for their departure. Tom had chafed at the seemingly endless wait while Mr. Steele supervised the packing of his bag and dashed off several notes cancelling his various engagements. The latter was apparently an onerous task, for Mr. Steele had emerged from his room to join Tom and Melody where they awaited him in the study with ink smudged on his hands, his hair in disarray as if he had clutched it in his search for inspiration, and a vaguely harassed look upon his pleasant face.

The true measure of Tom's impatience, however, could be taken from the fact that even the excellent breakfast which Mr. Steele insisted they eat before setting out on their journey failed to please him. He would, he gave Melody to understand, have been happier to leave at once with no more fortification than the bread and cider they'd been served earlier, although this declaration did not prevent him from feeding heartily on the ham and roast beef Mr. Steele's servant set before them. But Tom's misgivings had vanished the moment the greys had been hitched to the landau. When he had realized that he would, indeed, have the pleasure of seeing these prime bits of blood in action, his joy knew no bounds.

Nor was Tom disappointed in the performance of the horses or of Mr. Steele, who was, in Tom's freely expressed opinion, a crack whipster. He settled admiringly to watch the skill with which Mr. Steele handled the team, exchanging occasional smiles of contentment with Melody. And, indeed, it was a day to cheer almost anyone. The sun was shining; the skies were blue; it was unseasonably warm, the carriage was well sprung and comfortable, the horses splendid. Even Mr. Steele seemed to have shed the slight air of discomfort with which he had emerged from his session at the writing desk; he was conscious of doing a gallant turn for a lovely young lady, and he had pushed any misgivings about the wisdom of his actions firmly behind him. Bredon might have disapproved, but Bredon, for all that he was only five years older than Mr. Steele, had unfortunately got into a rather stuffy way of thinking. He did not understand the pleasures of the open road, the lure of escape, and the excitement of Adventure.

Disaster, when it came, came suddenly. The road took a sharp turn, but Mr. Steele held the horses firmly on track. Up ahead another carriage was approaching them, a high-perch phaeton drawn by a pair of spirited black geldings. The driver was going all out, and the speeding phaeton was swaying from side to side in a manner which Tom thought all the crack but which Mr. Steele observed with stern disapproval and Melody with a slight sensation of seasickness. Then, from nowhere, a dog ran out onto the road between the onrushing vehicles, and sat down unconcernedly to scratch at a particularly worrisome flea.

"Look out!" Melody seized Mr. Steele's arm and shouted, "He's going to hit the little dog!"

Indeed, the driver of the phaeton was aimed straight at the cur, and showed no signs of slackening his pace. Melody shook Mr. Steele's arm again in an agony of apprehension.

"Stop him!"

Mr. Steele had many admirable qualities, but quickness of mind was not among them. He gaped open-mouthed at Melody.

"Stop him," she repeated. "He's going to run down that little dog!"

This imploring cry was too much for Tom, at least, to ignore. Reaching between Mr. Steele and Melody, he snatched the reins from the former and pulled up hard. The greys, considerably startled at this unprecedented bit of cowhandedness, stumbled and swerved disastrously to the left, into the path of the phaeton. Mr. Steele swore fluently and wrested the reins back from Tom. He managed by an almost superhuman effort to keep his horses on the road. The driver of the phaeton was not so fortunate. His efforts to stop before the vehicles collided sent him into the ditch, his horses lurching awkwardly off the road, scrambling to keep their feet. The wheel of the toppling phaeton brushed alongside the unwitting cause of disaster, sending the little dog spinning across the road and the driver tumbling to the ground. A cloud of dust obscured the horrible scene for a moment, and Melody tugged again at Mr. Steele's arm.

"Get down, do, Mr. Steele! We've got to see how badly he's hurt."

Mr. Steele gave a little shake, as one emerging from a bad dream, then leapt down out of his carriage almost as precipitously as the driver of the other vehicle had left his. Placing his own interpretation upon Melody's words, he hastened to the side of the blacks, who stood shuddering and blowing in the ditch, still hitched to the phaeton which lay at a drunken angle behind.

"There, there, my beauties," Mr. Steele said softly. "You're all right." He unbuckled the horses from the disabled phaeton and very nobly led them up out of the ditch before hurrying to join Tom, who was crouched between the greys, anxiously examining their legs. Correctly discerning that this examination was bound to keep both men engaged for some time, Melody scrambled down out of the landau and ran lightly to where the dog lay upon the side of the road. To her relief, it greeted her with a soft whimper, and even wagged its tail wearily as she crouched over it. When she gathered the animal up into her arms, it trembled violently but made no move to get away. Speaking soothingly to the little creature, Melody gave it a quick examination and began to hope that it was not too badly hurt. Like Tom and Mr. Steele, she ignored the driver of the phaeton, whose own injuries, if any, were evidently not too extensive to prevent him from issuing an unabated stream of profanities from the ditch where he still lay.

Melody straightened, the injured dog in her arms, and joined her companions at the landau.

"Are your horses injured, Mr. Steele?"

Almost speechless with anxiety and indignation, her would-be rescuer glared helplessly at her.

"Apparently not," he managed finally. "Although they could have both been crippled, for all that you cared."

"Oh, no," she assured him earnestly. "I would be very sorry to see anything happen to your beautiful horses, Mr. Steele. Please believe me, sir, I had no idea that our sudden stop would cause such a commotion."

"A commotion!" Mr. Steele's voice rose in pitch. "Is that what you call this? Rather say a disaster!"

"Not a disaster," Melody said soothingly. "After all, your horses are uninjured. Of course, this little dog is wounded, but I do not believe mortally. If your horses are really unhurt, we must hurry on to the nearest town, where we can seek some sort of medical attention for him. And someone ought to see to the driver of the phaeton, I suppose, even though he was quite criminally careless. He could see the dog had wandered out upon the road, and he made not the slightest effort to slow down till Tom blocked his way with your landau, Mr. Steele. Which was very quick thinking on Tom's part, though, of course, rather hard on the horses."

Mr. Steele stared for a moment in horror at the lunatic with whom he had so unwittingly involved himself, but her words had recalled him to a sense of obligation, and he went to the assistance of the other driver without responding to Melody's remarks.

That gentleman, who had by this time struggled up out of the ditch on his own and was sitting desolately on the side of the road, holding his head as if to steady it, appeared to feel little gratitude for Mr. Steele's somewhat tardy expressions of concern.

"Am I injured?" he echoed indignantly. "I should say I am. It's a miracle I wasn't killed. What do you think you were doing? You blocked my way!"

"Terribly sorry," Mr. Steele said weakly. "Never done such a thing before, I assure you. But you were coming along too fast, you know. Even if we hadn't blocked the way, you'd have come a cropper around that curve."

"Are you claiming you blocked my way deliberately to prevent me from overturning on the curve?" the gentleman demanded.

"No, no, of course not. Not claiming anything of the kind, I assure you. Just pointing out you were going too fast for the road. Cowhanded way to behave. Ought to have more consideration for your horses.''

This was too much for the other driver to bear. He leapt to his feet, his injuries apparently forgotten in his indignation. His sandy-red curls stood out wildly about his rather round face, and his sharp eyes sparkled with anger.

"I ought to consider the horse!" he cried. "What about you? You could have killed us all, including the damned horses. That was the worst bit of driving I've ever seen in my life!''

"Here, now," Tom interrupted fiercely. "There's no call for you to be saying such a thing. Mr. Steele is a crack whipster, best I ever seen. And it wasn't him brought the landau round to block your way. It was me!''

"Indeed!" The man stood and advanced upon Tom, who danced warily back out of his reach. "Then it's you I have to thank for almost breaking my neck, not to mention wrecking my best carriage." He looked around at the road, and spied his whip in the dust where he had dropped it. Picking it up, he moved towards Tom again.

"Now, now," Mr. Steele said. He had been ready enough to box Tom's ears himself a few minutes earlier, but the red-haired gentleman seemed to have something much more serious in mind, and Mr. Steele overcame his own anger to come to Tom's rescue. "No need to be brandishing that whip, old man. Chuckle-headed thing for him to do, of course, but he's only a boy, after all. Very sorry about the damage to you and your vehicle. Only too glad to pay for the repairs. Least I can do.''

"I should say it is," the redhead replied indignantly. "Look at my phaeton! The axle's cracked, the wheel's off, the perch is knocked askew, the paint is scraped off the sides, the wood's all gouged out here.''

"Yes, yes," Mr. Steele soothed. "Damned shame. But I know just the man to fix it for you. Best in London, I swear. We'll have it brought round to him with my compliments and he'll have your rig back in prime shape before you know it. You'll never know it had been damaged."

"That's all very well," the man said, a little mollified. "But what about my clothes? Look at this coat. I got it from Weston himself, and now it's ruined. Split right up the back, and the sleeve torn half off. And my cape's covered in mud. It'll never come clean."

Mr. Steele's attention was engaged. "Weston, did you say?" he murmured. He rubbed a fold of the torn sleeve between his fingers. "Very nice," he pronounced. "I always use Stultz myself, but some people swear by Weston."

For just a moment it seemed as if the gentlemen's attention would be diverted by a discussion of the rival merits of two of London's most esteemed tailors. But Melody, who was growing more concerned at the amount of blood which the stray dog was loosing, chose the moment to interrupt.

"I really don't see that it matters which tailor one goes to," she began, thus horrifying and astonishing both men. "I'm sorry to be incivil, but we must get this animal somewhere so I can have its wounds attended to. And first we must do something to stanch the flow of blood. Mr. Steele, may I have your cravat?"

"My cravat?" Mr. Steele was not a dandy, but he was shocked at the notion of appearing in public without his cravat, and his hand went up instinctively to his throat to guard it. Melody sighed.

"Well, then your handkerchief, perhaps," she suggested. "Whatever you have that I may use. Quickly, please!"

Spurred into action, Mr. Steele produced a snowy white linen handkerchief and watched with a slightly regretful expression as Melody folded it and bound it around the dog's foreleg. She looked up from this operation with a strained smile.

"Thank you," she said. "That's much better. But I believe the leg is broken, and there may be other injuries as well that I have not discovered yet. May we please be on our way now?"

"And what about me?" the London gentleman protested. "Am I to be stranded here with no arrangements made for transporting my carriage or me back to Town?"

"I would hope you could make some arrangements yourself," Melody retorted. "You are not a helpless animal, sir."

The man bristled, but before he could respond, Mr. Steele forestalled him. "Terribly sorry," he explained kindly. "Hate to leave you in a lurch, but the young lady is concerned about the dog, you see. I'll send back a horse for you from the next inn; do please make any arrangements you wish about the carriage. I'll give you my card, and you can have it all laid upon my account. The suit and your cape, too, of course. Have new ones made, and charge it to me."

He was searching his pockets as he spoke, one after another. "The name is Steele," he continued. "Elliot Steele."

"Mr. Montgomery," the other gentleman replied automatically.

"Pleasure to make your acquaintance," Mr. Steele responded in kind. "I'll write the name of the carriage maker on the back of my card." He searched another pocket rather frantically, then shrugged. "I seem to have come away without my card case," he said apologetically. "But I assure you, I will take care of everything."

"Do please let us go now, Mr. Steele," Melody urged. "You can make the arrangements for this gentleman later;

I'm afraid the little dog will die if we don't have his wounds seen to soon."

"And who's to say I'll ever hear from any of you again, much less that you'll send help back for me?" Mr. Montgomery protested.

"No need to come over ugly," Mr. Steele said, genuinely shocked. "I promise you I shall take care of everything, Mr. Montgomery. But you don't want the little dog to die of its wounds, do you?"

"I don't care if the damned dog dies or not," Mr. Montgomery replied. "It shouldn't have been out on the road."

"How dare you!" Melody flared up. "You didn't have to run the poor little thing over. If you'd slowed down you could have avoided it easily enough. You're a horrible man, and I don't care if Mr. Steele sends anyone back for you at all. It would serve you right if you had to walk all the way back to Town."

"This is all your fault," Mr. Montgomery cried. "I doubt I'd have hit the cur if you hadn't pulled your carriage across the way like that, so that I had to skid all over the road to try to avoid you." He looked from Melody to Mr. Steele, a suspicious light dawned in his eye. "And I'll be damned if I'll let you go off and trust you to arrange things afterwards," he added. "There's something ramshackle going on here, and I don't trust any of you. How am I to know that you are a gentleman at all? I'm quite sure this is no young lady."

"Here, here," Mr. Steele protested, shocked to the core. "Assure you, not what you think. Travelling companions, that is all."

"Indeed." Mr. Montgomery's sandy eyebrows rose in disbelief. "Strange companions, if you ask me. Is the young lady related to you?"

Mr. Steele was at a loss for words, but Tom waded it in his stead.

"She's my sister," he declared stoutly.

Mr. Montgomery barely spared Tom a glance. "Yes, of course," he said witheringly. "And I'm her Uncle Alex."

Bewildered, Tom looked to Melody for help.

"I don't see that it matters who I am related to," she said firmly. "I wish to go now." She turned and started back towards Mr. Steele's landau, obviously hoping that her companions would take the hint. Tom turned to follow her, but before he had gone more than a step, Mr. Montgomery spoke.

"Hoyden!" he said contemptuously. "Regular brazen one, too, giving herself such airs and travelling about the countryside with no chaperon. If you are a gentleman, and I have my doubts, for all your fine clothes and expensive carriage, it's clear you're up to no good. Captain Sharp, that's what I reckon you are, and that little doxy your bit of muslin."

Astonishment at hearing himself described as a confidence trickster paralyzed Mr. Steele, preventing him from rising to the defence of Melody's honour. But Tom showed no such hesitation. He rushed Mr. Montgomery, arms flailing wildly. Montgomery, whose burly form must have weighed twice that of Tom's, fell back a step or two in confusion, then rallied and began laying about Tom's back and shoulders with the handle of his whip. Mr. Steele cried out in protest, and attempted to drag the contestants apart while Melody, who had reached the landau and realized that she was alone, ran back to the others, crying out for them to stop.

Mr. Steele had Tom by the shoulder and was struggling to pull him off Mr. Montgomery, while attempting to dodge the whip with which Mr. Montgomery continued to flail about, shouting "Take that!" again and again. Tom was silent except for his gasps for air; his attention was focused on raining as many blows as he might upon Mr. Montgomery's midriff.

"Tom! Stop that!" Melody cried. "There isn't time for you to be fighting now! We've got to see to the dog. Mr. Steele, make them stop!"

Mr. Steele, who was doing his very best to accomplish that very objective, spared no words for Melody. He gave a mighty tug which dislodged Tom finally from Mr. Montgomery's body. Before he could congratulate himself, however, Mr. Montgomery's whip slammed up against his head, a wild blow that made his ears ring. Mr. Steele had a great deal of patience, but the afternoon's events had exhausted it. He gave a great bellow of protest at the blow, and swung his fist at his excited opponent. Mr. Montgomery staggered back, both hands to his nose, which had begun to leak blood. Tom whooped loudly with delight, Melody cried out again for them all to stop fighting, and Mr. Steele danced around, his fists upraised, waiting for Mr. Montgomery to recover himself and re-enter the fray. So absorbed were they all in the action that none of them heard the approaching carriage, even when it pulled up alongside them.

"Ah, Elliot," came a coolly ironic voice which was familiar to three of them, at least. "Is there something that I may do to help, or do you have everything in hand?"

All four swivelled to meet Lord Dake's mildly enquiring gaze. He was seated in a sleek phaeton, pulled by a pair of glossy bays who tossed their heads restively at the delay. He was wearing a dark brown superfine riding coat which was fitted tightly across his broad shoulders and chest and tapered down snugly at his narrow waist. His collar, though only moderately high, was exquisitely starched and of the purest snowy white, as was his neatly tied cravat. His trousers were of soft brown doeskin, molded tightly to his powerful legs. No spot of dirt marred the rich gleam of his Hessians. Over it all he wore a severely cut surtout with one single, ankle-length cloak attached. His only ornament was a gold signet ring and one simple gold fob. He looked powerful, completely at ease, and inexpressibly elegant, a vision which provided a startling contrast to the four bedraggled travellers who stood looking up wordlessly at him. It was Melody who finally broke the spell and stepped forward.

"Lord Dake! I'm so glad you are here. This little dog has been run over and he's badly hurt. Please, won't you drive us to the nearest inn where we might find someone to take care of him?"

"Certainly. Elliot, won't you please help Melody up into the carriage? If you are quite done with your fisticuffs, that is. Thank you. Tom, please take the dog until Melody is settled in—there, you may give it back to her now, I believe. Are you ready, Melody?"

"Oh, yes, thank you." Melody looked up into Lord Dake's face wonderingly. His voice had remained polite and quiet, and yet Tom and Mr. Steele, both of whom had ignored her increasingly frantic pleas for help, had moved instantly to obey him. Lord Dake smiled at her reassuringly, and she was aware quite suddenly of what a handsome man he was.

"Please calm yourself," he said kindly. "You look quite agitated, and there is no need for it. I'm sure we'll find someone up ahead who can see to the animal's wounds." He looked back down at the still-silent Mr. Steele. "I'll leave you to finish your business with this gentleman, Elliot, and wait for you to join us at the next inn up the road. Please forgive me for not lingering, but we must not leave Melody in a state of anxiety any longer."

He nodded politely at them all, then urged his horses on. Melody settled back against the cushion and let out a small breath of relief. In her arms the little dog sighed as if in sympathy and squirmed as if to settle himself more comfortably. Lord Dake looked over at her with another smile.

"I suppose it would be impolite to ask how you have come to acquire that dog," he said.

"We rescued him," Melody replied. "Mr. Montgomery struck him with his carriage, and I believe his leg is broken. The dog's, I mean," she added for the sake of clarity.

"Mr. Montgomery being, I presume, that rather dust-covered gentleman whose face was as red as his carroty hair?"

"Yes. He ran his phaeton off the road, you know. That is why he was so very dusty."

"I thought he might have. I could not help but notice the vehicle in the ditch, but I did not like to ask about it. People can be so touchy about a trifle such as being tossed into a ditch, and Mr. Montgomery did not look to be in the best of humour."

"I am very sorry for Mr. Montgomery's misfortune," Melody said untruthfully. "But I do think it is all his own fault. He was driving his carriage straight at this little dog, and he wasn't making the slightest effort to slow down. If he hadn't gone off into the ditch, I believe he'd have run straight over the poor little thing instead of merely giving it a glancing blow."

"How fortunate, then, that he went into the ditch," his lordship murmured.

"Well, yes, I think so," Melody admitted. "But I don't believe Mr. Montgomery would agree."

"His opinion is bound to differ," Lord Dake said tolerantly. "How exactly did Mr. Montgomery come to end up in the ditch, by the way?" he added.

Melody stole a quick look up at him. Lord Dake's eyes were on the road ahead, his expression one of courteous interest, but she thought he was smiling a little.

"When I saw that he didn't mean to pull up to avoid hitting the dog, I asked Mr. Steele to stop him. Mr. Steele didn't quite know what to do, but Tom pulled the carriage across the road to block Mr. Montgomery's way. He was going too fast to stop in time, and went into the ditch in order to avoid colliding with us. I thought it was very clever of Tom."

"I see." There was definitely a smile lurking on Lord Dake's well-formed mouth now, though he kept his voice devoid of any emotion other than polite interest. "Was Elliot as impressed as you with Tom's quick thinking?"

"Well, no, he was not," Melody admitted. "In fact, he was very angry. He was afraid that his horses had been injured, you see, and he was very concerned about that."

"You will have to forgive him," Lord Dake said in defence of his cousin. "He is very attached to his horses, you know."

"I do understand," Melody conceded graciously. "I would have been very unhappy if anything had happened to Mr. Steele's horses, even though he did say I wouldn't have cared. But I was concerned about the little dog, too, and once it was clear that the horses were not injured, I hoped Mr. Steele might turn his attention to taking care of this poor animal. But instead he and that horrible man went on and on, discussing carriages and tailors and arguing about whose fault the accident was. And Mr. Montgomery was most provoking, and said he did not believe Mr. Steele was a gentleman. He acted as if Mr. Steele could not be trusted to reimburse him for his expenses as he had promised."

"Very churlish," Lord Dake said. "Is that why Elliot was pummelling him when I came upon you?"

"No. At least, I don't know precisely why the fight started."

She spoke absently, her attention obviously elsewhere, and Lord Dake slowed the horses and turned his own attention for a moment to the dog in Melody's lap. She watched his face during his brief examination.

"Do you think he will be all right?" she asked anxiously when he had finished.

"I feel certain of it," he said bracingly. "He's breathing normally, and his eyes are quite bright. I believe you are right; the leg does seem to be broken. But he seems fairly comfortable now, and I see no fresh blood on that bandage you've made him."

"It's Mr. Steele's handkerchief," Melody confessed. "He was kind enough to give it to me, and I'm afraid it's quite ruined."

"A small sacrifice was obviously called for. I'm sure Elliot does not mind at all."

"I hope you are right," Melody said. "I did ask for his cravat first, and he did not seem at all willing to sacrifice it."

"His cravat?" Lord Dake arched one eyebrow in spurious shock. "That would be a sacrifice, indeed. You must know, Melody, that my cousin is quite proud of his skill in tying his cravat. It's one of his few vanities. I have seen him affect a bewildering variety of knots, according to the dictates of fashion—though never one quite like what I saw just now. What was that one called, do you suppose...the Quizzical?"

Despite her worry, Melody could not help but laugh. "Poor Mr. Steele. He looked quite elegant when we set out. I'm afraid his cravat was disarranged in his battle with Mr. Montgomery."

"Ah then, in that case I suppose we should christen his new style the Fisticuffs. I quite liked it; there was something rather endearing about its asymmetry, don't you think?''

Melody laughed again, but carefully, so as not to jar the dog. After a moment Lord Dake prompted her.

"You were going to tell me about what started the fight between Elliot and Mr. Montgomery, I believe."

"Oh, yes. But I'm afraid I really don't know. That is, I was on my way to the carriage, and I'd hoped that Mr. Steele and Tom would follow. But when I looked back at them, Tom was boxing with Mr. Montgomery, who was lashing him about with the handle of his whip. Mr. Steele was only trying to separate them."

"Going to the defence of the young and helpless again!" Lord Dake marvelled. "Do you know, Melody, I am beginning to be quite pleased to have encountered you and Tom. I never suspected before what a perfect pattern of chivalry my cousin Elliot was. It puts an entirely new light on his character."

Melody laughed a little shyly, not at all taken in by the solemn expression on Lord Dake's face.

"Well, at first he was only trying to separate Mr. Montgomery and Tom; however, after Mr. Montgomery caught him on the side of his head with his whip, Mr. Steele entered into the battle instead of trying to stop it."

"I see." Lord Dake's grey eyes danced with laughter. "I imagine even a man as chivalrous as Elliot would take exception to that sort of thing."

"He is truly a chivalrous man, even though I know perfectly well you are making fun of poor Mr. Steele now," Melody protested laughingly. "He was very angry at Tom for pulling the horses over that way, and at me for causing him to. But he defended Tom against Mr. Montgomery, and he gave me his handkerchief for the dog's leg. And he is trying to help me by taking me to Yorkshire; the kindest thing of all.''

For once Lord Dake's voice was devoid of any ironic undercurrent. "Oh, yes, Elliot is truly kind. He's a good man, the best of all of my relations, and I'm quite fond of him.''

"I believe he's very fond of you, too," Melody said gently. "He was very flattering when he told us about you last night. He seemed to think you'd know exactly what to do. Of course, that was before..." She paused uncertainly, and Lord Dake grinned at her wryly.

"Before this morning when I was so very unhelpful, you mean," he prompted her amiably.

Melody blushed, but said shyly, "Well, yes. But you changed your mind, didn't you? You must surely have been coming after us. Or were you coming to make Mr. Steele bring us back?" This last was obviously a disturbing thought, but Lord Dake reassured her.,

"No, not at all. I had repented of my hard-heartedness and was coming to lend Elliot a hand."

"Why?"

"I am a very fickle fellow," Lord Dake said carelessly.

"I don't believe that is why at all," Melody said softly. Lord Dake made no reply, so she did not pursue the matter, occupying herself with stroking the injured dog's head and crooning soothingly to him instead. Yet her thoughts were not on the dog, but on Lord Dake, whose behaviour she found very intriguing. She had turned to him instinctively as an ally when he'd ridden up, one who might help her to make order out of the angry, confused scene in which she found herself. And somewhat to her surprise, he had immediately done just that, and had done it so easily and charmingly that she could scarcely recognize in him the man who had been so angry and uncooperative at their first meeting. She had not liked him then, had suspected him of

cruelty when he'd teased Mr. Steele and of indifference when
he abandoned them all. But now he seemed a different man,
and she could not help but wonder about him.

"There's a signpost ahead," he said suddenly, breaking
the spell of silence. "We may not have much farther to go
before we can find someone who can help that little fellow."

The signpost read *Grampton* and pointed the way down
a lane which led off of the main road. The lane was narrow, winding through uninhabited fields for some distance.
At length, however, it passed through a small village, and
here Lord Dake was able to stop and enquire for someone
who might be skilled in setting a broken bone. Somewhat to
his surprise, his query met with immediate success. The
burly villager to whom he had put his question nodded vig-
orously and gestured expansively to the north.

"Yes, sir. Dr. Simms lives up the hill there; regular London sawbones he be, come to live here in the quiet, like." He
shot an avidly curious gaze at Melody, who, with her torn
and bloody gown and her hair tumbling down around her
strained, white face, did look like a likely victim. "Is the
young lady hurt?" he asked sympathetically.

"Fortunately not," Lord Dake said. "There has been a
carriage accident, but the young lady seems to have escaped without serious injury. Her little dog, however, has
broken its leg, and we need to have it set."

"Dr. Simms wouldn't be thanking you for calling him out
to see to no dog, sir," the burly man explained with a laugh.
"He's a high and mighty one. He don't take to doctoring
animals."

"We shall have to see if we can persuade him in this
case," Lord Dake said calmly. "Is there an inn nearby where
we might spend the night? Also, it would be very helpful if
we could arrange for someone to go to the scene of the ac-

cident on the main road; there is a gentleman there who could use some help to pull his phaeton out of the ditch. It's lost a wheel, I'm afraid.''

"That's no problem," the man replied cheerfully. "Me and the Brison twins will go pull the gentleman out of the ditch. We can repair his wheel for him too, likely, so he can get back on his way."

"Thank you." Lord Dake gave the man a coin. "Please let me know if this is not enough to recompense your time and trouble."

The burly man looked down at the coin in his hand and laughed. "This will cover it, sir, and very generously, too. And as for a place for you to spend the night, that's no problem, either. Joshua Pitt's widow keeps an inn now. She lets rooms and has a little public parlour. Not much business through this way—we're too close to Town—but sometimes folks want to change their horses or stay the night. Just go on down this road a bit; the inn's off to the right, sir, you can't miss it."

"Thank you. My cousin is also at the scene of the accident; if you could direct him to the inn as well, I would be grateful."

The villager promised to do just that, and with a final word of thanks and a request that someone be sent to ask Dr. Simms to attend to them at the inn, Lord Dake turned his horses in the direction the man had indicated.

CHAPTER FOUR

JOSHUA PITT'S WIDOW did not operate the inn which her late husband had left her because she was fond of people, nor did she particularly enjoy seeing travellers come and go. A small, skinny woman with grey hair and a face wrinkled from the accumulated effects of advanced age and bad temper, she regarded her patrons as necessary but highly undesirable adjuncts to her trade. Had she been asked to think about it, she might well have admitted that it was not possible to run a posting inn, even one so small and so unfortunately situated as hers, without the presence of individuals who wished to bespeak one's horses, one's rooms, and one's meals. But as Mrs. Pitt was not given much to thought, she had no difficulty reconciling her dislike of visitors with her desire that the inn should provide enough income to support her. So when Lord Dake and Melody appeared at the threshold of her inn, she had greeted them both with barely concealed impatience and a minimum of civility. The gentleman, she grudgingly admitted to herself, looked respectable and, more importantly, wealthy. There was nothing to fault in his impeccably neat trousers and well-cut riding coat, nor in the pure white of his shirt and cravat, nor in the rich leather cape which hung from his broad shoulders. Nor was anything lacking in the polite smile which he wore upon his handsome face, nor his manner, which was quiet and gentlemanly. Looking up at him, Mrs. Pitt unbent to the full extent her nature permitted and bestowed a reluctant, wintry smile upon him. The smile disappeared immediately, however, when she took in the young lady—if, indeed, she *was* a lady—who accompanied him. She was another matter entirely. Her hair was dishevelled, her bonnet hanging down her back by the string around her throat. Her dark blue travelling dress looked as if it had been well enough once, but it was dusty now, the seam in one shoulder was ripped, and there was blood all down the front of the gown. Worst of all, she was holding a filthy, flea-bitten animal in her arms, looking for all the world as if she intended to bring it into the inn. Mrs. Pitt hastened to disillusion her.

"That animal is not to come in here," she began abruptly. "I don't allow such filthy creatures in my inn."

Melody opened her mouth to reply, but Lord Dake was before her. "Of course not," he replied calmly. "It is quite unfit to be allowed inside now. We shall leave the dog outside while we wait for the doctor to arrive and set his broken leg."

"Doctor?" Mrs. Pitt was momentarily diverted. "What doctor would that be, now?"

"Dr. Simms, I believe his name is. I have sent someone to direct him to your inn."

Mrs. Pitt was not generally inclined to laughter, but she could not repress a chuckle as she pictured the face of Dr. Simms once he was confronted with his patient. "He won't like that," she predicted with some relish.

"I am sorry to hear it," Lord Dake replied carelessly. "But we shall not worry about that now. What we need at the moment is two rooms for the night. You can provide that, can you not? And a hot dinner?"

"I can," Mrs. Pitt admitted grudgingly, as if she did not want word of this weakness to get about.

"Splendid." Lord Dake paused, and smiled charmingly. "But I am forgetting Elliot," he added. "I believe we require three rooms. There will be a gentleman joining us later; my cousin."

Lord Dake watched as Mrs. Pitt considered this new piece of information. She plainly did not like it. Apparently the presence of another gentleman in their party rendered it even less respectable in her eyes. After a moment she spoke.

"Two rooms only," she said. "That's all I have available at present."

"That will do nicely," Lord Dake conceded. "My cousin and I can share a room, and my ward can have the other." He glanced briefly down at Melody, half-afraid that she would thwart his concession to convention by pointing out that she was not his ward, but she appeared to be preoccupied with her burden and made no comment. Lord Dake breathed a silent prayer of thanks and looked back to Mrs. Pitt.

"Your ward?" She made the words sound insulting, and Lord Dake allowed the pleasant smile to fade from his face, fixing her with a level gaze which was designed to discourage presumption on her part. Apparently it worked, for Mrs. Pitt nodded and stepped back from the door. "I'll have the rooms made up," she said sourly. "But mind your ward don't try to bring that cur in here."

"No. Is there somewhere we might take the dog while we wait for the doctor?"

Mrs. Pitt looked as if this simple question were an enormous imposition. "Stables, I suppose," she said carelessly. "I don't know why you're taking so much trouble over it, though. Better have one of the stable-boys put it down for you."

Melody looked up in sudden outrage, but Lord Dake took her arm and gently guided her away from the open door.

"Thank you," he said calmly. "But I don't believe that will be necessary."

Mrs. Pitt disappeared wordlessly within. Melody started towards the stables, but Lord Dake's hand steered her in another direction. She looked up at him, puzzled, and he smiled.

"I believe it would be better to wait outside, unless we intend to provide a lantern by which the doctor can examine him," he said. "There's a bench here in the back."

"Oh, yes," Melody agreed. "This is much nicer. Not that I have anything against stables, but they are dimly lit and noisy, and these don't seem to be particularly clean. Besides," she added with a smile, "I seem to be spending rather a lot of time in them lately."

"You'll be more comfortable here," Lord Dake said firmly. They were in a small kitchen garden at the back of the inn. The afternoon sunlight warmed the wooden bench upon which Lord Dake had settled her, and streamed down richly on the flagstones. The noise from the stable-yard was dimmed and the air was scented with herbs. Lord Dake perched atop the low stone wall which marked off the garden space and smiled at her. In the sunlight his dark hair had a coppery gleam; looking at it, Melody was reminded of the rich copper coat of the chestnut horse she had admired in Mr. Steele's stable. It was almost impossible to believe that that had been only this morning.

"I hope the doctor is not long," she said.

"I'm sure he won't be," Lord Dake replied. "It sounded as if his house were quite near here, from what the villager said."

Melody gave a little sigh and settled back on the bench, careful not to jar the injured dog in her lap. It was a scruffy, underfed little thing, with droopy ears, long, tangled fur, and earnest brown eyes which it kept fixed upon its saviour's face. Its encounter with the carriage had injured its right front leg, which it held tucked up against itself protectively. But it was a patient sufferer, lying still in Melody's lap. Melody caressed its head and spoke soothingly to it. It wagged its tail again and even licked half-heartedly at the blood on its fur. Melody bent her head over it, hushing it softly, and ran her hands gently over its body. The bandage she had wrapped round its leg was stained with fresh blood, and she began to fear that the animal would bleed to death before the doctor came. A shadow fell across her, and Lord Dake's hand came gently around the dog's injured leg, brushing her fingertips in passing. Melody removed her own hand from the dog's body and sat back again, her eyes upon Lord Dake's face as he bent to examine the animal in her lap. His expression was abstracted, his grey eyes fixed upon his task.

"There, little fellow," he said softly. "Let's have a look. Yes, I know that hurts, doesn't it? You're a very brave little fellow. And you've found a very kind benefactress. Nothing for you to worry about now, is there?"

The dog whined softly, as if in agreement, and Lord Dake straightened and smiled down at Melody.

"He'll be fine," he said reassuringly. "You're quite right, the leg is broken, but it seems to be a simple break, and the bleeding is very sluggish. Once the doctor comes he'll be right as rain in no time."

"Thank you." Melody could feel the relief, as sure that things would be well as if Lord Dake's words had made it so. He was so kind. Looking up at him, Melody found herself wanting to tell him everything: the name of her guardian, her fears for the future. Surely a man who would take such pains over an injured animal, who was so concerned to reassure her, would see her own need and would help her.

Melody wanted to believe that it was true. She opened her mouth, poised to tell him her whole story, then paused.

"You never did say what made you change your mind about helping Mr. Steele, my lord," she said instead.

He smiled at her ruefully. "Nothing as noble as chivalry, I assure you, Melody. Mere habit, most likely, and a strong inclination to disoblige the rest of my family."

He said it lightly, as if he were making a joke, but Melody regarded him gravely, and with an apologetic shrug he continued. "Elliot's family believe I am a bad influence on him. He has been used to coming to me for advice, you see, since his father died when we were both quite young. And the advice I give him does not generally fit the tastes of his mama or the rest of his family."

"You said this morning that you knew what it was like to have a guardian who did not understand you. Did your father also die when you were young, my lord?"

"My parents both died while I was still a schoolboy. Elliot's father was my guardian, but then he died a few years later, when Elliot was only twelve, and another guardian was appointed for us both. Since his father's death I'm afraid Elliot has been in the habit of turning to me for advice. As our Uncle Leigh had died several years before my parents, I am afraid I am Elliot's oldest living male relative, God help him. To do him credit, Elliot tries not to bother me if he can help it."

"But if he needs you, he knows you will do your best to help him," Melody said quietly. "It must be very comforting, to have someone to turn to in such moments."

Lord Dake's smile was tinged with irony. "It depends upon the quality of the help, I suppose," he said. "Elliot's mama believes that I am selfish and unprincipled and that I encourage Elliot to follow my example. I am never quite sure whether I do what I do to help Elliot or merely to infuriate my Aunt Clarice.''

"I'm sure you do what you think best for Mr. Steele, my lord,'' Melody said. "It must have been difficult for you to be thrust into such a role of responsibility in your family when you were only a boy yourself.''

His handsome face lit up with another of his rueful smiles.

"Yes, that's the rub, isn't it? Elliot will have it that I have always been older than my years. I'm afraid, however, that all it really boils down to is that I have always taken myself too seriously.'' His grey eyes twinkled wryly. "And when I do try to help,'' he continued, "I can only do what *I* think best, not necessarily what Elliot or his mama would think best. I'm afraid that's what happens when everyone in the family insists upon coming to you for help and advice; you begin to think that you know better than everyone what is best for them.''

Melody looked up at him, raising one hand to shield her eyes from the sun. "As you did with me this morning, my lord,'' she said.

"Exactly.''

"But now you have come to help us, and we are in agreement as to what is best for me, are we not?''

Lord Dake frowned slightly and turned his head towards the stable-yard. "I think I hear a carriage,'' he said. "I must see if it is Elliot. Or perhaps it is the doctor. If you will excuse me, Melody, I shall be right back.''

He stood and went out through the garden gate, and Melody went back to her own thoughts. She was interrupted after a few minutes by an elderly man's high, querulous voice.

"What's going on? Where is my patient? Why is he out here and not in the inn?''

"Doctor?" Melody called eagerly to the unseen man, and heard him making his way through the garden gate towards her.

"Well, young lady," that gentleman began, though from his tone it appeared he doubted that the term described the dishevelled young woman he now beheld. "What is wrong? Are you my patient? You don't have a broken leg, do you?"

"No, no," Melody assured him. "I am unhurt. It is this little dog—he was run over by a carriage and I believe his leg is broken."

The sour-faced man regarded Melody with puzzlement which turned swiftly to rage as her words penetrated. "The dog! You expect me to minister to a *dog?* That fool Eban Varley told me there'd been a carriage accident and someone had broken a leg. He never said it was a dog. Why has my time been wasted? I should never have been disturbed for such a matter."

"But I'm sure his leg is broken, and it must be set," Melody pointed out reasonably.

"I am a physician, young lady. Not a veterinary surgeon. That animal is an obvious stray. Have the stable-boy put him to death. It would be a mercy, and there are hundreds of other strays to take his place. He is not worth the trouble of saving."

"How dare you decide whether he is worth saving or not!" Melody cried, enraged. "You are a horrible man, and don't deserve to call yourself a doctor. This poor little dog has been in pain all this time waiting for you, and now that you are here you can do nothing but tell me to have him killed. Shame upon you, sir!"

Her antagonist turned an alarming shade of red. He was a self-important man with a strong sense of what befitted his position, and he did not intend to be berated by a hoydenish girl over a dirty little stray. He turned without a further

word to go, but a firm hand upon his shoulder stopped him
in his tracks.

"Dr. Simms, I presume," Lord Dake said mildly.

Dr. Simms started. He and Melody had been so intent
upon their dispute that neither of them had seen Lord
Dake's approach. "I am Dr. Simms, sir," he said at last.
"And who, might I ask, are you?"

Melody looked up at the gentleman who stood towering
over the diminutive physician, and found her spirits rising
unaccountably. "Lord Dake," she cried. "Please, tell this
awful man that he must help me. He refuses to set the little
dog's leg."

Lord Dake smiled down into the passionate face raised
imploringly to his. "I am sure you misunderstand, Melody," he said softly. "Dr. Simms is no doubt merely pro-
testing the conditions under which you are asking him to
work. I know it is primitive here, sir," he added, turning to
the doctor, "but we could hardly bring the cur into the
house. Our hostess does not approve of the dirty creature
tracking blood and fleas into her establishment."

There was nothing but civility in Lord Dake's manner, but
his hand was propelling the doctor gently but inexorably
back towards Melody and the injured animal as he spoke.
Whether because he sensed the determination behind that
gentle pressure or because Melody's identification of this
noble gentleman had impressed him, the doctor's trucu-
lence lessened visibly. He dropped down to his knees, took
the dog from Melody's lap, laid it upon the wooden bench,
and proceeded to examine it.

"Well, of course," he said sourly, "if you had told me
that the animal was of some importance to Lord Dake,
young lady, I would have been prepared to make an exception. Though I do not cater to animals as a rule, you know.
I thought it was merely a stray. Such animals' lives are cheap

enough, and with no one to care for them they seldom survive an injury even if it is dealt with. Let me see what condition the little dog is in.''

The doctor bent over the animal, and Melody turned her attention back to him. Lord Dake was conscious of a brief feeling of regret when her eyes left his face, but he settled himself patiently to await the doctor's verdict. He was becoming very intrigued with Melody. That morning, in Elliot's stable-yard, she had seemed to him to be a rather conventional young schoolgirl, lovelier than most, perhaps, and definitely more strong-minded. But her appearance and manner had been that of a gently bred young lady. When he had come upon the scene of the accident he had found a Melody who was dishevelled but self-possessed, trying her best to restore order between Elliot and Mr. Montgomery and to get attention for the wounded dog. When he had invited her up in his carriage he had expected reluctance, embarrassment, or even a feminine indulgence in a fit of the vapours, but she had been grateful, pleasant and calm. During the ride to the inn and here in the garden while awaiting Dr. Simms, she had responded courteously to his attempts to distract her with conversation. She was evidently a young lady who might have seemed conventional in a drawing-room, but whose behaviour under the circumstances in which she found herself was extraordinary enough to suggest a strong character and unusual composure. Now he'd found her engaged in a furious dispute with the doctor, her brown eyes flashing rage, a rage which had quickly vanished in her concern for the animal. At no time did she display the self-consciousness or confusion which one might expect to see in a gently bred young lady who found herself the centre of such public scenes. Lord Dake thought he could understand a little of his cousin's scandalized reaction to such composure on her part, but he did not share it.

The little dog whimpered as the doctor ran his hands over his body, but a soothing word from Melody elicited a few feeble wags of his tail, and he lay quietly enough beneath the doctor's touch. After a moment the doctor sat back on his heels and looked back up at Lord Dake. He seemed determined to ignore Melody.

"Well, my lord, there's some damage here, no mistaking that. The right front leg is broken, but it's a clean break. All the other injuries seem to be quite superficial. I've never set a dog's leg before, but no doubt I could do it if your lordship desires."

"I do indeed, Dr. Simms."

"If you'll pardon me for saying so, your lordship, I cannot be blamed for failing to realize that the dog was yours. His condition is hardly that of a pampered pet."

"He has strayed from home for some time," Lord Dake replied blandly. "You can imagine how glad I am to have him back. It would be tragic to lose him again now, so soon after we have found him."

"Yes, of course, my lord. I understand completely. And young ladies are so easily attached to their pets, aren't they? This young lady is perhaps a relative of yours, sir?"

Lord Dake's face assumed a decidedly less amiable expression. "I beg your pardon, sir," he said softly, "but I hope you will excuse me from discussing my family with you now. The dog has waited some time for your attention. Perhaps you could see to it with no further delay?"

Once again the words were spoken pleasantly enough, but there was something behind them which put an end to Dr. Simms's desire to ask personal questions of the baron. He turned his attention to the dog, and after some harrowing minutes, during which Melody, though pale, remained beside the little animal, holding its head and speaking sooth-ingly to it, the doctor stood and faced Lord Dake.

"That's done it, sir," he said brusquely. "He'll be all right now, but someone will have to watch him, to keep him from worrying the splint off before the bone heals properly."

"Thank you; I am sure that we can provide the care the animal needs. And thank you for your help, doctor."

Dr. Simms accepted the coin his lordship held out to him and nodded abruptly. He took his leave of the baron and left without a backwards glance at Melody or at his patient. After he had gone, Melody looked up at Lord Dake, who was surprised to see that her eyes were bright with tears.

"Thank you," she said simply. "I do not seem to be able to make anyone do what I wish, but whenever I find myself in difficulties, you appear as if by magic and make every-thing go well. I am very grateful for your help."

"I am afraid that you, like the doctor, have overesti-mated my importance," Lord Dake said lightly. "But it is true that money talks, and Dr. Simms was more ready to listen to it than to your altogether-more-deserving argu-ments. It is often the way of the world. But enough of re-flecting on man's frailties. I think you'd profit a lot more from a good, hot meal."

"You don't mean for us to leave the poor dog alone, do you?" Melody asked, fixing him with an alarmingly direct gaze.

"No, of course not," replied his lordship, who had, in fact, intended doing that very thing. "We shall have Tom settle him comfortably in the stables and see to him. You'd feel more comfortable about that, would you not?"

"Oh, yes, indeed," she said. "That would be just the thing. Tom is kind-hearted, and very good at taking care of things, even if he did give our money to that odious man. Which I don't believe was his fault at all," she added darkly.

"You can't be expected to treat every stranger with suspicion, can you?"

"Apparently *you* cannot," his lordship replied, reflecting not for the first time that Melody would be considerably safer if she could find it in her heart to entertain a bit more suspicion of her fellow man. He took her arm once again and made as if to lead her out of the garden and into the inn. But she stood where she was, lifting one slender hand to his coat sleeve.

"I did not thank you properly before," she said. "But I am very grateful for what you have done. And I have not forgotten how rude I was to you this morning, or how I accused you of doing nothing but criticizing others. I see now how wrong I was about you. You are a very kind man, and a very good one."

Lord Dake was suddenly conscious of how close together he and Melody stood. Her bright eyes were fixed on his face, and the look she was giving him was warm and approving. He looked down at her for one dizzy moment, then seemed to come to himself and pulled back gently from her, so that her hand slipped from his arm.

"I am not so kind or so good as you think, Melody," he said firmly. "It cost me nothing but a coin to convince the doctor to help you. I was not required to show the sort of heroism you did; even poor Elliot went to battle for you at considerably greater cost to himself."

"But I know you would have done more if it had been needed," she said, not taking her eyes from his. "And you didn't have to tell the doctor you were responsible for the dog or make any effort on its behalf. But you did."

She smiled up at him, and Lord Dake began to understand the extent of his folly in jaunting about the countryside in Melody's company. He had been thinking of her as a mere child, but she was a woman, or dangerously close to being one. How could he have contemplated, even for a short time, encouraging Elliot to continue serving as her escort? He wondered whether Elliot, Miss Otterleigh notwithstanding, was in danger of succumbing to Melody's charms. The situation was clearly even more complicated than he had realized, and Lord Dake was determined that after she had dined he would convince Melody to tell them the name of her guardian so that they could return her to his protection as soon as possible. He quite understood Elliot's initial chivalrous impulse and the ease with which he had given in to it. Escorting a damsel in distress, especially one as lovely as Melody, was an irresistible prospect, and one that was infinitely more attractive than attending the engagement dinner his mother had planned to celebrate his alliance with the terribly proper and steel-willed Miss Otterleigh. And Lord Dake himself had thought he'd understood his own motives well enough. He had sustained a visit from Elliot's mama which had reminded him anew of how ruthlessly that redoubtable lady dominated Elliot and how she looked to her protegée, Miss Otterleigh, to carry on in her tradition. He had been inspired partly by his fondness for his cousin and partly by his dislike of Elliot's mama to encourage his cousin's rare act of rebellion. But now, looking down into Melody's lovely face, Lord Dake was not entirely able to acquit himself of other, less noble motives for involving himself in her affairs. This was all more complicated than the romp he'd considered it to be, and he could no longer absolve himself from blame for aiding Melody in compromising herself. It was time that this little adventure came to an end, Lord Dake reflected sadly, before any real harm was done.

So resolved, he tried once again to lead Melody towards the inn door, and this time she followed him willingly enough. Tom came up to them in the stable-yard and reported that Mr. Steele's team had been stabled and that their owner was inside the inn.

"And has Mr. Montgomery gone on his way?" Lord Dake enquired.

"Yes. The men you sent pulled his phaeton out of the ditch and fixed the wheel up well enough for him to get back to the city," Tom said. "But he wasn't happy about it."

"And my cousin's team? Are they intact?"

Tom frowned. "I hope so, sir. Mr. Steele would have it that Champion's right foreleg has been strained. I don't see any signs of it yet, but it does feel a bit warm. I promised I'd keep an eye on it for him."

"I'm sure it is not a grievous injury, or Elliot would never leave him, not even in your capable hands," Lord Dake observed. "May we take advantage of your good nature and place Melody's dog into your care as well? We left him in the courtyard behind the inn, but I believe you could settle him more comfortably in the stables with Champion, if you would."

"I'd be glad to," Tom said willingly. "No trouble at all. I'll fix him up a nice pad in the stall with me, Melody. I'm staying there all night to be sure the horses are all right anyway, and it's no more trouble to keep an eye on him as well."

"Thank you." Melody demonstrated her gratitude with an impulsive kiss on Tom's dusty cheek. She did not seem to notice his blush, but Lord Dake did; it served to confirm his suspicion that Elliot was not the only one in grave danger of falling under the spell of Melody's unconscious charm. The sooner she could be got safely back home, the better for them all. He thanked Tom courteously for his help, and he and Melody proceeded to the threshold of the inn, where they were once again greeted by the aggrieved Mrs. Pitt.

"That cousin of yours has come, sir. He's in the parlour. Wanting a room immediately to change for supper, he was. I told him they weren't ready yet. I can't have people barging in here at all times demanding rooms. Your cousin will have to wait till his room is ready, and that's all there is to it."

"I'm sure Elliot will survive, Mrs. Pitt. But I hope you have my ward's room ready; she will definitely want to change before dinner."

Lord Dake accompanied his remarks with what Melody was coming to think of as his quelling look, and the landlady's gaze shifted away. Melody tried not to be glad of her discomfort. She had not quite forgiven Mrs. Pitt for her lack of sympathy for the injured dog or for the rudeness with which she had spoken to Melody herself. In her heart she knew that it was only Lord Dake's title and his bearing which had brought about the change in Mrs. Pitt as well as Dr. Simms, but it was hard not to feel just a little triumphant, as if she herself had somehow been vindicated by Lord Dake's companionship.

Mrs. Pitt picked up Melody's one bandbox, which had been sitting in the entrance hall since the stable-boy had unloaded Mr. Steele's chaise. "The young lady's room is ready," she said sullenly. "I can take you up if you like, miss."

"Yes, thank you," Melody replied. She looked up at Lord Dake and smiled warmly at him. "I shall be down shortly," she said. "Please don't suppose I shall keep you waiting long for dinner."

"There is no hurry," he assured her. "Mr. Steele and I shall share a pitcher of ale while we wait, and I am sure he will find enough to say about his horses and the rigours of the accident to fill the time."

She smiled at him, and turned to follow the plainly disapproving Mrs. Pitt up the stairs. Lord Dake watched until she was out of sight, then shook his head ruefully and made his way to the kitchens to arrange for some bread and cheese to be sent to Tom in the stables. He also arranged for dinner to be served in the private parlour after Melody had had time to wash and change her clothes, and for more ale to be brought to him and Elliot in the meantime. Then, having accomplished all he could for the moment think to do, he went to join Elliot in the parlour.

CHAPTER FIVE

THE PARLOUR WAS A COOL and dimly lit refuge from the
heat of the day, and Lord Dake made his way to it appreciatively. It was some seconds before his eyes had adjusted
to the dimness and he was able to see his cousin Elliot sitting at a small table in a corner of the room with a tankard
of ale before him. He took his own ale from an unsavoury,
sallow-faced minion, and went to join his cousin. Elliot appeared to be lost in a fit of brooding, but he looked up when
his cousin sat down across from him, and he smiled warmly
at him.

"Bredon! Thank God you're here."

"Do you know, that has been your habitual greeting to
me lately, Elliot. I can't think why you are always so pleased
to see me."

"Of course you know why, Bredon," his cousin replied
with a rueful grin. "It's because you're the best man I know
for getting a fellow out of a scrape. But I was never so surprised as when you drove up on us. I thought you said you
were washing your hands of this one."

"So I did. And I meant it, too. But then it occurred to me
that you were very likely making a muddle of things, and I
thought I'd better come along and see what needed to be
done to set them to rights."

His cousin smiled gratefully at him, not at all offended by
Lord Dake's ironic tone. "Just as always, Bredon," he said.

"I've lost track of the number of times you've come by the rescue for me."

Lord Dake took a deliberate drink of ale, then set his tankard down. "Only for the sake of family honour, I assure you, Elliot. If our relationship were not so well-known, I'd leave you to muddle through on your own, but word would get round that I had a black-sheep cousin, and that would be a black eye for the family. And speaking of black eyes, are you aware that you are developing a fine one?"

Elliot, who did not always understand his cousin's jests but who did know when he was being teased, merely grinned again. "Aware of it! I should say I was aware. Hurts like the devil."

"No more than you deserve, I'd say, for provoking the phlegmatic Mr. Montgomery into fisticuffs. However did you come to block the road and cause such a disaster, Elliot? My faith in your skill as a driver is badly shaken."

"I didn't!" Elliot said indignantly. "I didn't do it at all. It was that dratted boy!"

"Tom?"

"Yes, Tom, devil take him. Not that I should blame the boy. Melody saw that sapskull in the phaeton about to run over the cur, and she shouted for me to stop him. Well, I would have done my best, Bredon, especially since I could see she'd never give me a moment's peace otherwise. But I didn't stop quick enough for her and she shouted again, and before I knew what was going on the boy grabbed the reins and dragged on them. Pulled the chaise right across the road, and I'm afraid it's lamed one of my team."

"That would be a pity," Lord Dake agreed. "I'm surprised that Tom would be so reckless with your safety and that of your cattle."

"Well, I'm not," Elliot said firmly. "That boy would do anything Melody asked him to do. You may have been right after all about them being runaway lovers, Bredon. He's plainly besotted with her."

"Yes, I thought so," his cousin replied calmly. "But she doesn't seem as besotted with him, does she?"

"Lord, I don't know. I don't understand women. I never have, and as for knowing what one of them is thinking, I gave up on that long ago. I thought Melody was a gently bred maiden in distress, but she can take care of herself, believe me."

"Is your fit of knight errantry over so soon, then, Elliot?" his lordship asked.

Elliot had the grace to blush. He was a kind man, but he was also a conventional one, and the morning's activities had shocked him to the core. Melody's innocent reliance upon him had given rise to a surge of chivalry on his part which had led him to throw caution to the winds and embark on what he knew to be a reckless escapade. But reckless escapades were not characteristic of Mr. Steele. His mama had trained him well, and he had as great a horror of offending the strict conventions of Society as she. He drained his tankard dry, then looked up frankly into his cousin's eyes.

"You were right, Bredon," he said. "I was a fool to get mixed up with the two of them. I thought Melody needed my protection, but if the truth be known it's I who has a greater need of protection from her. After she made Tom cause the accident, she jumped down before I knew what she was at and ran to where that damned dog had been thrown. Took him up in her arms despite the blood and the dirt, and carried him back up to the chaise when she found out he was still alive. And you should have heard her demanding to be taken to where we could have a doctor see to the dog, just as cool as you please. I was trying to see if Champion had been hurt, and the driver of the phaeton had just climbed up onto the road and was trying to assess the damage to his rig, and all she could think of was that dog.''

"She seems to be a rather single-minded young woman," Dake agreed. "I noticed it during our first conversation."

"Single-minded! She's as stubborn as a mule! And as wild as a tiger. You should have seen her," Elliot went on, plainly shocked. "Mr. Montgomery had come up to us, and was berating us for blocking the road. As well he might! I was never so embarrassed in my life, Bredon, but it didn't bother her at all. She flew out at him, telling him it was no more than he deserved for running down a poor little dog. He was furious, naturally, and you can't blame him for that. But the way he eyed me when he'd got a look at us all fairly froze my blood. You could see it in his face plain as day that he thought we were up to no good. You should have heard what he said to her, too. That is to say, no, you should not have. You'd have knocked his ugly words right back down his throat. Which is what I would have done, too, only young Tom got to him first. Still, I did draw his cork.''

"So I saw," his cousin replied. "But the point is that you can hardly blame the man for thinking anything else, not if he is to judge from appearances, at least."

"Exactly. The thing is, Bredon, I didn't stop to think how it looked. But then when that bacon-brained fop looked us over, and I saw what he was thinking, you could have knocked me over with a feather. Of course, Melody didn't understand what he was implying. It went right over her head, and would have done even if she hadn't been too caught up with that damned dog to notice anything else. But I noticed, and I didn't like it at all. But before I could so much as say a word, Tom threw himself on Mr. Montgomery—just waded in with his fists flying.''

"Quite a champion," Lord Dake observed, barely able to hold back his laughter at the shocked look on his cousin's face.

"You may think so, Bredon," Elliot retorted. "I could only think he's gone mad. And the upshot of it was that Melody started crying out to me to help Tom, and when I went to his rescue the three of us ended up in a brawl. And there was Melody, as cool as you like! I'd have thought a gently bred female would swoon at such a scene, but not she! I was never so glad to see you in my life when you came up and took her away with you."

"You looked more thunderstruck than glad," Lord Dake teased. "I hope you didn't think I was trying to dim your lustre as knight errant."

Mr. Steele shook his head wonderingly. "I'm not the brightest man in the world, Bredon, but I know when I'm in over my head. This is all too much for me."

"The situation is somewhat complicated," Lord Dake agreed. "Aside from everything else, there is the appearance of it all to consider. Do you know, I believe Mrs. Pitt was about to refuse us a room for the night when I spoke to her. I had to become very firm and flourish my wealth and position before her eyes in order to make her relent. And even now I don't think that is going to be enough to keep her quiet indefinitely."

"You're probably right," his cousin agreed gloomily. "Though she ought to be able to see that Melody's a mere child herself, and as innocent as—as a little kitten. Mrs. Pitt ought to trust her even if she doesn't trust us."

"I'm not sure that Melody is such a child as you perceive her to be, Elliot," Lord Dake replied. "But even if Mrs. Pitt shared your view of the girl, that would probably only make things worse. I do not want to be thought to be abducting a child too innocent to know what danger she is in, and I don't suppose you do, either.''

''No, no! Absolutely not,'' Elliot cried in horror. ''You're quite right, Bredon. I can't imagine why I couldn't see it this morning. All I could think of was that Melody was unhappy and that Tom couldn't be trusted to take care of her himself. You'll admit yourself he couldn't, after the way he let that Captain Sharp separate him from their travelling funds, and couldn't think of anything else for them to do but spend the night in my stables.''

''I have said from the beginning that Tom was not an adequate escort,'' Lord Dake pointed out. ''Where we differed was over *your* suitability for the role.''

''Well, we don't differ any more, Bredon. I know I'm not suited for it. God, I thought it would be easy. I'd just quietly take Melody North, and when we got close enough to where we were going that she'd have to tell me her destination, I'd take her there and hand her over to her aunt, no questions asked and no one the wiser. But I ought to have known it wouldn't be that easy. Even if the aunt did take her with no questions asked, and now that I think about it I can see that she would not be likely to, I'll never get Melody that far without half the world knowing about it. She's hardly inconspicuous, especially if she goes on causing scenes like the one today, and I'm bound to run into half the people I know on the road.''

''Do you anticipate a mass migration of your acquaintances northwards?'' his lordship could not resist asking.

''Yes, laugh at me if you wish, Bredon,'' his long-suffering cousin replied. ''But you know I'm right. That's simply the way it is. Whenever I go anywhere I always run into just those people I want most to avoid, and I've no reason to suppose this trip would be any exception. Why, just last week I was at Almack's, and who should I run smack into but our Aunt Adelia. Last person in the world I wanted to see, but there she was. Not that I'm not fond of Aunt Adelia," he added piously. "It's just that she asks so many questions, and she's so deaf she shouts and makes you shout back. It's embarrassing talking to her in public at all, but at a place like Almack's you think that half the world is listening while you bellow out all the answers to the most personal questions she can think of to ask. And she always asks personal questions."

"She doesn't ask me personal questions."

"That's because she knows you won't answer her anyway," his cousin retorted. "You're very rude to her, Bredon."

"Nonsense. You are simply too kind, Elliot. You've got to learn to say no. That is why you are in this scrape, come to think of it. Let that teach you what happens when you are overly kind."

"And what about you, Bredon?" his cousin retorted. "Why are *you* in this scrape?"

The baron's eyes lit up with irrepressible laughter. "I believe it must be a judgement upon me," he said with a chuckle. "I came to join you from the most uncharitable motives, and now I'm being punished for it."

"Why say your motives are uncharitable? You came to help me out of a scrape, didn't you? I call that charitable."

"Unfortunately, Elliot, I came more to disoblige your mama than to oblige you. And as I should know by now, my sins will always find me out."

"Mama! Has she been to see you?"

"You must know that she has, Elliot. She always does when she has fault to find with you, and I had scarcely returned from your apartments this morning when she turned up at my doorstep to complain that you had not kept your appointment with her the evening before. She's convinced all of your failings can be attributed to my influence, you see, so it is only fair that I should be responsible for you."

He spoke lightly, but Elliot coloured and gave him an apologetic glance. "It is very wrong of her to do so, Bredon. I cannot understand why she thinks you responsible for me. I have told her many times it is not so, but Mama is hard to convince when she fixes an idea in her mind."

"Which happens rarely," Lord Dake murmured sweetly.

Elliot's flush deepened, and he looked away. "I don't blame you for not getting along with Mama, Bredon," he said quietly. "I know she can be difficult. Her nerves, you know. She's very sensitive. And she's overly protective of me since my father died. I suppose she feels I'm all she has to rely on. But I won't make excuses for her. I know how hard it is for you to have your many kindnesses to us returned with such ingratitude. No wonder you are tired of us all."

"Don't be absurd," said Lord Dake, who perceived that his teasing had genuinely disturbed his kind-hearted cousin at last. "I'm not in the least tired of you, and I won't be unless you insist on taking me seriously when any looby should know it's only my devilish levity. But I should not have spoken that way about Aunt Clarice, and I am sorry. Am I forgiven?"

Mr. Steele took his cousin's outstretched hand with both his hands and shook it heartily. "Idiot," he said fondly, which Lord Dake correctly took as a sign of forgiveness. He dropped Dake's hand to pour them both more ale, evidently finding apologies a thirsty business. They drank in silence for a few minutes.

"Was my mother very angry?" Mr. Steele asked at last. "She must have been. I'm missing the engagement dinner this evening."

"Engagement dinner?" Lord Dake queried innocently.

"You know, Bredon," Elliot prompted. "We were supposed to dine with Miss Otterleigh and her parents. In formal acknowledgement of our engagement."

"Oh, yes," his lordship answered carelessly. "I believe she did mention something of the sort."

"I quite forgot that Mama was coming into Town last night to make the final arrangements," Mr. Steele confessed. "Melody and Tom showing up in my stables put it right out of my head. And this morning, I tried to write a note to Mama and to Miss Otterleigh explaining why I could not keep our engagement this evening, but no matter how many times I started I could never write anything that seemed to make the least sense. I decided I'd better wait till I returned to Town and explain it to them in person. Mama will be quite angry, and justly so. She's gone to a great deal of trouble to see that things go well between Miss Otterleigh and me. And Miss Otterleigh will be very upset, of course. But no doubt she will understand when I explain," he ventured hopefully.

"Oh, do you think so?" enquired his lordship with polite surprise. "You must know the young lady better than I, of course. I admit I had not thought her the understanding type."

Elliot's eyes narrowed thoughtfully, but he said nothing. Lord Dake sipped at his ale, wisely allowing his cousin time to think. After a few minutes Elliot looked up and noticed Lord Dake's gaze upon him. He blushed again, and took another swallow of ale.

"I'm sorry, Bredon," he said with an attempt at briskness. "If you said something, I didn't hear. I've been thinking about Champion's leg," he added.

Lord Dake accepted this obvious excuse with a polite nod.

"I'm afraid he may have strained it when Tom pulled them up so sharp," Elliot went on. "I've put a fermentation on it, but we'll have to stay the night at least and see whether it's swollen in the morning. I've got nothing against dogs, Bredon, and you know I'm as soft-hearted as the next fellow, but when I think of a horse like Champion possibly lamed just because of a mangy little cur, I can't believe it. But I suppose it might have been worse," he added gloomily. "It's a wonder that phaeton didn't plunge right into us, and Lord only knows how badly the horses might have been injured then."

"Or the passengers."

"Yes, of course," his cousin agreed perfunctorily. It was plainly a less horrifying thought to him.

"Elliot, you're as single-minded in your way as Melody is," Bredon laughed. "With you it's the horses, though, and not the dog."

"Well, horses are valuable animals," Elliot said defensively, and Lord Dake laughed again.

"You are right, of course," he admitted. "Come, have some more ale. I've ordered dinner for Melody and us in here, and have had something sent out to Tom in the stables. He tells me he is spending the night with the horses."

"Yes. I'd have done so myself, but I can't take any more of young Tom's company for a while. No matter what I say, I can't get him to see that he or Melody has done anything amiss."

"Poor Elliot! It's a wonder you haven't strangled them both. Put it out of your head for now, and drink up. We'll tackle the problem of what's to be done next after we've had something to eat."

CHAPTER SIX

THEY HAD NOT FINISHED their second tankards of ale when Melody came into the room to join them. She had managed to transform herself during the short time since she had parted from Lord Dake. Her hair was no longer tumbling down her back; her soft curls were carefully combed and subdued, twisted into a neat knot at the back of her neck. She had changed the blood-stained blue gown for a simply cut dress in soft dove grey, trimmed with cherry-coloured ribbons at the throat and bodice. She looked clean and neat and demure. She smiled warmly at both of them as they rose, and Lord Dake pulled out a chair for her.

"I feel so much better now," she said as she sat. "Knowing that that little dog is safe, and Tom is watching over him. Did you send some food out for him, my lord?" she added with a slight return of anxiety.

"I did indeed. Tom has no doubt dined well by now, and here is Mrs. Pitt with our dinner as well."

"Lovely. I'm very hungry, for all that Mr. Steele served us an enormous breakfast before we set out this morning."

Mrs. Pitt, placing a platter of cold ham before them, sniffed audibly. Mr. Steele began to blush a rosy red, and Melody shot him an apologetic look. She turned to Lord Dake to find him once again looking correct and remote, but she was becoming more adept at reading him and had no difficulty in recognizing the fugitive laughter in his eyes. She felt an answering laughter within herself, but for Mr.

Steele's sake she choked it back and said nothing until Mrs. Pitt had made her exit. Then she smiled and helped herself to a roll and a thin slice of Cheshire cheese. Mr. Steele, who found himself succumbing anew to her charm, peeled and sliced an apple for her in a feeble attempt to cushion the blow which he knew was to come. Melody, unsuspecting, thanked him warmly. He poured a glass of lemonade for her, then felt his cousin's sardonic eye upon him and subsided, blushing.

"What do you think we should call him?" Melody asked suddenly. Both gentlemen looked at her in confusion, and she gave a bubbly laugh. "Oh, I'm sorry. I was thinking about something and just burst out as if you would know what I was speaking of. I am always doing that, and people are always complaining of how shatter-brained I am. Why, my guardian, Mr. Stan—" She broke off suddenly and coloured, throwing them a guilty look. Encountering nothing but further bewilderment from Mr. Steele and a blandly attentive gaze from Lord Dake, she hurried on as if to persuade them that the near slip had never occurred.

"My guardian always says I shall convince people I am feeble-minded if I don't stop bursting out with things like that. He says that the art of conversation involves sharing one's ideas in an orderly sequence, and not just producing the conclusion of one's silent reasoning out of thin air, so to speak. He's given to sarcasm, though. Rather like you, Lord Dake. It's one of his greatest faults," she added candidly.

Mr. Steele choked back a startled guffaw, but Lord Dake maintained his air of polite interest. Melody realized what she had said and blushed unhappily, putting down the slice of apple at which she had been nibbling in order to explain.

"Oh, I didn't mean it that way," she said. "I mean, you are very sarcastic sometimes, but I wouldn't call it one of your greatest faults."

"No doubt it is eclipsed by many others," Lord Dake agreed amiably.

"No, that is not what I mean at all," Melody said in dismay. "I mean it is not a fault in your case. Some people are sarcastic in order to hurt other people; that is what my guardian does. But your sarcasm just comes from your sense of irony, I think. It is not a sign of ill nature. Please believe I did not mean to criticize you. Why, you're kindness itself."

"You must have me confused with my cousin, Melody," Lord Dake said calmly. "He is notoriously kind-hearted. And I am not."

"I don't believe that. You are indeed kind-hearted. Only think how Mr. Steele's first thought after Tom and I turned up at his stables was to ask you what he should do. He would not have thought to do that if it were not natural for him to turn to you when he finds himself in difficulty. And look how you did come the very next morning. And even though you were cross because I would not tell you what you wanted to know, you changed your mind and came after us to rescue us on the road. And when I needed your help with Dr. Simms you were quick to give it. Our little dog owes his very life to your kindness, you know," she added with a blinding look of gratitude. "And that brings me to what I meant to say before. What do you think we should call the dog?"

Lord Dake looked down at her thoughtfully for a moment. He wondered again if Elliot was falling under her spell. She was undeniably lovely. Small wonder if Elliot was smitten again, but Lord Dake regretted to think that he might lose his ally in the argument which he sensed was coming. He looked at his cousin now, but he could read nothing in Elliot's rather blank expression. He turned back to Melody.

"Lucky," he said.

She wrinkled her nose charmingly. "Lucky? That seems odd for a dog that was almost trampled to death."

"Ah, but he wasn't trampled, was he, and by all rights he should have been. And he was rescued by you, which makes him very lucky indeed."

She laughed delightfully. "Very well," she said. "Since he owes his life to you, my lord, it is only fitting that he should owe his name to you as well. Lucky he is."

She went on with her meal then, chatting happily about Lucky and about a dog she had had as a child. Watching her, Lord Dake marvelled. She was poised right at the brink of womanhood, possessing initiative, a sense of responsibility, and a concern for others that were all the mark of maturity. But she possessed as well an almost devastating candour and a curious unconsciousness of her own beauty and the effects it might have on others. There was in her a complete absence of the tendency to achieve her will by a flirtatious display of her attractions which Lord Dake had so often perceived in other young ladies of his acquaintance. In fact, that was precisely the problem. She was all too unaware of her own charm, and of the dangers into which her trust and innocence might lead her. He felt a moment of very real fear at the thought of what might have befallen her if she and Tom had ended up in the stables of someone less honourable and kind than Elliot. The fear made him interrupt her chatter brusquely.

"If you have finished your meal now, Melody, we must talk of what we are to do next."

"Oh, yes," she said seriously. "It's always best to have a plan. I suppose if Mr. Steele's horses are injured—and I certainly hope they are not—he must leave them stabled here for some time. Shall we stay here with them, or do we proceed northwards and leave them behind?"

"Neither," Lord Dake said grimly. "We turn round first thing in the morning and take you back to London."

"London! But I don't wish to go to London," she protested.

"I know," Lord Dake said. "Unfortunately, one is not always able to have what one wishes in this life. And what you must do now, child, is tell us the name of your guardian and where you live. Then we shall take you to him and I shall explain things as best I can. I promise you that I shall tell him that you have been unhappy and shall ask whether you might go to live with your aunt if that is what you wish. He may listen to me, though he's more likely to blast me for my impertinence," he added fairly. "Still, I shall try. But you must tell us his name now."

"No, I shan't tell you," Melody said quietly but firmly. Her brown eyes looked up at Lord Dake very directly, and he could see her disappointment in them. "I thought you were my friends," she said. "I thought you had changed your mind and agreed to take me to my aunt."

"I told you that I had changed my mind and agreed to help my cousin," Lord Dake countered gently. "I believe I can best do that by helping him to take you home before you endanger your life and reputation further."

"I see." Lord Dake steeled himself against the sorrow in her voice. "But Mr. Steele, you will still help me, won't you?" she added anxiously.

Elliot looked miserably down at the table. "You must listen to my cousin, Melody," he said. "You must go back home to your guardian before your reputation is ruined forever. It may already be too late, but perhaps Bredon and I together can make your guardian see that this has just been a youthful prank and not the sign of real wickedness on your part."

Melody pushed her chair back from the table, and shook her head. "I can't go back, not now," she said. "You don't know what he is like. He'll preach to me, and he'll keep such a close guard over me that I'll never have a chance to be free again."

"That is what you must expect, after the way that you have behaved," Lord Dake said, hating himself as he said it. "In time, though, perhaps you can earn his trust again. But either way, you must go back to London tomorrow, child."

"No! I *won't* go back. You can't make me! And I'm not a child," Melody added, and proved her point by running from the room and up the stairs. Lord Dake followed her out into the passage, and listened for her bedroom door to slam shut. Satisfied, he returned to Mr. Steele.

"Cheer up, Elliot," he said. "She'll come round in the end, and we really have no choice in the matter."

"No, of course we don't," Elliot agreed listlessly. "But I feel like a traitor anyway." He bid his cousin good-night then and went up to their room. Lord Dake sat alone in the parlour for some time, finishing off the decanter of brandy Mrs. Pitt had left. But even when it was gone, he thought that Elliot was right. He had Melody's best interests at heart, but he, too, felt as if he had betrayed the girl.

CHAPTER SEVEN

MELODY AWOKE well before dawn. She had gone up to her room and to bed so early the night before that she felt quite alert and refreshed. She sat up in the bed, pulling the bed-covers into a snug nest around her. It was time to consider her position and what she should do next. She would not return to London as Lord Dake wished. He did not understand, and Melody could not really blame him for that. Lord Dake was a kind man, a very kind man, and very handsome, too—though, she reminded herself sternly, that was hardly relevant. Melody had been disappointed with him and with poor Mr. Steele the night before, but now she was not.

If she had been abused, if her guardian had neglected her welfare or stolen her inheritance or treated her badly, Melody was sure that Lord Dake would have come to her rescue. Lord Dake, she was beginning to understand, was very good at coming to one's rescue. But he did not understand what it was she needed to be rescued from. Lord Dake could not know how it felt to watch the certainty of an unhappy future swallow one up. He could not know how it was to feel helpless to make those who had the power to make decisions which would affect the rest of your life understand what it was you wanted. Her guardian, Mr. Stanhope, was a kind enough man, but he was so sure that he knew what she needed and what was best for her that he could not stop to see how different she was from his notion of her. Mr.

Stanhope's view of a suitable match for his ward was nothing like her own and was bound to end with her wed to a man who was as unsympathetic and ignorant as he himself was of Melody's real nature. Melody thought she knew how it would be to be married to a man who did not share her sense of humour, who frowned at her wit, who believed that book learning was largely unnecessary and ideas almost deadly in a woman. Mr. Stanhope was such a man, and so were the men to whom he had introduced her over the Christmas holidays.

Melody knew how difficult it could be for a young girl to determine her own future. She knew how unstoppable the machinery of engagement and marriage was once a public announcement had been made. Marriage was a finality, and she did not harbour the illusion that once wed she could do anything to save herself. She had seen other girls at Mrs. Beehan's, girls whose parents had compelled them to accept the hand of a man who could never please them, girls whose eyes were bright with fear as they smiled and went through the public rituals of engagement and courtship. No, if she was to be rescued it had to be now, before any match had been settled upon, before a connection was made public. And since only she could understand how abhorrent marriage to the wrong sort of man would be for her, only she could rescue herself. She could not rely on Lord Dake, kind though he was.

And he *was* kind. Melody thought of how she had misjudged him. Yes, he could be autocratic and he knew how to rebuke pretension with a cold stare, and he was stubborn, and convinced that he knew best. But he was also a kind and caring man, and she had seen in him a thoughtfulness and a concern for others that surprised her after that first unhappy meeting in Mr. Steele's mews. And even then, Melody was sure, she had seen flashes of laughter in his grey eyes, and an appreciative acknowledgement of another's points well-made even during an argument. And if he was managing, was it any wonder? From what he and Mr. Steele had told her, Lord Dake's family were in the habit of turning to him with all their difficulties. He had had a lot of practice at managing the affairs of others, a fact which did him far more credit than indifference would have.

Wistfully, she wondered why Mr. Stanhope could not have invited a man like Lord Dake to dine with them last Christmas. Of course, Lord Dake himself had shown no signs of being interested in her as a future wife or even as a woman. He called her child, and it was clear to Melody that that was how he thought of her. But she was not a child. And she could not deny to herself, at least, that she was very attracted to him. Nor was Lord Dake too old for her. Why, he surely could not be as much as thirty years old, and Lord Ashburne, whom Mr. Stanhope had seated next to her at dinner one night, must have been nearly fifty and deaf as a post into the bargain. He had stared rudely at Melody, answered her few conversational gambits with a grunt, then proceeded to talk about his estate and his lands for the rest of the evening, all the while gobbling his food as if he had been starved for weeks. Lord Dake would never have been guilty of any of these failings.

But Lord Dake was not an unattractive and self-absorbed elderly peer. He was young and handsome and intelligent and rich. He could have any young lady he desired, just for the asking. He had been charming to her in the carriage as they rode to the inn, never once even pointing out the disastrous consequences of her actions. And in the courtyard where he'd sat with her while she was waiting for Dr. Simms, his words had indicated a generous and sensitive nature, as well as a lively wit and appreciation of the ridiculous. He was a wonderful man, but his kindness to her had been simply that: kindness and nothing more. It was useless to imagine that he would be interested in a hoydenish runaway given to disastrously candid statements, impatient with the circumscribed role which young ladies were expected to play, ignorant of how to charm or attract a man. Useless and a waste of time. And Melody had no time to waste. Resolutely she put the futile thought of Lord Dake aside. She had plans to lay.

On the whole, Melody thought it would be best if she proceeded quite alone. It would have been quite comfortable if the four of them could have travelled on together, but Lord Dake had declared an end to their adventure, and Melody knew that Tom would be unhappy and worried if she tried to convince him to defy Lord Dake. Tom was diffident by nature, like poor Mr. Steele, and neither of them was capable of outright rebellion against Lord Dake. Besides, Tom would not like to leave Mr. Steele's horses until their injuries were quite healed. No, it would be best if she went on by herself.

Melody felt quite sad at the prospect of leaving the others behind. She would have liked to take Lucky, at least, along with her to keep her company, but she was practical enough to see that a young woman travelling alone might find her progress seriously impeded by the companionship of a crippled dog, and she consoled herself with the thought that she had consigned Lucky to Tom's care. She realized a little sadly that her splendid adventure was turning into a rather lonely and humdrum journey, and one that she had best resume as soon as possible.

IN THE ROOM he and his cousin were sharing, Lord Dake slept several hours later than Melody, though he woke shortly after dawn. He rose and dressed quickly, taking no care to be particularly quiet, but Elliot did not stir until Dake tossed a boot onto his bed.

"Come on, sleepyhead," he chided. "Do you plan to lay there snoring all day?"

Elliot sat up, yawning mightily. "I don't snore."

"Then some wild animal spent the night with us," his cousin retorted, "because the sound of something snoring kept me up half the night."

"Lord, I didn't know you were so delicate, Bredon," Elliot said with a grin as he climbed out of his bed. "Did the bedlinens chafe your skin, too?"

Lord Dake smiled at his cousin's sally, but only briefly. The thought of the day's activities to come, activities in which he could not help but feel he featured as chief villain, had lowered his spirits considerably. He turned back to the cracked and none-too-clean dresser mirror and began to arrange his cravat as he spoke.

"We must lay our plans, Elliot."

"Yes, indeed," his cousin agreed, suddenly stirring into vigorous activity as he gathered up his clothes and began donning them. "I must go out first thing and see how Champion's leg is doing."

"Indeed you must. But I warn you, Elliot, even if the horse is lame I believe you must accompany us back to Town. It would not do for one of us to travel alone with Melody; we shall have enough explaining to do to her guardian as it is. And I need not tell you that Tom scarcely comprises a suitable chaperon."

"Yes, of course. I suppose I can leave Champion in the care of these villagers for a day if I must. I don't like to, of course, but you are quite right. It will look bad enough as it is, there's no use to make it worse. But Bredon, what will we do if the girl refuses to tell us who her guardian is?"

"I will have to make some discreet enquiries when we return to Town. A gently bred girl cannot disappear without causing some excitement, after all. And in the meantime, we'll have to take Melody to stay with your mama and sisters."

"With Mama! Are you mad, Bredon? Do you know what Mama would say if I explained that I had missed the engagement party because I was squiring a young girl about the countryside and that now I would like her to keep the girl with her until we can find where she belongs? We cannot take her to my Mama."

"Well, to Aunt Adelia, then."

"Just as well hire a town crier, Bredon. Aunt Adelia would spread the news all over Town faster than you can say scandal. If you want the matter handled discreetly, Aunt Adelia mustn't get a word of it."

"Then it will have to be your Mama, Elliot. But don't worry. I doubt it will come to that. Once the girl sees we are adamant, she will have no choice but to tell us who her guardian is. Now, I shall order up some breakfast and have Mrs. Pitt rouse Melody. You go and look in on Champion. If he can travel, then you can have your team harnessed and can take Melody and Tom up with you again and I'll ride along behind. If his leg is too bad we can hitch my team to your landau and leave my phaeton here with your greys. We shall all have to fit in your landau together. It'll be tight, but Tom can ride up behind and we must manage."

"If Tom rides up behind, who'll look after the dog?" Elliot asked suspiciously.

"We'll leave it behind with the horses. I don't mind forcing four people into a vehicle best meant for three, but I'll be damned if I'll have an injured dog shoved in with us."

"Melody will never consent to leave the dog behind," Mr. Steele predicted.

"Melody will be obliged to accept it," Lord Dake said grimly. "I doubt her guardian will allow her to keep the cur anyway."

Mr. Steele looked for a moment as if he would protest, but then he caught his cousin's eye in the mirror and wisely decided to forbear. He finished his toilet hurriedly, though he did take the time to tie his cravat in a precise Mathematical, then set out for the stables to check his horse's injuries. Lord Dake rose from the dressing-table, eased himself into his snugly tailored riding coat and set off to complete his part of the preparations for travel. Mrs. Pitt promised to have breakfast laid for them in the parlour within the hour, but when he asked her to rouse Melody, she came back shortly to report her mission had been unsuccessful. The young lady's room, she reported, was quite empty.

Lord Dake felt a moment of panic. He ought to have realized that Melody had acquiesced too readily the night before. Obviously she had been planning some mischief. But then reason reasserted itself. She would not have set off alone in the night. No doubt she was in the stables right now, seeing to that wretched dog. She would come in with Elliot and Tom for breakfast.

So certain was he of this that Lord Dake was quite surprised when Elliot came in alone to breakfast. He sat across from where his cousin was waiting at the table, and poured himself a cup of tea.

"I knew it," he said gloomily before Lord Dake had a chance to say a word. "Champion's in no condition to travel. I shall have to leave him here and come back for him after we get Melody to London. I've given orders for your team to be harnessed."

"Is Melody not coming to breakfast?" Lord Dake asked.

"Melody?" Mr. Steele looked around the parlour vaguely, as if he suspected that she might be hiding in one of the corners. "Isn't she down yet?"

"Do you mean she was not in the stables with that dog?"

"No. I haven't seen her. I thought she was in here with you."

"Mrs. Pitt says her room is empty," his lordship said grimly. "I told myself she had merely gone out early to see to that cur, but I should have known it could not be anything so simple. The chit has given us the slip!"

"She can't have gone far," Elliot protested. "Surely she wouldn't have set out alone before dawn."

"Where is Tom?"

"He's in the stables with Champion. You know, Bredon, he's not as simple-minded as he seems. He's very good with horses, and he spent half the night applying fermentations to Champion's foreleg. Good job, too; there's no telling how much worse the injury might have been this morning without them. I'm thinking of leaving Tom here with Champion when we go; I trust him more than I do the local lads."

"I'm not as interested in his knowledge of horses as I am in his knowledge of Melody's whereabouts, Elliot," his cousin said repressively. "I'll wager that if anyone knows where Melody has gone, it'll be Tom."

But in this he was proved wrong, as Tom declared himself completely ignorant of Melody's departure from the inn. There was no doubting his sincerity or his concern when he was made to realize that she had gone. Lord Dake, looking down at him sourly, saw what a conquest Melody had made in him. No doubt the chit didn't even realize what a *tendre* the boy held for her. And who was she befriending now? The thought brought a greater urgency with it, and Lord Dake grimly organized a thorough search of the inn and the neighbouring area. Melody was not to be found, but a little of the mystery surrounding her disappearance was cleared up by Elliot, who came hurrying up to the yard where Lord Dake was supervising the harnessing of his team.

"Bredon! One of the kitchen girls says that Melody asked her where the nearest place was that one could catch the stage. She told her the coach came through Grampton. It's about ten miles down the road. Said that Melody thanked her very nicely and slipped out the kitchen door. Thought she was going to take a little walk in the kitchen gardens, she says. Says she thought it was strange, because it was before dawn."

"Damn the girl!" Lord Dake cried. Mr. Steele was not sure whether his curse was meant for Melody or for the overly helpful kitchen maid. "Get in, Elliot, and let us go. If she's still on foot we should catch her up before she reaches Grampton."

"What if she's been picked up by someone?" Elliot asked as he climbed up into the landau.

"Then you'd better hope that it's someone with her welfare at heart. If she's fallen into the hands of someone unscrupulous enough to offer her any harm, I swear I'll see him dead before nightfall!"

Elliot stared at his normally pacific cousin. Bredon sounded downright melodramatic, which was not in his line at all. The effect was somewhat spoiled, however, by Tom, who had run off into the stables as soon as Elliot had delivered his news, and who returned now with Melody's dog in his arms. He started to scramble up into the chaise, but Lord Dake barred his way.

"Get rid of that dog, you fool," he snapped. "This is no time to be burdened with that cur."

Tom glared up in anger, his normal awe of Lord Dake forgotten. "Melody told me to take care of him," he cried out. "I promised, and I won't break my promise to her. I'm coming after her, and so's Lucky."

For a few seconds the issue hung in the balance. Then, with a muttered oath, Lord Dake pulled Tom up into the chaise and took up the reins. Tom settled in, Lucky securely in his arms, and Elliot braced himself as Lord Dake sent the horses hurtling through the stable-yard gates and onto the road to Grampton.

CHAPTER EIGHT

GRAMPTON WAS A market town, and as it was market day there were a great many vehicles coming and going, and a throng of men, women and children on its two main streets. Lord Dake was forced to slow the chaise to a walk as they entered the town, and as he surveyed the crowd around him he swore again under his breath.

"Tom, jump down and find out where the coach stops," he directed.

Tom thrust Lucky into Mr. Steele's unwilling arms and obeyed. He was back in a moment to direct them to the coaching inn. There was no sign of Melody in the coach yard or in the inn, and as the coach was not due for some hours, Lord Dake commended the landau to the care of one of the ostlers and jumped lightly down into the dusty yard.

"We'll have more chance of catching sight of her on foot," he said grimly. Mr. Steele and Tom climbed down without a word. There had been few words exchanged among them on the ride to the town. As each mile went by and there was no sight of Melody's familiar figure trudging along the road, their moods had grown more and more so-ber. Lord Dake appeared to be in a black rage, and both Elliot, who knew him well, and Tom, who did not, could see that it would be foolish in the extreme to aggravate his mood. They were all sure by now that Melody must have been taken up in someone's vehicle. If no harm had come to her, she would be somewhere in Grampton, and most likely

would be at the posting inn when the coach was due. Lord
Dake set Elliot to await her at the inn, and he and Tom set
off on foot to search the streets of the town. Mr. Steele secretly hoped that Lord Dake was not the first to find Melody. He was not afraid of his cousin, not really, but he knew
how vicious his tongue could be when he was this angry, and
he shrank to think how Bredon might lash out at the child
when he found her.

But it was Tom who put them on Melody's trail. He had
caught a glimpse of her in a wagon with a man who looked
to be a farmer. Tom had only seen them from behind, but
the slender figure of the girl and her grey travelling dress
trimmed with cherry red bows was unmistakable. For a few
minutes he chased down the street after the wagon, dodg-
ing human and animal traffic wildly, till reason returned.
The wagon was plodding along the road out of Grampton.
The road was straight, and the wagon would be in sight for
some time. Tom turned and ran back the way he had come,
searching for Lord Dake. He found him almost immediately, and the two of them hurried back to the posting inn
and their waiting carriage. As they rushed Mr. Steele in between them and Lord Dake set the horses off again, they
explained what Tom had seen to their companion.

"But why did she ask about the stage if she was planning
to travel away from Grampton in some farmer's cart?" Mr.
Steele asked querulously.

"I don't know," his lordship said grimly. "But I can
think of at least one possibility. Melody appears to have
forgotten that it takes more than a winning smile to pur-
chase a seat upon the stage. Or did she have money that I
don't know about?"

Both Tom and Mr. Steele shook their heads. "All of her
money was stolen. And since I was travelling with her and

paying for everything, it never occurred to me to lend her any.''

"Just as well it did not. She must have realized she could not pay for her passage, and has set off with this farmer in desperation. We should be able to catch up with him in no time; she cannot get away now."

Yet, as though he did not quite believe his own words, Lord Dake urged the horses on at a greater speed than the traffic on the streets could accommodate. He swerved to avoid a small child which ran out into the road, and Mr. Steele became aware for the first time that he was still holding the dog which Lord Dake had scooped up from the stable-yard and thrust into his arms when they were leaving the inn. Mr. Steele passed the animal unceremoniously to Tom and held on tightly to the carriage, which was swaying ominously. In just a few minutes Lord Dake had fought his way out of town, and on the open road he set the horses to galloping after the wagon, the cloud of dust in the wake of which was still visible up ahead.

When they had pulled up nearly behind the wagon, its driver pulled it politely to one side, as if to allow them room to pass. Tom was calling Melody's name, but she did not turn round. Indeed, she seemed unconscious of any possibility of pursuit, which surprised Lord Dake. He guided the team alongside the wagon and looked down at its occupants, a red-faced farmer and a slender, brown-faced young girl who, for all that she might have been wearing Melody's clothes, bore no other resemblance to the girl they were seeking. Tom, who had also seen the girl, gave a hoarse cry of surprise, and the farmer glanced up curiously at him without further slackening his horse's pace.

"Pull up, please," Lord Dake called out, and the farmer obeyed placidly. He gazed up at them without a word, but Lord Dake thought he saw a glint of amusement in his sharp blue eyes. If so, he thought it understandable; the three of them—four, counting Lucky, who was barking enthusiastically for no apparent reason—must have presented an odd appearance. Tom and Elliot were both gaping in surprise, and Lord Dake was afraid that his own expression was as comical.

"How may I help ye?" the farmer said, his deep voice definitely holding a current of barely suppressed laughter. Lord Dake began to speak, then subsided momentarily at a new wave of frenzied barking from the dog, which squirmed eagerly in Tom's arms.

"I beg your pardon," he tried again. "Tom, can you quiet that cur? We are looking for a young lady, and I'm afraid we've mistaken your companion for her. She wears a dress very like one belonging to the young lady we are seeking."

"Oh, aye, I'll wager she does," the farmer said comfortably. "Like my daughter's dress used to belong to your young lady. If she be the young lady we picked up on the road outside of Harley, that is."

"It seems quite likely," Lord Dake admitted with a smile. "Our young lady was making her way to Yorkshire; her name is Melody. I take it you and your daughter have taken her up?"

"That we did, sir. Saw the young thing trudging along on the side of the road, carrying her little bandbox with her. Well, naturally I stopped to see where she were making for, and when she said she wanted to go to Grampton to catch the stage, we took her up with us, seeing as we were going that way ourselves. Very sweet young lady she was, and as friendly as a little puppy, sir."

The farmer's words implied no commentary on the strangeness of Melody's circumstances nor of her curious pursuit by three men, but his shrewd eyes were watching

Lord Dake closely, and it was clear that he had his reservations about them. Lord Dake wondered what tale Melody had told her benefactor and whether he himself had figured in it as the villain. He smiled down ruefully at the farmer.

"Too friendly, I'm afraid," he said. "She has no notion of why it is not safe for her to go gallivanting about the countryside on her own, and is likely to regard everyone she meets as the most delightful companion imaginable. She is very young and inexperienced, you see, and I only hope we can find her before her innocence leads her into trouble."

The farmer looked up at Lord Dake and his companions for a long moment, then a smile lit his ruddy face.

"Well, sir, I'm bound to say if you intend the lass harm yourself you're going about it in a strange way. Most men don't bring a boy and a dog along when they're bent on such mischief."

Lord Dake perceived that Lucky's presence in the chaise might not be the unmitigated mistake he had until then thought it to be. His glance moved to take in Tom, still holding the dog tightly to his chest, then returned to the farmer.

"I assure you, sir, I wish the child no harm at all, no matter what she may have told you. And I apologize for our rather noisy companion. He had an encounter with a phaeton on the road yesterday, and Melody rescued him. He seems to have given her his heart completely from that moment, and I'm afraid that all of this ruckus now is because he has caught the scent of his new mistress on that dress your daughter is wearing."

"Aye, she told us about the little dog, sir. Seemed very sad to be leaving him behind. She told us about the rest of you, too, in her way. But she said nothing against any of you, sir; just that she had left her travelling companions behind because you'd come to a parting of your ways. She said she was going on to Yorkshire and the rest of you were returning to London, so she'd decided it would be best to take the stage the rest of the way. That's where we took her, sir. Left her off at the inn, we did. I offered to stay with her till the stage had come, but it wasn't due for hours, and she insisted she'd be all right waiting on her own. So we left her there and came on; we're going on to visit my brother and his family, and he was expecting us early, just as soon as we'd left our load of fruit there in the market. That's where we're making for now, sir."

"I see. It's no business of mine, I realize, but would you take pity on my curiosity and tell me how your daughter comes to be wearing one of Melody's gowns? Did she sell it to you in order to raise money for her fare, perhaps?"

"Lord, no, sir. It were a trade, so to speak. Your young lady was chatting away with us when we took her up in the wagon, as friendly as if we'd all known each other for years. And she was complaining how hard it were to walk in her gown. My Sarah Jane here told her how pretty it was, and she said she'd rather have Sarah Jane's clothes and shoes as they were stouter and looked more comfortable to travel in. Well, the next thing you know, sir, both girls have got it into their heads to exchange clothes. Nothing I could say would change their minds; you know how women are when they get a maggot in their heads, sir. Once we got to the inn, your Miss Melody insisted that Sarah Jane come in with her so they could switch, too. So now Sarah Jane's got this fancy get-up. Though what she's going to do with it besides show it off to all her friends is what I don't know, sir, nor what my wife will say when she lays eyes on it. No telling with a woman, sir, what way they'll take things."

Lord Dake agreed gravely that there was not, and after thanking the farmer and bidding goodbye to him and to his still-silent daughter, he turned the horses back towards Grampton, Lucky giving one last despairing yelp as they rode away from Melody's beloved scent.

"Never mind, boy," Lord Dake advised him. "We're on our way to the real thing, now, and you'll like that much better."

"But why was she not at the inn when we were there?" Mr. Steele asked.

"Your guess is as good as mine, Elliot. As our departing friend says, there's no telling what a woman will do. But she must still be in Grampton, and either she hasn't thought yet about her fare or she has hatched some plan. No doubt she will explain it all to us when we next see her. And that, if we are lucky, should be soon. I believe the coach will be coming through town in a few hours, and she will not be able to board without our seeing her."

MELODY STOOD in the market-place. The noise and clamour did not disturb her. She looked about happily, searching for the right person to approach. So far, she felt, things were going well. Leaving the inn before breakfast had proved to be easy, and the farmer and his daughter had taken her up in their cart almost the moment she reached the road. The farmer had been kind, and his daughter shy but admiring. The farmer—Mr. Felts, his name had been—had obligingly taken her right to the coaching inn in Grampton, even though it was out of his way. And he'd insisted upon waiting while she determined when the stage left and what the rate of passage was. Melody had not had the money to buy passage, of course, but she had a plan which she believed would allow her to solve that slight difficulty very handily. Not that she had told Mr. Felts. He'd turned out to be disconcertingly fatherly, and she was sure that if he had known she did not have the money she needed, he'd never have left her there. Nor had he been very enthusiastic about Melody's notion of switching clothes with his daughter. But he'd accepted her explanation that his daughter's gown was much more suited to travel on the stage than her own dress. He seemed to regard such judgements as the province of females, and had made no real protest when Melody had coaxed Sarah Jane out of the cart and into the inn where they prevailed upon the landlord for a private place in which to exchange their garments. Sarah Jane was overwhelmed into complete inarticulateness by the elegant new dress which she now possessed, but Melody was even more satisfied with the trade. The plain cotton dress with a wide skirt and no petticoats, the thick hose, and the sturdy leather boots were comfortable and practical, and Melody felt less conspicuous in them. And after she had waved goodbye to Mr. Felts and Sarah Jane, Melody had felt an enormous sense of freedom and anonymity as she'd made her way to the market-place. There was a crowd of people there, and Melody was certain that one of them would want to buy her pearl necklace and ear-bobs at a price which would enable her to buy a ticket and travel comfortably to Yorkshire in the stage.

At first Melody was a little disconcerted at how few women there were in the market-place, except for the farmers' wives selling vegetables and other foodstuffs. But there were several tradesmen and businessmen, plus a few young bucks who seemed to be out for pleasure. These latter she avoided carefully, but finally she did find a pleasant-looking middle-aged man who looked prosperous and comfortable, just the sort of man, she thought, who might want to buy a set of pearls for his young daughter or wife.

"Excuse me, sir," she began politely, "I wonder if you'd care to buy some jewellery. I'm in need of some money to book passage to Yorkshire, so I would be willing to take any fair price.''

The portly gentleman she had accosted swung round and gazed down at her in some surprise. After a moment he glanced at the pearl set which she held out towards him, then shook his head. ''Sorry, lassie,'' he said pleasantly. ''I've no need for such baubles, I'm afraid.''

''Oh.'' So strong was the image Melody had formed in her mind of the gentleman's loving wife and young daughter, that she could scarcely believe he'd turned her down. ''Wouldn't you like to buy them for your wife?'' she persisted.

The man laughed, not unkindly. ''No, dear, for my wife's been gone these twelve years, bless her. And if I did have a wife, I'd not buy her a set of pearls that's more suited for a young girl than a grown woman.''

Melody opened her mouth to thank him and to apologize for her own persistence, but before she could speak she was jostled rudely from behind and almost lost her balance.

''Here! Watch where you are going!''

Melody turned to take in the man who had shoved her. ''It was you who bumped into me, sir,'' she pointed out truthfully. ''I was not going anywhere.''

''Mind your impertinent tongue,'' the man snapped, and Melody's eyes widened in surprise. Apparently, in the simple attire of a farmer's daughter she was not even entitled to common courtesy. Before she could reply, however, the rude man, a small but very aggressive individual with a florid face and an aggrieved look, snatched the pearl necklace from her hands.

''What is this? Where did you get such trinkets, girl, and what are you doing with them here in the market?''

Melody reached for the pearls and tugged them urgently out of the man's hand. He seemed as if he would fight her for a moment. He glanced at the prosperous-looking man as if for support, but evidently he failed to find it, and he loosened his grip and let them slip from his fingers. "Is this young lady with you, sir?" the newcomer asked.

"No, I don't know her. She asked if I wished to buy the pearls for my wife, but as I told the young lady, I have no wife, and I am in no need of a set of pearls."

"And where did *you* get them?" the florid man demanded, turning back to Melody. "Those pearls aren't the sort of cheap bauble a girl like you might own. Did you steal them? Are you trying to sell stolen goods?"

"No!" Melody was indignant. "They are mine. My guardian gave them to me for Christmas three years ago. And I can sell them if I wish."

"Your guardian?" The man laughed unpleasantly and gave Melody a quick, avid glance that seemed to cover her from head to toe and brought an uncomfortable blush to her cheeks, though she could not have said precisely why. "And what sort of a guardian do you have, who lets you run free in the market-place selling his gifts? An unlikely story, if you ask me!"

"Well, I did not ask you," Melody pointed out with some asperity. "And though I don't wish to be rude, I must say that it is none of your business. It was you who bumped into me and shoved your way into what was none of your affair. I was merely asking this gentleman…" Here Melody paused in some confusion, for the pleasant-looking man was gone, evidently considering that since he did not wish to buy her pearls or become involved in an unseemly brawl, his presence was no longer required. Curiously, though she had not known him, Melody felt a slight sense of panic at his absence. He might have been an ally of sorts, at least, against the rude man, who was even now talking loudly enough to begin to draw a crowd.

"I shall tell you what business of mine it is, girl," he was saying pompously. "My brother-in-law, Mr. Lacey, is the mayor of this town, and he will be very interested to know about brazen young girls peddling stolen jewels in the market-place, you may be sure. It is a disgrace that decent folk should be subjected to such things, that's what I say!"

Melody tried to slip back into the crowd, but she was by now surrounded by an avid audience, trapping her in the unpleasant scene. A sense of panic began to overcome her. Her original plan of selling her jewels and boarding the stage before her former travelling companions could catch up with her was temporarily forgotten. All she wanted for the moment was to escape from this loud, bullying man and the increasingly hostile onlookers. The man was still talking loudly, seeming to enjoy the attention he was drawing. He was proposing that Melody should be taken before the authorities so that the possession of the pearls might be verified, and more than one voice in the crowd around them was raised in assent. They were rapidly becoming the sensation of the day, and Melody realized that alone, and a stranger as she was, she might very well have a difficult time proving her innocence. Visions of being clapped in jail, of being interrogated by the magistrate, of having to send word to Mr. Stanhope, to beg him to come and free her from this humiliating tangle, were beginning to run through Melody's mind when, to her enormous relief, she saw a familiar figure approaching through the crowd.

"Lord Dake!" she cried happily.

"What is going on here, Melody?" he asked sternly, and several participants in the scene, none of whom had witnessed his approach, whirled round to face him. He looked assured and calm, as if he found nothing to surprise or shock him in her predicament; the same could not be said of Mr. Steele, who stood aghast at his side. Melody gave them both a sunny smile of relief.

"Lord Dake, I'm so glad to see you. And you, too, Mr. Steele," she added politely. "Now you can explain to this horrid man that I am not a thief."

"Yes, of course I can," Lord Dake agreed promptly. "What I cannot explain to him is how a young lady such as yourself comes to find herself dressed in those extremely unsuitable clothes and embroiled in what appears to be a very vulgar argument in a public market-place."

"Well, I can explain *that,*" Melody said with a gurgle of relieved laughter, "if you will simply explain that I am not a thief and that I have every right to sell these jewels if I wish, because they belong to me. They do, you know," she added, displaying a simple strand of pearls and a pair of pearl ear-bobs with a touch of anxiety.

"Yes, I do know," replied his lordship with a flash of enlightenment. "There is no doubt that the jewels are yours. Whether that excuses your selling them in the market-place is another matter."

Melody's eyes sought his face uncertainly, and Lord Dake found it difficult to maintain his stern air. Now that he could see that she was safe and unharmed, the desperate worry which had oppressed him all morning was lifted, and even his anger at her recklessness began to dissipate in his lively appreciation of the absurd. One glance at his cousin Elliot's shocked face sent the rest of Dake's anger packing, so that he had to struggle to maintain his own disapproving air. But when the red-faced man who had been arguing with Melody began to speak, all inclination towards laughter fled immediately from his lordship.

"What I say is, it's a disgrace," the man declared roundly. "Look at her, sir. Dressed like that, and displaying those jewels for sale. Why, any fool can see those jewels and those clothes don't match. Don't be taken in by that pretty face— it's the young ones that are the worst, that's what I always say. She's stole those jewels, I'll wager, from her mistress. Like as not she cut her throat in the night and ran off with them. She's no gentlewoman, for all her airs. Gentle-women don't dress like that, do they, and they don't stand out in the market-place, bold as you please, for everyone to see their wares. She's no better than she should be, that's what I say. Thinks to pull the wool over people's eyes, but she can't hide what she is. The truth will out, sir, that's what I always say."

Melody turned back to him with an outraged gasp, but Lord Dake checked her with his glance.

"I have little interest in hearing any more of what you always say," he pointed out to the pugnacious man. "No doubt you may find a more appreciative audience else-where—might I suggest that you do so, and leave us to attend to our business without further interference?"

"Them that conduct their business in the market-place needn't ask for privacy," the little man pointed out indignantly. "I was just doing my duty, sir. This young woman approached me with her stolen jewels, and it's my duty to call down the law on her for it!"

There were appreciative murmurs from several of the spectators, but Lord Dake noticed that many of those who had gathered round had already slipped away, apparently not wishing to become involved in what promised to be an ugly debate. He brushed the stout man aside, and reached to take Melody's arm possessively.

"I have already told you that my ward's jewels are not stolen," he said quietly, "and that your interference is no longer needed."

"No, nor was it ever!" Melody declared vehemently. "I didn't approach you with my jewels anyway, as anyone can see you are not the sort to appreciate them. I was showing them to another gentleman, and I don't know why you felt you had to push your way into what was no business of yours."

"That will do, Melody," Lord Dake said. There was a flash of anger still in the eyes she raised to him, but she subsided, blushing slightly. Lord Dake smiled approvingly at her, and began to lead her towards the chaise. Mr. Steele trailed along as one in a trance.

"The gentleman is quite right on one point, however," Lord Dake was saying firmly. "We shall not conduct any further business in the market-place. Your jewels are not for sale, my child, and there is nothing more that we have to say that cannot better be said in private."

He half expected some protest from her, but once again she surprised him.

"You're quite right," she said as he handed her up into the chaise. "I was not entirely comfortable in the market anyway, especially after that nasty, interfering man came up. He was very rude. I'm glad you came along just then, though I don't know how you found me so soon. He was threatening to call the law, and several of the people in the crowd seemed to agree with him. I can't think why they all seemed to believe him instead of me."

Lord Dake might have enlightened her, if he could have found a way to make her see how disreputable her behaviour had been, but Melody's attention was claimed by Lucky, who along with Tom had been left to guard the chaise. He flung himself rapturously into his mistress's arms as she joined him in the chaise, and she caught him up to her in a gentle hug.

"Lucky! I'm so glad you brought him with you. I knew you wouldn't abandon him. Tom, he looks so much better. And you've bathed him, haven't you? How good of you." She broke off, laughing, as the dog began to cover her chin with enthusiastic licks, and Lord Dake took advantage of her preoccupation to drive them all back to the inn. The coach was already in the stable-yard, but Melody barely gave it a backwards glance, and once she was assured that she could bring Lucky with her, she came along with no further protests to the private parlour where Lord Dake ordered a luncheon to be served. Once they were settled, and the gentlemen had been provided with ale and Melody with lemonade to sustain them until their meal arrived, Lord Dake began the speech he had prepared.

"Melody, what you did today was very wrong," he began sternly. "You must give us your promise that you will not try to run away from us again. I assure you it is not safe for you to do so, and if you will not give us your word, you will force us to make you our virtual prisoner until we can return you to your home."

"But I don't want to be returned to my home," Melody pointed out reasonably. "And all I did was set out on my own and try to sell my jewels to pay for my passage. I did not cheat or steal or lie or do anything wrong. Why, you did worse than I, my lord," she added with a smile. "You told that man a lie when you claimed I was your ward."

"My child, I told the truth. A guardian is one to whom a minor's care has been entrusted, and providence has entrusted you to me. I am as responsible for you now as is your legal guardian. You don't know the things that can happen to a young woman who travels unprotected. Don't you see, if you slip away from our care and something dreadful happens to you, we will hold ourselves accountable, even if the law does not?"

"I hadn't thought of it that way," Melody admitted. "It didn't seem wrong to slip away from you all. Not so very wrong," she amended.

"Not so very wrong!" Mr. Steele's feelings had been pent up too long, and they exploded now. He had been genuinely concerned about Melody, but finding her unharmed and apparently cheerfully unrepentant had replaced his concern with anger. He was a serious-minded young man, and was genuinely shocked by what he had seen.

"How can you say such a thing?" he demanded. "You slipped away from us this morning and set out all on your own. You cadged a ride from that farmer and talked his daughter into exchanging clothes with you. Then you tried to sell your necklace and ear-bobs in a public market-place in front of half the rustic louts in the county. No wonder your meddlesome friend back there thought you were a thief. What gently bred female would behave as you have done? Have you no understanding of propriety? A young lady should never draw attention to herself. You could scarcely do more if you hired a musical band to accompany you wherever you go!"

Melody was visibly distressed by Mr. Steele's words. Even Tom, her self-appointed champion, seemed quashed by the tirade, and Lord Dake, who had earlier harboured a wishful fancy to box Melody's ears, found himself irrationally coming to her rescue again.

"You sound more like your mother every day, Elliot," he pointed out, wounding his cousin deeply. "Melody understands now why what she did was wrong. There is no need for you to scold her like a fishwife."

"Are you saying my mother sounds like a fishwife?" demanded the much-tried Mr. Steele.

Lord Dake had no desire to say any such thing, no matter how much he might privately think it, but before he

PLAY THE

LUCKY

CARNIVAL WHEEL

scratch-off game
and get as many as
SIX FREE GIFTS...

HOW TO PLAY:

1. With a coin, carefully scratch off the silver area at right. Then check your number against the chart below to find out which gifts you're eligible to receive.

2. You'll receive brand-new Harlequin Regency Romance™ novels and possibly other gifts—ABSOLUTELY FREE! Send back this card and we'll promptly send you the Free Books and Gifts you qualify for!

3. We're betting you'll want more of these heart-warming romances, so unless you tell us otherwise, every other month we'll send you 4 more wonderful novels to read and enjoy. Always delivered right to your home. And always at a discount off the cover price!

4. Your satisfaction is guaranteed! You may return any shipment of books and cancel at any time. The Free Books and Gifts remain yours to keep!

NO COST! NO RISK!
NO OBLIGATION TO BUY!

You'll look like a million dollars when you wear this elegant necklace! It's a generous 20 inches long and each link is double-soldered for strength and durability.

More Good News For Subscribers Only!

When you join the Harlequin Reader Service®, you'll receive 4 heart-warming romance novels every other month, delivered to your home. You'll also get additional free gifts from time to time, as well as our subscribers-only newsletter. It's your privileged look at upcoming books and profiles of our most popular authors!

If offer card is missing, write to:
Harlequin Reader Service, 3010 Walden Avenue, P.O. Box 1867, Buffalo, NY 14269-1867

BUSINESS REPLY MAIL
FIRST CLASS MAIL   PERMIT NO. 717   BUFFALO, NY

POSTAGE WILL BE PAID BY ADDRESSEE

HARLEQUIN READER SERVICE
3010 WALDEN AVE
PO BOX 1867
BUFFALO NY 14240-9952

NO POSTAGE
NECESSARY
IF MAILED
IN THE
UNITED STATES

◀ MAIL THIS CARD TODAY! ▶

could think of a suitable reply, Melody interrupted them both with a shuddering cry.

"Oh, please, don't argue, I beg you. Not over me. I can't bear to cause arguments between you, when you have both been so kind to me, and you are both such good friends. Please, I'm very sorry that I behaved badly, and I see now that I must have worried you. I didn't mean to. I will give you my word as you have asked. I won't try to run away from you again. I promise."

"Thank you, Melody," Lord Dake said gravely. He looked down into her distressed face. Unshed tears filled her eyes and sparkled in her long lashes. He reached out one finger and flicked her gently on the chin.

"Don't cry. Elliot and I will not argue anymore. But we must take you back to London, child. Will you not tell us your guardian's name so that we may take you to him?"

For a moment Lord Dake thought that he had won. Melody regarded him unblinkingly, apparently unconscious of the single tear which slipped down her cheek, her concern still evident in her expression. The smile she gave him was twisted, but it was a brave effort nonetheless.

"I'm sorry. I can't tell you. I know you mean well. It's just that you don't understand what is best for me. If you take me to London, I suppose I must go there, because I have promised you now that I will not run away, and I will not break my word. But I will not help you by telling you my guardian's name."

"We will find out once we reach Town, child. You must see that. It would be much more discreet if you save us making our enquiries."

"Yes, I understand," she said, and this time the smile, though rueful, was more genuine. "Perhaps I'm being foolish. All I know is that I cannot help you to ruin my chance of happiness."

Lord Dake stared down at her in silence. Once again, Melody had caught him by surprise with her reaction. He had thought that he could withstand her blandishments, her pleas, her anger, even her bitter reproaches, in order to do what he conceived to be his duty to her. But this new mood of brave resignation left him with no defences. He had hobbled her with the promise he had wrung from her, but even so she would not fully surrender. For the first time a new thought occurred to Lord Dake. What if Melody were right? What if she, despite her youth and inexperience, knew better than he how oppressive the life her guardian wished to arrange for her would be? What if she were being the more realistic, facing the unpleasant future and taking what action she could to change it? He had approved Elliot's faltering attempts at self-determination. Why had he been so determined to thwart the girl's? Besides, he reflected ruefully, Melody, like Elliot, had burned some bridges behind her. It was too late now to hope to return her to wherever she belonged before her absence could be discovered. Why not take her to her aunt, if an aunt there was? He had to escort her somewhere, after all; why not where she wished to go? As long as Melody promised not to elude him, he would see that she came to no harm.

Besides, he reflected, his sense of mischief asserting itself once more, if he did keep Elliot involved with Melody's affairs long enough, he might just prolong the breach between his cousin and the rich and insufferable Miss Otterleigh to the point where even Elliot's interfering Mama could no longer heal it. So what if Elliot did lose his heart to Melody? Lord Dake thought he knew how unlikely it was that Melody would reciprocate his feelings, and in the meantime there were worse things that could happen to the mild-mannered Mr. Steele. It might even do him some good to be involved in an utterly unsuitable affair of the heart.

Lord Dake glanced from Melody to Mr. Steele. They were both regarding him intently. He began to shake his head in mock despair.

"I fear I shall regret what I am about to say," he said at last. "But I know when I am defeated. Tell us where you want to go in Yorkshire, child, and we shall take you there. I give you my word on that, and I, too, will not break my word."

Melody cried out in delight, and Tom gave a loud cheer. As if in sympathy, Lucky greeted the commotion with enthusiastic if uncomprehending barking. Mr. Steele was the only dissenter to the general joy.

"Bredon, do you know what you are doing?" he demanded.

"Yes, Elliot, I do," his cousin assured him with a smile. "That is the worst of it; I'm afraid I know precisely what I am doing."

CHAPTER NINE

THE REMAINDER OF THE TRIP to Melody's Aunt Augusta's home in Ilkley was, to Mr. Steele's great relief, accomplished with no further adventures. Melody had kept her word. She seemed relieved to have the source of contention removed, and relations between them became completely amiable, and so comfortable that Lord Dake believed she must have come to regard him as an unofficial older brother or, more likely, uncle. Tom was delighted to have matters brought into the open as well. He would have guarded Melody's secrets with his life, but secrecy was not natural to him, and he had feared that he might accidently blurt out some information which would have betrayed her, a circumstance which had left him almost completely dumb. With the terrible burden of the secret removed, he became much more his natural self, and soon grew so talkative that Lord Dake yearned to see his former taciturnity restored.

Tom's chatter, however, proved to be a consolation for Mr. Steele, as most of Tom's conversation revolved around horses and their peculiarities, and there was no topic nearer to Mr. Steele's heart. It was well that Mr. Steele had the consolation of equine talk to sustain him, for he was truly scandalized by Melody's behaviour and increasingly appalled by the thought of what his mama and Miss Otterleigh would have to say about his recent activities. His mood was not improved by what he thought of as his cousin's whimsical approach to the situation. Having once made his decision, Lord Dake had put aside all his misgivings and had entered into the expedition with what appeared to his cousin to be an entirely uncalled-for levity of spirits. He and Melody spent many hours talking, and though Mr. Steele was often shocked by Melody's unconventional opinions and what he considered to be the unbecoming forwardness with which she expressed them, Lord Dake seemed to find no fault with the girl. Mr. Steele turned naturally to Tom, who partly shared his conventional outlook, and the two of them often formed a sort of disapproving Greek chorus to the conversation of their companions.

For Melody the leisurely trip was a precious interlude between her unhappiness with Mr. Stanhope and her uncertainty about what the future with Aunt Augusta might hold. The journey was pleasant, the weather lovely, and the company most congenial. Lord Dake was an excellent conversationalist, his opinions were informed and courteously presented, and he listened to Melody as no one had ever listened before. Lord Dake never told her she was too young to know what she was about or said that her curiosity about so many topics was unseemly. He did not quell her, as Mr. Stanhope and the mistresses at Mrs. Beehan's Academy had done, with the charge that a young lady should not concern herself with matters of public policy or social controversy or learning. He was well-read himself, and saw nothing to condemn in Melody's interest in books, nor did he exclaim in wonderment, as had the other young ladies at Mrs. Beehan's, that she should have read anything more than the sensational novels of the day. And while he did not always share her opinions, he listened to them with patience and, often, with a good deal of appreciative amusement. But Melody never minded when Lord Dake laughed at her, because he did so very kindly and without the slightest trace of condescension, and she sometimes found herself making deliberately outrageous remarks just for the pleasure of seeing his eyes light up with laughter. The longer she and Lord Dake travelled together, the greater was Melody's dejection at the thought of parting from a companion who was becoming very dear to her. She avoided the topic of their parting, however, as carefully as he, and nothing was allowed to mar the quiet contentment of their remaining time together.

Indeed, the greatest excitement of the latter stages of their journey came the evening before they were to arrive at their destination. They had decided to find their lodgings for the night in the afternoon, so as to time their arrival in Ilkley the next morning rather than late at night. There was a charming little inn on the road, with ivy-covered stone walls, a thatched roof, and a cobblestone courtyard through which swaggered a small flock of self-important geese. These creatures charmed Melody, excited Lucky into a frenzy of barking, and thoroughly disgusted Mr. Steele. He watched with ill-concealed disapproval as Melody set off into the inn to ask for bread to feed the geese, while Tom attempted, at her instructions, to restrain Lucky from giving chase. Lord Dake, having given instructions to the ostlers for the care of the horses, joined his cousin just in time to be made the recipient of Mr. Steele's discontent.

"Why did we stop here, Bredon? That damned dog will be barking half the night, take my word on it, and the geese themselves are making enough racket to wake the dead. Stupid creatures. We'd have been better off to continue on to Ilkley tonight and have Melody off our hands that much the sooner."

"Are you so anxious to get rid of her, then?" his cousin asked quizzically.

"Lord, yes. Aren't you? I know she hasn't tried any more hare-brained schemes since she gave you her word not to bolt, but I can't be easy in my head about her, Bredon. I keep feeling that at any moment she'll change her mind and we'll be off on another wild-goose chase." It was an unfortunate choice of words, since it recalled him to his present complaint, and he watched with a sense of gloomy vindication as the scene in the courtyard grew noisier and more confused. Melody had reappeared with several loaf ends of stale bread which she was feeding to the geese, who responded by becoming more raucous and quarrelsome than ever. Nor was the situation improved by Lucky, who eluded Tom's grasp and darted among the birds, little hampered by the splint which held one leg rigid, setting them into flurries of retreat and advance which quite overwhelmed a rather timid elderly parson who had alighted from a newly arrived carriage and stood, blinking and tentative, in the midst of the fray.

Mr. Steele turned indignantly to his cousin, but whatever he had been about to say—and Lord Dake assumed it would be some variation of "I told you so"—was lost in the din around them. Lord Dake's eyes shone with a light which seemed to Mr. Steele to indicate a lack of proper concern for decorum, but before he could intervene, order was restored by Melody, who gave the remains of the bread to Tom and sent him off to lure the geese away, scooped up Lucky herself, and turned her attention, with a charmingly apologetic air, to soothing the ruffled clergyman. He revived considerably under her ministrations and allowed her to take his arm and lead him into the cool refuge of the inn, chatting all the while. Lord Dake grinned at Mr. Steele.

"There. Are you happy now?" he asked lightly.

"I shall be happy when we have delivered Melody to her relations," Mr. Steele replied. "Not before. Surely you are as anxious as I to give her safely over."

"Am I? Yes, I'm sure you are right, Elliot," his cousin replied. "I must be, after all."

Mr. Steele, who was not given to subtlety, seemed to accept Lord Dake's assurances unreservedly, and did not appear to note any absence of enthusiasm in his cousin's voice. He and Lord Dake followed Melody into the inn and set about the business of ordering a meal and rooms for the night. As it was some time till dinner would be ready, Mr. Steele excused himself in order to visit the stables, and Melody and Lord Dake were left to amuse themselves in the public parlour along with the elderly clergyman, who immediately launched into a gentle and largely incoherent monologue about the state of the church in present-day society. Melody settled herself to listen, her rapt expression intended to make amends for the earlier incident with the geese. Lord Dake, while heartily wishing the old gentleman at the devil, summoned his reserves of patience and assumed an air of courteous attention.

The proof that virtue was rewarded, had Lord Dake been seeking any, was not long in coming. The Reverend Mr. Nieman had apparently been much struck by his encounter with the flock of geese in the stable-yard. It now appeared to him that while in ancient times a spiritual leader might most logically model himself upon a shepherd, leading a passive if often misguided flock, the contentious nature of modern times was such that a gooseherd might well be a more fitting model. No sooner had he formulated the thought than the Reverend Mr. Nieman began to see a series of analogies by extension, all of which he brought forth with great earnestness and a growing sense of intellectual excitement. Whereas sheep were earthbound, geese were liable to fly off at once in any direction, thus increasing the difficulty with which the attentive gooseherd watches over them. Modern man, the cleric asserted, with ever better roads, faster carriages, and even the wondrous new hot-air ascension balloon at his disposal, was as flighty as geese and as difficult to control. Sheep were placid and patient animals, while geese were contentious, aggressive, and vocal. Tactfully, the Reverend Mr. Nieman left his listeners to draw their own comparisons with the present-day congregation.

As the clergyman's comparisons became more convoluted, Lord Dake abandoned his earlier hopes of having the opportunity for a private conversation with Melody and gave himself over to a lively appreciation of the absurd. Nothing in his blandly courteous expression gave him away, but when at one particularly outrageous remark he could not help but look to Melody, he found in her dark eyes a laughter which echoed his own. The shared glance was brief; Melody primmed her mouth to stifle her smile, and they both looked back to the Reverend Mr. Nieman. But the moment of inward laughter they had shared was like a bond between them. Listening to the elderly clergyman, Lord Dake thought only of Melody; he was as conscious of her sitting demurely across from him on the worn settee in the inn's public parlour as if the two of them were alone together, and though they seldom dared to glance at each other, whenever they did both could see their amusement reflected in the other despite the carefully correct expressions they both wore.

By the time the Reverend Mr. Nieman had exhausted his thesis and himself and had benignly bid them good-night in order to retire to his room for a bit of supper before his early bed, Lord Dake and Melody were half-giddy with suppressed laughter. Lord Dake, who had courteously risen with the older man's departure, turned to Melody, but before he could speak Mr. Steele hurried in the room. Resigned, Lord Dake settled back down in his chair.

"Bredon!" Mr. Steele burst out. "You must let me have some money."

"Certainly, Elliot," Lord Dake drawled carelessly. "Nothing gives me greater pleasure than to serve as your banker."

Mr. Steele shot him a startled look. "I don't mean for you to give it to me outright, Bredon," he explained. "I shall pay you back."

Lord Dake raised an eyebrow dubiously. "Shall you, indeed?" he murmured. "I wonder why I ever doubted that."

"Well, and so do I!" Mr. Steele exclaimed indignantly. "I've never been one to sponge off you, Bredon. I'm not our cousin Rawleigh, you know."

"I should hope not. If you were I would not have been able to endure the last several days in your company."

"Lord, yes," Mr. Steele agreed. "Young Rawleigh is a coxcomb and a greenhead," he added, reflecting upon his nineteen-year-old cousin with the full sophistication of his own twenty-three years. "But I hope you will acquit me of his sins. You're as closely related to him as I, after all."

"And yet," Lord Dake continued in a dreamy voice, "Rawleigh has never burst in upon me in an inn and demanded that I give him money."

"Lend him money," corrected Mr. Steele, who was beginning to understand that his cousin was making sport of him. "And don't try to play the fool with me, Bredon. You know perfectly well that you've always spared me a bit of blunt when my pockets were to let, and I've always paid you back promptly."

A smile twitched at Lord Dake's lips, and Mr. Steele gave a relieved grin. "You oughtn't to scare me like that, Bredon," he complained amiably. "It ain't sporting of you."

"You took me by surprise," he cousin objected. "I would never have believed someone with your experience and maturity would set off on a trip like this without sufficient funds.''

"I *had* sufficient funds, as you know very well," Mr. Steele retorted. "But I had to give almost all of it to that precious dandy Mr. Montgomery to buy him a new outfit and repair the damage to his carriage."

"Ah, yes. Well, certainly I shall be glad to lend you whatever you want, Elliot. May I ask the reason for your sudden need?"

"Livestock!" Mr. Styles cried triumphantly. "I've found some real beauties, Bredon, and I must have them now, before someone else buys them out from under me."

"Livestock? Oh, yes," Lord Dake said calmly. "Geese, I suppose?"

"Geese!" Mr. Steele stared at him, thunderstruck. "Why the deuce would I want to buy geese?" he demanded.

Lord Dake looked down to brush a bit of lint from his coat sleeve. His expression was sedate, but Melody caught the glint of laughter in his eyes.

"How can I say, Elliot? Your motives are, as always, your own. I can only assume that our exposure to the animals this afternoon has given you a new appreciation for poultry."

"Poultry?" Mr. Steele echoed in shock. "Bredon, have you run mad? What is all of this nonsense about poultry?"

"That is coming it too brown, Elliot," his cousin chided him. "It was you who brought up the subject of buying geese in the first place, after all."

"I never did anything of the kind!" Elliot protested.

"I am sure you did," Lord Dake replied. "Melody, did you not hear my cousin mention poultry?"

Melody bit back a smile. "I believe I have heard geese mentioned several times this afternoon, my lord," she said demurely. "Apparently they are all the rage."

"Which would explain Elliot's interest in them. Always in the height of fashion, my cousin."

"Bredon," Elliot begged. "Please tell me what you are going on about."

"Geese," Melody explained helpfully. "Lord Dake is expressing his willingness to lend you the money you need to buy your geese."

Mr. Steele's patience was beginning to wear thin. "It's horses I want," he cried. "Not damned geese, not chickens, not ducks, not any sort of poultry at all. I don't care about poultry."

"And yet I believe in poultry we may find a metaphor for our modern life," Lord Dake said ponderously.

"One far more fitting than sheep," Melody agreed mischievously.

"Sheep!" cried the much-tried Mr. Steele. "I don't want sheep, either. Nasty, smelly, stupid creatures. What have sheep to do with anything?"

"Well you may ask," Lord Dake said, having pity upon his cousin. "If you had joined us earlier you would have been privileged to hear the Reverend Mr. Nieman expound for some time upon the relevance of sheep and geese to modern life."

"Well, I'm glad that I didn't join you earlier, in that case," Mr. Steele retorted. "It's bad enough having to listen to you and Melody trying to be amusing at my expense."

"Not at your expense, Elliot," Lord Dake said kindly. "You were simply so unfortunate as to be the next person we encountered after making our mighty effort to listen courteously to the clergyman. Anyone in such a position would have provoked a similar outburst, I'm afraid."

"Lord, I don't mind you laughing at me, Bredon," Mr. Steele said generously. "Only do please let me have some money now, so I may settle up. There's the sweetest pair of matched mares I've ever seen in the stables, and their owner is willing to sell them. It's too good an opportunity to miss."

Lord Dake tossed him his coin purse carelessly. "Do try to leave me enough to pay for our lodging, Elliot," he murmured.

His cousin merely grinned and headed for the stables. The landlord came in to announce that dinner was served, and Lord Dake and Melody made their way into the dining-room. With the Reverend Mr. Nieman taking his own meal upstairs, they found themselves quite alone except for the servants who came and went hurriedly upon their duties.

"Ought we not to wait for Mr. Steele and Tom?" Melody asked as they took their places at the table.

"Not unless you wish to wait all night," Lord Dake replied. "I know Elliot when he is involved in a transaction of this sort. He will be the next several hours in the stables, unless I am greatly mistaken, and from what I have observed of Tom he is likely just as bad."

"It was very kind of you to let him have the money he needs to buy his horses," Melody said.

Lord Dake shrugged and served her a thin slice of ham. "Elliot is welcome to whatever I have," he said. "He knows that. Not that he would take advantage of it. He has occasionally borrowed a small sum when he is temporarily embarrassed, but he has never failed to pay me back promptly."

"Still, it must be very pleasant for him to know he can depend upon you if he needs to," Melody said rather wistfully. "Not just for a loan, I mean, but for whatever help he requires."

"I wish you would refrain from casting me as benevolent hero," Lord Dake complained mildly. "I assure you that I do not fit the mould at all. I'm afraid I bullied Elliot rather mercilessly for most of our childhoods, and when I finally reached my majority and was free of my guardian, I became very stiff-necked and proper for several years. Luckily I more or less outgrew the worst of it, but poor Elliot suffered through so many snubs and set-downs it's a wonder he didn't wash his hands of me entirely. And even now, though we are good friends, I cannot seem to resist annoying him. He is rather easily agitated, and I'm afraid I derive altogether too much amusement from driving him to distraction."

Melody laughed. "It was really too bad of both of us to confuse him about the geese," she admitted. "But after staying sober throughout the whole of the Reverend Mr. Nieman's talk, I'm afraid I had exhausted my self-control."

"Lord, yes. I don't know what I would have done if he had not finally excused himself to retire for the night. I envisioned the monologue continuing throughout our meal."

They laughed again, almost overcome by the memory. But after a moment Melody's laughter faded, and she smiled a little sadly at Lord Dake.

"It is so good to have someone to laugh with," she said.

"Who do you usually laugh with, child?" he asked gently.

"No one." Her smile was bitter. "My guardian does not approve of laughter, especially in young ladies. He thinks it frivolous. And my friends in school do not seem to find amusement in the same things I do. It makes me feel very lonely at times."

"I know just what you mean," Lord Dake admitted. "My friends and family are more likely to deplore my sense of the ridiculous than to share it. And if my guardian had even the rudiments of a sense of humour it was undetectable to me. I think prosiness must be the most important requirement for the position of guardian."

Melody laughed again with him, then turned her attention to her plate. After a moment, however, she raised her eyes to Lord Dake again.

"My father used to laugh with me," she said shyly. "But he's been dead a very long time."

Lord Dake nodded. "Elliot's father was my guardian for several years," he said. "He was a wonderful man, with a great capacity for laughter. Poor Elliot takes after his mama as far as his sense of humour is concerned, I'm afraid, but his father was one of the most jovial men I've ever met. He died four years after my father's death, however, and Mr. Vaughn was appointed my guardian then. Not a sympathetic man at all. But it comes to an end, you know. And once I was no longer chafing under Mr. Vaughn's control, I could even see that he had some other fine qualities which compensated for his dryness."

Melody nodded, and said no more. She made a valiant attempt to smile cheerfully, but Lord Dake could see the pensive mood overcome her. He cursed himself mentally for introducing the subject of guardians. After a long silence, he decided upon a more direct approach.

"I wish you will tell me what is bothering you," he said gently.

Melody, who had been gazing in apparent abstraction at the nearly untouched bread and ham on her plate, looked up at him in surprise.

"Nothing is bothering me," she protested.

"That is nonsense, child, unless that slice of ham has done something to annoy you. You have stabbed it repeatedly with your fork, and directed many dark glances at it, but I have yet to see you take a bite. It is obvious that there is something on your mind."

"Well, yes, I suppose there is," Melody admitted. "But please do not bother yourself about it. It will all work for the best."

"Are you sure that there is nothing I can do to help it work out well? I would be glad to listen to your problem and to advise you if I find I have any ideas upon the subject. I am generally thought to give excellent advice," his lordship added somewhat plaintively. "At least my family are always anxious to solicit it."

"I'm sure you do," Melody replied warmly. "And if I ever stand in need of any you may be sure I shall come to you. But I was really only wondering what Aunt Augusta's home is like."

"Have you never been there?"

"Oh, no. I've never been this far north before, and Ilkley is only a name to me. I know nothing about it, or about Aunt Augusta's estate."

"I don't believe I've actually been to Ilkley before, but I have been to Yorkshire many times, and I believe the town is right out among the moors. Very romantic, no doubt, or don't modern young ladies believe in romance?"

He said this last with a deliberate lightness, but Melody blushed rosily and looked away.

"Oh, yes, they do," she said in a strangled voice. "Or at least those of my acquaintance do. But I was not thinking of romance now; I was thinking more of Aunt Augusta and what she will say when I knock upon her door."

"I see." Lord Dake abandoned the subject of romance a little reluctantly, and assumed what he was coming to think of ruefully as his avuncular look. "Your coming is likely to be somewhat of a surprise to your aunt, I surmise?"

"There was no time to write," Melody explained defensively. "My decision to visit her was made a trifle precipitously," she admitted, but a tentative smile seemed to tremble on her lips as she spoke the last word.

"Yes, I see," Lord Dake said blandly. "And, of course, there was always the fact that had you written to her of your plans, she might have written back to tell you not to come."

The smile grew, and a very charming dimple appeared in Melody's cheeks. As usual, Lord Dake's teasing had restored her good spirits, and her eyes were alight with mischief as she allowed that what he said was true.

"But do you not expect your aunt to welcome you?" he asked. "Were you and she not close?"

"Not really," Melody explained. "That is to say, she seldom visited us when my parents were alive, though Lily went to stay with her a few times when we were very young."

"Lily?"

"My sister. After my parents died she was sent to live with Aunt Augusta, and I went to live in my guardian's household. My father's estate was leased until I should attain my majority and decide whether I should like to return there to live."

"It seems odd that sisters should have been separated in such a manner," Lord Dake ventured.

"It is because Lily is actually my half-sister, you see. She inherited a small bequest from my mother, but my father's estate passed to me. Lily was not his child. I don't know much about Lily's father except that he was much older than my mother and died of a fit of apoplexy soon after Lily was born. My mother was a recent widow when she met my father, and after a time they married and had me—I'm nearly four years younger than Lily. And Aunt Augusta is really only Lily's aunt," she added in a burst of candour, "but I have always thought of her as my aunt, too."

Lord Dake regarded her thoughtfully. "And has she always thought of herself as your aunt, too?" he asked.

"That is what we are about to see, isn't it?" Melody's tone was light, but he could sense the uncertainty behind her words. He felt a stab of pity and a fierce resolution that she should be protected from any hurt, including that which might be meted out by an indifferent pseudo-aunt. But he said nothing of it, merely smiling at her and reminding her teasingly that he had maintained from the beginning that the aunt was a creature of her imagination.

"That is not kind, sir," Melody protested with an answering twinkle. "And Aunt Augusta would not care to be described as a creature of my imagination, or as any type of creature at all, if I remember her correctly. She was a rather formidable woman; quite frightening to a child."

"But not to the young lady you have now become," he reminded her gently, and she smiled her gratitude at him.

"No, of course not," she agreed. "But will you come with me when I go to her house? Just to help me explain?"

Lord Dake, who perceived more clearly than Melody how much there was to explain, agreed readily. They finished their meal with no further conversation, and Melody excused herself to go up to bed. Bidding her good-night, Lord Dake thought it was just as well that she retired early. The next day was likely to prove trying for them all.

Their departure the next morning was delayed somewhat by Lucky, who had wandered off after breakfast and had to be retrieved by Tom, but eventually they set off for the last leg of their journey. Lord Dake's memory had served him well. The moors did surround Ilkley, and the ride seemed to further depress Melody's normally buoyant spirits. By the time they had reached the town she sat, a silent, subdued little figure, tucked between Lord Dake and Mr. Steele and looking very much more like a schoolgirl than a young lady of Quality. Mr. Steele might well have approved the change in her demeanour, but Lord Dake found the transformation not at all to his liking. He much preferred the lively, unexpected, and disastrously candid Melody he had come to know on their journey together. Unlike Mr. Steele, he was not at all shocked by her. He found her directness and her courage and her willingness to enter into the outspoken defence of others a refreshing change from the conventional insipidity of those young ladies with whom he had formerly come into contact.

Looking down at her now, as she sat with her chin raised bravely, but with fear evident in her dark eyes, Lord Dake reflected on the irony of his earlier concern that Elliot might be infatuated with Melody. She was not Elliot's type at all—his mama had trained him too well for that. No, Lord Dake reflected ruefully, it was he himself who had tumbled head over heels in love with Melody. He was nearly as besotted as young Tom, and the chastening truth was that Melody was as indifferent to him as she was to the stable-boy. But if he could not make her love him, at least he could have the satisfaction of knowing that he had done her a service, and if he could best do that by playing favoured uncle to her trusting child, then so be it. Lord Dake was not vain, and he did not find it incomprehensible that the only woman with whom he had ever fallen in love showed no sign of reciprocating his feelings. He merely found it damned frustrating.

CHAPTER TEN

AUNT AUGUSTA'S HOUSE was a solid-looking Georgian manor on the outskirts of the town. Tom directed them to it, but bade Lord Dake stop the horses before they came too near so that he could slip out of the carriage and away from the dangerous area. He was not quite ready to face his father yet, and seemed to sense that to come upon him unexpectedly in his present company would be a mistake. Tom conferred briefly with Mr. Steele, then waved goodbye and slunk off down the street. Lord Dake, Mr. Steele and Melody, the latter clutching Lucky to her bosom as if he were an animate good-luck token, approached the house with varying degrees of trepidation. Lord Dake had time only to bestow a reassuring smile upon Melody before he advanced to the door and beat a tattoo with the knocker, feeling as he did so rather as a medieval knight approaching a dragon's lair might have been supposed to feel.

The butler who answered the door informed Lord Dake, after a supercilious look at his companions, that his mistress was not receiving visitors, as it was the hour of her afternoon nap. Upon learning that her niece had come to visit, the butler admitted them rather grudgingly to the house. His eyes flicked down disparagingly at the dog which Melody still clutched to her bosom, then to the faces of both gentlemen accompanying her. He looked away from Lord Dake's face without any visible reaction, but winced at the sight of Mr. Steele's still slightly bruised eyes. Then he went abruptly to fetch Miss Lily Napier, leaving them standing in the hall.

Lord Dake looked down at Melody. She was clinging tightly to Lucky and looking as timid as a mouse, though he noted approvingly that her chin was still held high, and she did not allow herself to shrink behind him or Elliot as he felt sure she wanted to. He smiled enquiringly at her.

"Is Napier your name as well, or did your half-sister not take your father's name?"

"Oh, no. She is Napier, but I am Maitland. Melody Maitland," she added, in case he should be confused.

"A very great pleasure to meet you, Miss Maitland," he said suavely. "I am Anthony Bredon Fennimore Steele, Lord Dake, though my friends call me Bredon. And may I make you known to my cousin, Mr. Elliot Steele?"

Melody smiled a little at this levity, and her mood seemed to lighten slightly. But Mr. Steele declined to enter into the frivolity; the stern elegance of Aunt Augusta's residence was having a depressing effect upon him. He was suddenly overwhelmed by the folly of what he and his cousin had done. He thought they must have both been mad. What would Melody's aunt think? What *must* she think, when two strange men turned up upon her doorstep with her niece in tow? Wild thoughts of prison and disgrace flitted through Mr. Steele's mind. He would not have been at all surprised if Melody's aunt had them arrested, or ordered them driven from the house and horsewhipped. The more he thought about it, the more likely such an eventuality seemed. And he could not blame her. He looked at Melody standing demurely between him and Lord Dake and was barely able to suppress a shudder. She looked so young, and so innocent. How had she led him into such folly?

No, to be fair, the folly was his alone. Bredon had warned him at the very beginning that he must be mad to think of aiding Melody in her escape from her guardian. And he, Elliot, had ignored that warning, had thrown aside every other consideration, leaving his mother and his fiancée to be disappointed and no doubt distracted with worry, and had set off on this wild escapade. Now he had ended up here, in this old-fashioned, austerely correct dwelling place, sneered at by the butler, waiting like a child called upon the carpet to receive the reckoning which was his due. Mr. Steele was not generally a fanciful man, but it seemed to him as the moments passed and Melody's sister did not appear, that some horrified uproar must be going on in the far reaches of the house. Perhaps the sister had fainted at the news of what awaited her. Or perhaps she was even now summoning official help to deal with the men she must believe had abducted her younger sister. The as-yet-unseen Miss Napier was rapidly beginning to assume the form of a frightening ogre in Mr. Steele's mind.

So strong was the hold that these imaginings had upon Mr. Steele that when Miss Lily Napier joined them at last he was astonished to see she was a dainty blond woman, very pretty, and looking barely older than her schoolgirl sister. She was frowning a little, true, but it seemed more in puzzlement than in anger. She cast a look back over her shoulder as she hurried down the stairs towards them, as if in fear that her aunt's nap might have been disturbed, and when she reached them she spoke in a half whisper which seemed to confirm this fear.

"Melody! Darling, what are you doing here?"

"Lily!" Melody thrust Lucky at the startled Mr. Steele and flung herself enthusiastically into her sister's arms. She began to pour out her story, but after a few complicated sentences Lily shushed her gently.

"Wait, wait. We cannot stand here in the hall. Aunt Augusta will hear, and if we wake her she'll be even more cross.

And these gentlemen will think we are both sadly lacking in manners. You have not even presented me to them yet, my dear."

"Oh, yes, Lily, I must make you known to them," Melody agreed, "but do let us go in out of the hall if you think our voices will carry to Aunt Augusta's room. She is going to be very cross with me already, I'm sure, and there's no need to make it worse by waking her." She bustled her sister into the first room off the hall, very much as if she were at home there and her sister a stranger. Mr. Steele and Lord Dake followed them into the room, which proved to be a small sitting-room. Mr. Steele, very conscious of the ambiguity of his position and of the ludicrous picture he felt he must present, clutching Melody's dog and with the remnants of his black eye still visible, murmured disjointed apologies to Miss Napier, who was herself nearly inarticulate with embarrassment at the informality of the proceedings. Melody, however, seemed to be regaining her equilibrium rapidly, and Lord Dake, who was perfectly at ease, settled down to enjoy the interview which must follow.

"There," Melody said with a satisfied nod as she closed the door firmly but quietly behind Mr. Steele. "Now we may talk. Lily, may I present to you Lord Dake and his cousin, Mr. Elliot Steele."

Lord Dake bowed over Miss Napier's hand with exaggerated courtesy, but he saw no answering flicker of amusement in Miss Napier's gentle blue eyes. Indeed, he could scarcely see anything at all in them, for she gave him only the briefest, timid glance before looking away in embarrassment. Lord Dake found himself comparing the glance unfavourably to Melody's characteristically frank gaze.

Mr. Steele, however, did not feel that Miss Napier suffered in any way from a comparison to her sister. Quite the contrary; he thought her shyness and her embarrassment over the awkwardness of the meeting spoke well for her gentility. He was nearly as awkward himself as he set Lucky abruptly down and bowed over her hand, and the quick, bright look she gave him before turning back to Melody almost dazzled him. Melody took her sister's arm and drew her down to sit on the sofa beside her. Lily obeyed, and gestured to Lord Dake and Mr. Steele to seat themselves opposite them. Lucky, who had been wandering about the room sniffing several interesting objects, returned to throw himself at Melody's feet.

"I'm very glad to meet your friends, Melody," Lily said after they had settled in and declined her polite offer of refreshments, "but I do not understand how you come to be here. Is something wrong with Mr. Stanhope? Has some accident befallen him?"

"Merely that his name has finally become known," Lord Dake murmured. Lily glanced at him in puzzlement, then looked quickly away. His jest disconcerted her; Lily was rather frightened by clever men.

"Nothing has happened to Mr. Stanhope," Melody reassured her, with a reproving glance at Lord Dake. "I have simply decided that I do not wish to live with him any more."

"But you don't live with him, do you, Melody? I thought you were in board-school in London. Did you not write me from there just last month?"

"Very true, love," Melody said to her literal-minded sister. "But what I meant was that I do not wish to be under Mr. Stanhope's care any more, no matter whether I am actually living in his home or at the school."

"Oh, Melody, what has he done? He cannot have hurt you; he seemed a very kind man to me when I met him. Of course, that was years ago, but he cannot have changed so."

"He hasn't done anything unkind," Melody explained. "It's just that I knew I must leave him after seeing the men he invited to dine with us at Christmastime."

"Men? What men, Melody? Were they unkind to you? Did they behave badly? What did they do?"

"They dined with us!" Melody perceived that she was not making herself understood. "Mr. Stanhope invited them there particularly to meet me," she added helpfully.

Lily regarded her blankly. Lord Dake saw that she still did not understand and made a contribution of his own. "Perhaps it was their manners at table which gave your sister such a dislike of them," he suggested. Lily, understandably, looked more blank. Melody gave Lord Dake another reproving look, then turned back to her sister.

"It had nothing to do with their table manners," she explained. "Pay no attention to Lord Dake at all; he is merely being ironic. It was simply that they were so suitable. Only they weren't. Not for me. If you know what I mean."

Evidently Miss Napier did not. Her bewilderment appeared to be growing by the second, and Lord Dake's sense of the absurd began to prompt him to make another helpful contribution to the conversation. Before he could do so, however, Miss Napier took a course of action which proved that she had an old and intimate acquaintance with her sister.

"Now, Melody, stop that," she said with more firmness that she had yet shown. She set her slender hands on her sister's shoulders and gave her a little shake. "Explain in complete sentences, and from the beginning, if you please!"

"Mr. Stanhope spent the Christmas holidays at home with me," her sister responded obediently. "He told me it was time that he should give some thought to finding a husband for me. He invited several men he considered suitable to dine with us on different nights, so that I might meet them. But I did not find them suitable at all, Lily! And when I was to go back to Mrs. Beehan's, Mr. Stanhope told me that he would be taking me out of school after the next term so that I could make my entrance into Society and meet more suitable men. He said he expected to have made a match for me within the year.''

Lily looked thoughtfully into her sister's face. ''But, Melody,'' she said after a moment. ''Surely Mr. Stanhope is right. You are only seventeen, I know, but it is time for you to come out of the schoolroom and to make your entrance into Society. Why, many girls younger than you have already married. Don't you want to make a match? You haven't become one of those horrid bluestockings at that school of yours, have you?''

''Of course not!'' Melody said indignantly. ''Not that anyone could, not at Mrs. Beehan's. Most of what they teach us is comportment and etiquette and the other accomplishments suited to a lady of Quality.''

''It pains me to say so, love, but perhaps you should have paid more attention to those lessons. I cannot think you have behaved as you ought in this. Even if you did not care for any of the men to whom Mr. Stanhope introduced you over the holidays, that is no reason to set yourself against making a match. You should be grateful that Mr. Stanhope is giving so much thought to your future.''

''Well, I don't want him to think about it so much,'' Melody countered mutinously. ''I want to be allowed to think about it myself, and to make my own plans. And you should not talk, Lily. You are nearly four years older than I, and you are not yet married.''

Colour flared in Lily's cheeks. "If I am not married it is not because I have stubbornly set my face against it, as you seem to have done. No one has provided me with the opportunities that Mr. Stanhope has been good enough to offer you. And I do not think it kind of you to discuss my private affairs quite so openly," she added.

"I'm sorry, Lily," Melody said instantly. "I did not mean to be rude. And I should not have spoken of such things in front of Lord Dake and Mr. Steele. It is just that the three of us have become so close these last few days, almost like a family ourselves, and I've got into the way of saying anything I please with them."

Lily did not appear to find this explanation reassuring. She glanced uncertainly towards Mr. Steele, and far more uncertainly towards Lord Dake. "Of course, if you say so, Melody," she said at last. "It is only natural that you should be more comfortable than I in discussing things with your friends, since I have only met them. Only, I am sure you do not really mean that you say whatever you please to them," she added with an uneasy little laugh. "A young lady must stay within acceptable limits, even when she is speaking to gentlemen who are as well-known to her as these gentlemen are to you. And I am sure they must be very well-known to you, and very good friends of Mr. Stanhope," she added politely, "or he would never have allowed them to escort you here. Although I must confess that I am surprised that Mr. Stanhope would allow you to travel even with his trusted friends without some lady to chaperon you. Just for appearances' sake, you understand. I would have thought he would have come himself if he wishes you to stay with Aunt Augusta for a time. Surely there must be things he would want to discuss with her."

"One imagines there would be many things he'd wish to say," Lord Dake observed blandly.

Lily blushed a little as she turned to him. "I pray you do not think I was criticizing you," she said uncertainly. "I am sure it is quite proper for Mr. Stanhope to have entrusted Melody to your care and that of your cousin. Are you perhaps related to Melody's guardian?"

"Not to my knowledge," Lord Dake replied.

"Then you must be very old friends," Lily persisted.

"I have never met him. Nor has my cousin, I believe. Do you know Mr. Stanhope, Elliot?" he asked politely.

"You must know that I do not," Mr. Steele replied in a slightly belligerent tone. Lily gave an audible gasp of surprise or shock, and he hastened to try to make the best of a rapidly worsening situation. "We met your sister sometime after she had left Mr. Stanhope's care, Miss Napier," he explained. "As she and her escort had encountered some difficulties, my cousin and I thought it best to accompany her the rest of the way."

Lily appeared to find his polite manner reassuring, but she was plainly still puzzled. "But who did Mr. Stanhope set to escort you if not these gentlemen?" she asked her sister.

"You don't understand, Lily," Melody said. "Mr. Stanhope didn't arrange for anyone to escort me here. He did not know I was coming."

"He did not know!"

Melody winced a little at this near shriek from her older sister, but Lord Dake remained unmoved. "Mr. Stanhope was travelling abroad when Melody made her somewhat precipitous decision to remove herself from board-school and come to visit you," he explained kindly. "He is still abroad, and may very well still not have heard of it."

The blood seemed to drain from Lily's face, leaving her alarmingly pale. "Do you mean to say my sister's guardian has no idea where she is or what she is doing, and that she decided to make the journey to Yorkshire without consulting him?" she demanded.

"Had she consulted him, he must obviously have known. And, no doubt, he would have forbidden it as well. That is why she thought it best not to consult him."

Lily sat back weakly in her chair.

"Damn it, Bredon, this is difficult enough without your complicating things with your misguided sense of humour," Mr. Steele protested. Miss Napier gasped again, and he blushed rosily. "Very sorry, Miss Napier," he apologized. "Please forgive my language; I forgot myself."

"Well, I think you are right," Melody chimed in. "Lord Dake is making things much worse, and it's not kind of him because he promised he would help to explain things."

"My dear Melody," Lord Dake replied plaintively, "you are unfair; I have helped to explain several things so far."

"You haven't helped at all!" Melody gasped in outrage. "You're just being ironic again. And if you mean to do the same when we explain things to Aunt Augusta, she will never see why I felt I could trust you and Mr. Steele to bring me here even though I didn't know either of you."

"Melody!" The protest from Miss Napier was a wail of pain. "Are you saying that both of these gentlemen are strangers to you?"

"Well, not now they aren't," Melody temporized. "They were when we met, but now we have become good friends."

Mr. Steele sprang forward in his chair and caught at Miss Napier's arm just as she was apparently about to slide nervelessly to the floor. His touch seemed to bring her out of her near-swoon, and she sat back weakly.

"Miss Napier, I beg you," he said earnestly. "Please do not torture yourself with worry. Miss Maitland is quite unharmed, I assure you. Won't you let me order some tea before we go on with the rest of the story? I believe it would do you good."

"Yes, please, Lily," Melody said. "Don't take on. Let Mr. Steele order us some tea, and once you've had some you'll feel better and we can talk some more. Lord Dake is just being provoking. You musn't allow him to upset you."

"I apologize," Dake said. "And to prove my repentance, I shall order the tea and Elliot may chafe Miss Napier's hand. Miss Napier, please believe that my cousin is telling you the truth. Melody came to no harm on her journey. Despite my lamentable tendency to make light of things, I assure you that my cousin and I would never have allowed anything to happen to Melody."

Lily thanked him weakly, but it was obvious that even in his conciliatory mood she was unsure of him. She suspected him of irony even when he was not indulging in it, and felt that he was not a man to be trusted. Mr. Steele, however, had impressed her far more favourably, and once Dake had left the room and Melody and Mr. Steele combined their efforts to reassure her, she began to feel much more herself. Even Lord Dake's return failed to loosen the hold she had obtained upon her emotions, and once tea had been served and she had taken a few sips of the fortifying brew, she declared herself ready to hear the rest of the story.

Lord Dake, who had formed as dim an opinion of Miss Napier's spirit as he had of her intelligence, would have liked something rather more fortifying to face the task of making her understand all that had happened. But for Melody's sake he exerted himself to control his ironic tongue and to present Miss Napier with as bland and reassuring a demeanour as it was in his power to do.

Despite his best efforts, it proved a difficult task. Miss Napier was genuinely shocked by the experiences which Melody frankly described for her. She was dismayed by the reflection that Melody had run off with Tom, but the fact that she knew Tom to some degree allowed her to accept that part of the story relatively well. But she was almost overcome by the knowledge that Melody had met Mr. Steele when she and Tom had slept in his stables, and was aghast at the ease with which her sister had accepted Mr. Steele and Lord Dake as travelling companions. The story of the accident with the phaeton caused her to turn so pale that Mr. Steele was concerned again that she might faint, and took her cup of tea from her for a moment so that she might not burn herself with it if she did. The argument with the phaeton driver, the fight which gave rise to Mr. Steele's black eye, Melody's argument with Dr. Simms, and especially Melody's attempt to sell her pearls in Grampton market horrified her. Every escapade which Melody described was a new enormity, and at the end of the story Lily was tearfully disapproving of her sister's deportment.

"I don't understand how you could behave that way," she almost wailed. "I thought Mrs. Beehan's was supposed to be a superior school. What will Mr. Stanhope say when he finds out?"

"Perhaps he'll say that he does not wish to be my guardian any more, and that I may stay here with you and Aunt Augusta," Melody said hopefully.

"Melody, how wicked of you! I doubt very much whether Aunt Augusta would allow you to stay. Mr. Stanhope is your legal guardian, and you are his responsibility."

"But, Lily, wouldn't you like me to stay here with you and Aunt Augusta? I was sure you would be lonely here; I thought you'd enjoy having someone else young in the house with you," Melody pleaded.

"How could I enjoy having you with us when I could never know how you were going to behave and whether you would take it into your head to do something outrageous?"

"But I wouldn't *have* to do anything outrageous, because I would be where I want to be," Melody pointed out.

"You say that now, but what if you changed your mind and decided you didn't want to be here any more? What if Aunt Augusta did something that displeased you as much as Mr. Stanhope has? She might invite someone to dinner, too," Lily countered bitterly, "and then who is to say whether or not you would take it into your head to run away from her? No, you must go back, Melody. You must stay here until Mr. Stanhope can arrange a suitable escort for you, and then you must go back to Mrs. Beehan's Academy, or to Mr. Stanhope's home, if that is what he prefers. He is your guardian, and you owe him your obedience. Don't you agree, Mr. Steele?" she added, as Melody turned impatiently away.

"Yes, I do, Miss Napier," that gentleman said earnestly. "I hope you will believe me when I say that both my cousin and I entreated Melody many times to tell us Mr. Stanhope's name so that we could take her back to him, where she belonged. We only consented to bring her here because she refused to tell us who her guardian was, and because we were afraid she would run away from us altogether and try to make her way here on her own. There is no saying what trouble she might have got herself into if that had happened."

"Oh, yes, Mr. Steele. Indeed, I perceive that Melody owes you a great deal, as do all of us who love her. You have behaved just as you should. It is Melody whose behaviour has put me to the blush. I shudder to think what might have happened if she had eluded you and Lord Dake a second time."

"Well, I wouldn't have," Melody said indignantly. "I promised Lord Dake I would not, and I always keep my promises, Lily. You know me well enough to know that."

"I don't feel that I know you at all, Melody. You must have changed a great deal in the years we have been apart. You were always a headstrong child, but I would never have believed that there was any wickedness in you. But only a very wicked girl would behave as you have."

Melody did not reply, and a gloomy silence settled over the room. After a moment Miss Napier looked up at the ormolu clock on the mantelpiece.

"It is time for me to go to Aunt Augusta. She likes me with her when she wakes, to help her prepare for dinner."

"May I see Aunt Augusta?" Melody asked.

"I'm sure she will see you," Lily replied. "Although you will probably wish she had not when she has said whatever she will have to say to you. Aunt Augusta is very plain-spoken. She says it is one of the advantages of advanced years that one may speak exactly as one wishes. I shall tell her you are here, and we must see what she says."

"After you finish telling her how wicked I am she will probably not wish to see me," Melody pointed out bitterly.

"I shall tell her as few details of how you came to be here as possible, Melody. I believe you should have the opportunity to explain to Aunt Augusta yourself. Though what you could say that would make your behaviour sound less disgraceful is beyond me. However, I promise you I shall not turn her against you. You are my sister, and I love you, even though I am thoroughly shocked by the way you have conducted yourself. If you will wait here, I shall see what Aunt Augusta wishes to do."

She rose, and Mr. Steele and Lord Dake rose with her.

"Had we better leave, do you think, Miss Napier?" Mr. Steele asked with some little trepidation.

"I think you had much better stay, if you will, Mr. Steele. Very likely Aunt Augusta will wish to talk to you as well."

Mr. Steele's heart sank, but he nodded and politely expressed his willingness to wait upon Aunt Augusta at her convenience. He felt Lord Dake's ironic eye upon him as he spoke, and he was aware that his cousin knew how eagerly he would have avoided the coming ordeal. But Lord Dake said nothing, and after Lily excused herself the three of them sat down again to wait.

"Melody, may I pour you another cup of tea?" his lordship asked as calmly as if he were entertaining a small party in his own home.

"Thank you." She smiled shakily at him, but he was startled and angered to see the tears in her eyes when she looked into his face. She tried to blink them back, but a few crept down her cheeks. She brushed them away impatiently and reached for the cup of tea Lord Dake was holding out to her.

"Thank you," she said again. "I'm sorry to cry. Only it's very hard to hear Lily call me wicked. You told me what I did was wrong, and after I considered what you'd said, I could not but agree. Still, I did not feel that I was being wicked. I thought Lily at least would be pleased to see me," she added sadly.

"Your sister seems quite easily shocked, Melody," Lord Dake said gently. "To do her justice, she was very surprised to see you here so unexpectedly, as anyone might have been, and upset as well by the thought of what harm might have befallen you. And my tiresome attempts at levity did not help matters, as you pointed out. I am sure that once she recovers from the initial shock she will be very pleased to have you with her once again."

"Do you think so?" Melody asked wistfully. "It is very kind of you to say so, even if you are only saying it to make me feel better. And it was wrong of me to complain that you were not helping. After all you and Mr. Steele have done for me, you must think I am not only wicked but ungrateful as well."

"I think you are tired," Lord Dake said firmly. "And rather easily bothered as a result. You must not refine so much upon what your sister said. You could not expect to escape without a scolding, after all."

She smiled at him gratefully, and sipped her tea. Mr. Steele was silent, absorbed in his contemplation of the interview to come with Aunt Augusta, an old woman whom he had heard described as formidable. It was not a prospect which he found pleasant, but he was not left to contemplate it for long. The butler soon appeared at the door to announce in tones of gloomy relish that Augusta Napier would join them all at dinner. Mr. Steele had a feeling that the meal would prove to be an ordeal.

CHAPTER ELEVEN

MISS AUGUSTA NAPIER was a tiny, frail-looking woman with soft white hair elaborately arranged with feathers and jewels in a style that might have been fashionable in her youth but certainly had not been for many years. She appeared to have shrunk and dried out as she aged, and her skin was so wrinkled and hung so loosely upon her that it was impossible to tell whether she had ever been pretty. But her eyes were a bright, piercing blue, and her posture was aggressively upright. She was dressed all in black, with tiny black lace mittens, and carried an ebony cane topped with a huge ruby. Rubies were evidently her favourite jewels; they twinkled at her scrawny throat, in her ears, and in the heavy rings which seemed to weigh down her tiny hands. She was the smallest woman Mr. Steele had ever seen, and the most frightening.

She came down to dinner with Lily at her side, and though Lily herself was of diminutive stature, she seemed to tower over her aunt. But there was no question as to who was dominant in the relationship and in the household. The supercilious butler who had greeted the new arrivals hovered anxiously over her as she approached the table, but she ignored him. She allowed Lily to seat her, then maintained a complete, and to Mr. Steele extremely harrowing, silence until the soup had been served. But her bright eyes were avidly and disapprovingly fastened on Melody and her companions, until Mr. Steele felt that he had endured the most horrible ordeal of his life, and even the normally composed Lord Dake found himself experiencing some of the sensations of a schoolboy called into the headmaster's office after some piece of adolescent mischief. When finally the old lady spoke, though, it was Melody she addressed.

"So, miss, what have you been up to now?"

"I've been wanting to explain, Aunt Augusta," Melody began pacifically. "I do not wish to remain under Mr. Stanhope's guardianship, and I was hoping that you might persuade him to let me live with you instead."

"Ha!" The crack of bitter laughter was so abrupt that Mr. Steele's spoon shot from his hand and clattered down into his soup plate, earning him a bright, scornful look from Aunt Augusta. "And why should I do any such thing, missy?"

"I thought perhaps you'd like to have me live with you," Melody said reasonably. "I could do errands for you and make myself useful. I've learned a good deal at Mrs. Beehan's school, Aunt Augusta. I could play the pianoforte for you and sing and read to you and anything else you'd like."

"I've got your sister to do all that, girl," her aunt retorted. "She's clumsy and stupid, but even she can run errands, and read to me, though why she bothers when there's nothing worth reading nowadays is beyond me. She tried to read me some of that rubbishing new poetry just last week— terrible stuff. What was it, Lily?" she demanded, turning so abruptly to her other niece that Mr. Steele, now thoroughly demoralized, almost dropped his spoon again. Lily Napier seemed more used to her aunt's characteristic style of conversation, however, for she simply murmured softly, "It was Lord Byron, Aunt. *Childe Harold's Pilgrimage.*"

"Childe Harold's Rubbish, that's what it was. Should have been put out for the dustmen. But I don't suppose you'd show any better taste in reading materials, Melody.

Yes, and Lily can play the pianoforte, too, if I want to hear such a thing—I usually don't, mind you—and sing well enough if you like the insipid songs young girls sing nowadays.''

"I thought perhaps you'd allow me to live with you because I'm not happy living with Mr. Stanhope,'' Melody said, perceiving quite clearly that practicality was yielding few results and hoping for a better return from an appeal to sentiment.

"Nonsense, girl! Of course you're not happy. Lily's not happy either, are you, Lily? Always wanting something other than what they have—that's what young girls are like. Lily would like me to take her to Town and racket all over to a bunch of humdrum parties with mazey-brained loobies who have no notions of the proper way to dress or behave, simply so that she could meet some romantic young fool who'd break her heart and probably lead her into total disgrace. That's what *she'd* like, and if she thinks that that would make her happy, she's even more foolish than I think. And you no doubt think you'd like to live here, at great additional expense to me, and for no other reason than that you're not happy where you are. Well, if you think living here would make you happy, you're even more foolish than your sister. What do you have to say to that, girl?''

"I think perhaps you are right,'' Melody said quietly but firmly. "I don't believe I would be happy here, and I don't believe that Lily is, either.''

Aunt Augusta's eyes flashed, but she laughed harshly. "Always were a truthful little thing, weren't you?'' she said. "Too truthful, perhaps, missy. A young lady should watch her tongue; good manners are more important than the truth, after all.''

"I don't believe they are,'' Melody said. "I don't believe anything is more important than the truth.''

"Oh, you don't, don't you? Then perhaps you will do me the courtesy of telling me the truth now. Your sister is too mealy-mouthed—I couldn't get a thing out of her. How do you come to be here, missy, why has your guardian let you come without escorting you himself, and who are these fine gentlemen you've brought with you?"

"This is Lord Dake and his cousin, Mr. Elliot Steele," Melody said, taking the easiest first. "They were kind enough to escort me. Mr. Stanhope could not do so because he is abroad, and because he does not know I planned to come to see you."

"Do you mean to say that you came halfway across England in the company of these gentlemen, if they are indeed gentlemen, with no other chaperon?"

"Yes, I did," Melody said defiantly. "Except for Tom Baxter. And they are gentlemen; you have no cause to doubt that."

"If they were gentlemen, they'd never have consented to take you anywhere without your guardian's permission," Aunt Augusta retorted.

"They had no choice. I had started on my journey before they met me, and once we did meet they wanted to take me back to my guardian, but I refused to tell them who he was. They did not learn his name, or my last name, until today."

Aunt Augusta choked on the morsel of bread she had placed in her mouth. She gasped, alarmingly red in the face, but struck out at Lily petulantly when her niece would have patted her back. Lily subsided wordlessly in her chair, and after a moment Aunt Augusta regained control of her breath and her voice. But it was evident that she was genuinely outraged by Melody's words.

"You ran away from Mr. Stanhope's care," she cried, "and took up with these two strange men! Quiet, girl! Don't say another word. You there!" Here she lifted her cane and poked it across the table at Mr. Steele, completely unnerving him. "You, sir, what do you have to say for yourself?"

"N-nothing!" he stammered. "That is to say, very sorry for the irregularity. Most awkward, of course. Assure you that Miss Maitland came to no harm. Terribly sorry."

"Bah! Stop babbling, man," Aunt Augusta demanded. She removed her cane and her attention from Mr. Steele's vicinity and turned to Lord Dake. "And you—claim to be a lord, do you? I suppose you think that entitles you to do as you wish to foolish, innocent schoolgirls?"

"I have made no claims of any kind," Lord Dake said calmly, though he was pale with anger. "I am Lord Dake, though it is Miss Maitland, and not I, who has said so. And though I hesitate to offend you, I cannot but point out that if Miss Maitland's family were as concerned with her wellbeing as they are with her reputation, it would not have fallen to strangers such as myself and my cousin to see that she was not left to wander about the countryside on her own like the innocent child she is."

"Ha! Innocent child. A hoyden, that's what I call her. Shameless chit of a girl. Not that she has any harm in her," she added inconsistently. "Too foolish to know what she is about. That's what comes of sending girls off to board-schools; too much book learning and not enough common sense. I knew no good would come of Stanhope packing her off to board-school for years while he travels about the world free as a lark."

"It is a pity you did not act upon your knowledge," Lord Dake observed. "If her family had spoken up on her behalf, perhaps Mr. Stanhope might have provided for her better."

"I ain't her family," the old lady snapped triumphantly. "No relation at all. It's one thing to allow the girl to call me

Aunt Augusta, it's quite another to think that that gives me any legal rights or obligation to interfere with her upbringing. Mr. Stanhope was her father's choice as her guardian. Nothing to me if I disagree with his practices."

"You're quite right," Lord Dake said smoothly.

She eyed him for a moment as if to see whether there was any fight left him in him, then turned her attention back to her dinner as the next course was served. There was no further discussion during the meal, but after it was ended Aunt Augusta rounded on Lily.

"You, Lily, go up and show your sister to her room. Don't ask me which room, girl. That's the sort of detail you can handle by yourself. Better make it a good one, though, because she'll be spending the rest of her visit there. And as for you, Melody, go where your sister takes you, and stay in your room. I shall send for you when I have made my arrangements to escort you back to that school of yours. And you may be sure that I shall have something to say to them about letting you run away. What kind of supervision do they provide for their students?"

"They do not guard us as if we were prisoners," Melody said.

"Well, they will when I've returned you to them, my girl, make no mistake about that. I shall see to it that they do. Now go, and don't let me see your face again until I send for you."

Melody's cheeks were flushed with anger and humiliation. She looked at Lord Dake, but said nothing as Lily led her away. Lord Dake watched her go in silence; the strength of his own anger towards this little woman who was bullying Melody confused him; he did not trust himself to say a word. Once he and his cousin were alone with Aunt Augusta, however, she prodded him again.

"You, Lord Dake. I want you to escort Lily and me to the assembly tonight. We can talk further about what's to be done to prevent word of this scandalous situation getting out. The foolish girl's done her best to ruin herself, but perhaps we can think of something."

"I see no need to think of anything," Lord Dake retorted as calmly as he could. "You desired to see your niece, and as her guardian was travelling abroad and was not available, you sent me and my cousin to escort her to your house. It seems to me there is not the slightest occasion for scandal in that."

"Oh, so that's your idea, is it? Well, it might work. If you are really Dake, then I knew your father well. Knew your mother, too. A silly woman, but harmless, not like that sour-faced miss your uncle married. Clarice, she called herself. Always giving herself airs, that one was. We may be able to claim that you were acting on my behalf if that chit has not brought too much attention to bear on herself during her travels. And depending on what that Beehan creature has done about her disappearance. If she's smart, she'll have hushed it up discreetly, but I doubt you can count on her to be smart. She sounds like a fool to me; always has done. However, we'll discuss that later. Come back at half past ten. Lily and I shall be waiting for you. We'll discuss what's to be done in the carriage on the way to the assembly."

"Surely it would be better if we discussed it now," Lord Dake said. "A social occasion will hardly give us the privacy we need for such a discussion."

"That cannot be helped. I've accepted the invitation for Lily and myself, and unlike you, I believe that it is important to honour one's social obligations. That sort of thing is what distinguishes us from the harum-scarum riff-raff who feel free to do as they please. And it takes me longer to dress than it used to. Besides, I want to think about this for a bit while I'm getting ready. But we need to agree on our course of action as soon as possible, so I can get the gel back to Mrs. Beehan's and stamp out any rumours which may be flying in that quarter. Don't forget now—half past ten o'clock sharp, and don't bring your addlepate cousin with you. He won't be of any use.''

She rose abruptly and started from the room, leaning heavily on her cane. Mr. Steele, who had struggled to his feet, leapt back like a startled fawn when she nearly brushed up against him in passing, and she stopped to shoot him a sour look of disapproval before continuing out, trailed by the butler, and audibly muttering about the brainlessness of modern youth. For a moment after she left it seemed as though they would be left to find their own way out, but her butler reappeared at last and showed them to the door.

Once outside, Lord Dake took the badly shaken Mr. Steele's arm and drew him to the waiting chaise. "Come, Elliot," he said. "We must find rooms for the night, and if I am to escort that dragon and Miss Napier to an assembly, I shall have to change my clothes as well. Where do you suppose Tom has got off to?"

"I told him to secure a room for us at the best hotel in town," Elliot said. "He said it was the Royal Arms, and that he would meet us there."

"Excellent! The dragon is wrong after all—you are most definitely of use, Elliot. Courage, now. The worst of the ordeal is over for you, at least. All you have to do is avoid Aunt Augusta, and that should be easy enough. Just be thankful that she has taken such a dislike to you and that you will not be required to attend upon her tonight."

"Lord, yes," Mr. Steele said, climbing into the carriage. "I don't know how I could keep a civil tongue in my head if I did. Did you hear what she said about my mother, Bredon?"

"Yes, I heard," Dake said soothingly. "Do not let it bother you. I don't believe Augusta Napier ever had anything good to say about anyone in her life."

"She seems to like you, though," Elliot pointed out thoughtfully.

"A dubious honour," Lord Dake said, guiding the horses in the direction the groom had indicated. "A dubious honour, indeed."

CHAPTER TWELVE

LILY NAPIER brushed back a strand of soft, golden hair which had escaped from its pins and closed the door of Aunt Augusta's bedroom behind her. She paused for a short moment of peace in the quiet hallway. Since leaving the dining-room she had brought Melody up to her own room to wait while she arranged with the housekeeper to have one of the extra bedrooms prepared for her use, and had then immediately gone to attend to Aunt Augusta, who had barely reached the top of the stairs on the butler's supporting arm before she began pounding her cane loudly on the floor, a sign that she wanted her niece in attendance. Aunt Augusta's mood had been as difficult as Lily imagined it would be, and it had taken her several minutes to calm the old woman and settle her on a chaise lounge where she could compose herself for the coming ordeal of dressing to go out. Aunt Augusta seldom went out, and when she did, the process of getting ready was a prolonged and difficult one, requiring much tactful assistance from Lily. All too soon that process would begin, and in the meantime Lily would have to settle Melody in her room and to change her own gown prior to going out. Spurred by the thought, Lily hurried towards her own room. She had left Melody alone for over half an hour, and she was conscious of a good deal of anxiety as to what her sister might have got up to in that time. Lily normally considered her quiet routine in Aunt Augusta's household to be boring in the extreme and she had often longed for a bit of excitement, but this was more than she had bargained for.

When she reached her room, however, she found no further disasters awaited her. Melody was seated decorously in front of Lily's dressing-table, the little dog she called Lucky snug in her lap. Melody looked up at Lily's entrance, and Lily thought she saw traces of tears on her sister's face. Her quick sympathy deepened when Melody attempted a rather forlorn smile.

"Thank you for having Lucky sent up here to wait for me," Melody said. "I was as glad to see him as he was to see me."

"I'm pleased," Lily said. "But he can't stay, you must know. I had Jason bring him up because I didn't know what else to do with him. But he'll have to go out to the stables before Aunt Augusta finds out he's here."

"No!" Melody's voice was resolute. "If Lucky goes to the stables, so do I. It wouldn't be the first time, either," she added a little wistfully. "Besides, Aunt Augusta simply said I was to remain in my room for the rest of my stay. She said nothing against Lucky being with me."

"Only because she doesn't yet know that he exists," Lily said reasonably. "When she finds out, you may be sure she will make her objections known."

"*If* she finds out." Melody smiled tentatively.

After a moment, Lily smiled back. "Very well," she said, sitting down on the side of her bed. "Perhaps she won't find out. You will not be here that long, after all."

Melody said nothing, merely bending over Lucky and gently tugging the little dog's ears, to his evident enjoyment. Lily regretted her unfortunate observation, and tried to make amends.

"You wouldn't like it here, you know," she said gently. "You and Aunt Augusta would not suit at all."

"Oh, no," Melody agreed readily. "I can't imagine living here. It would be much worse than Mrs. Beehan's Academy or Mr. Stanhope's household. I don't know how you bear it, Lily."

"It's not so terrible," Lily said stoutly. "Of course, Aunt Augusta is rather difficult, but she isn't generally as horrid as tonight. If you never cross her and just ignore the unkind things she says, you can get on fairly well with her."

"Perhaps *you* can," Melody said frankly. "But I could not. I don't have your patience, Lily, and I could never let her bully me the way you do."

"And I could never stand up to her the way you would," Lily said with a smile. "It's just not in my nature. I cannot bear unpleasantness, and I'd do anything to avoid a scene. You must not think I approve of what you did, my dear, but I must admire your spirit, at least a little. I could never run away from my guardian and set off on my own the way you did."

"Not that it did me much good," Melody said wryly. "Aunt Augusta is determined to take me right back to Mrs. Beehan's, and if she does, things will be worse than ever, because they will keep such a guard over me I shall never get away again."

"You must have known how it would be," her sister said. "How could you think Aunt Augusta could do anything else? Even if she were likely to exert herself on your behalf, how could she keep you here against the wishes of your appointed guardian?"

Lucky began to wriggle restlessly, and Melody bent to set him down on the floor. She turned back to the dressing-table and rearranged her sister's toiletries absently for a few moments. At last she looked up and caught Lily's gaze in the mirror. She smiled and made a little face.

"I don't know," she said slowly. "I suppose I didn't let myself think about what would be likely to happen once I arrived here. I'd convinced myself that it would be best for everyone if I came to live here. I hoped Mr. Stanhope might have agreed to the scheme if Aunt Augusta wrote to suggest it. He could have paid her for my upkeep from my estate and would have been free of his worry about what to do with me. I thought Aunt Augusta might not mind, as long as I was no extra expense for her, and then you and I could be together. I've missed you, you know. I suppose I knew that neither Aunt Augusta nor Mr. Stanhope would be likely to agree to the scheme, but I didn't want to admit it, even to myself. Have you never convinced yourself that a thing would be so, simply because you wanted so badly for it to be?"

Lily smiled sadly and shook her head. She looked so unhappy that Melody tried to think of some way to comfort her.

"At any rate," she told her, "I am glad that I came, even for so short a time. At least I was able to see you again, after all these years. And I met Lord Dake. And Mr. Steele," she added. "That makes the whole thing worthwhile."

"They seem like very nice men," Lily ventured a little uncertainly. "When you think of it, they've done their best to rescue you and protect you. Rather like knights in shining armour."

Lily seemed serious, but Melody bit back a smile. The thought of Lord Dake in armour amused her. She imaged the bemused irony with which he'd regard himself in that role, the way his eyes would light with laughter when she repeated Lily's words to him—if she ever had the opportunity to do so. She realized suddenly that she might never again have the opportunity to speak to Lord Dake alone, and a great sadness came over her. But Lily was still talking, and Melody tried to attend to her sister's words. Listlessly, she agreed that both Lord Dake and Mr. Steele were handsome men.

"And very kind," Lily was adding quickly. "At least, I believe they must be, to have taken such good care of you. I admit Lord Dake seems a bit imposing. I don't always know when he is serious and when he is making a jest, but then I don't really know much about young gentlemen. I'm sure he's really quite charming."

"Yes," Melody agreed. She gave herself a little shake and exerted herself to overcome her self-pitying mood. "What about you, Lily," she asked. "Do you really not know any gentlemen?"

"Well, there is the vicar. He visits Aunt Augusta nearly every week, but he's very old and he's a trifle befuddled, I'm afraid. And, of course, there's Colonel Baylor. He and Mrs. Baylor come and play whist with Aunt Augusta every Saturday night, but the colonel is rather deaf, and he doesn't say much. I think he's a little afraid of Aunt Augusta."

"Is that all?" Melody asked. "Don't you know any young gentlemen?"

Lily blushed and looked down at the counterpane, plucking unhappily at a bit of thread. "Not really. We seldom go anywhere, you know, and when we do, Aunt Augusta likes me to be right at her side in case she needs me. Mr. Harleigh asked me to dance once at the assembly, but Aunt Augusta poked at him with her cane and told him I was too busy taking care of her to be twirling about the room in the sort of indecent embrace that passes for dancing with the modern generation."

"Oh, no!" Melody forgot her own problems in her sympathy for her sister's plight. "How awful! Did she really say that?"

"Yes, indeed. And it was even worse than that." Lily looked up unhappily at her sister. "She told Mr. Harleigh that he needn't be dangling after me anyway, because everyone knew he needed to marry a fortune, and I had only a modest pittance. She said it quite loudly, too, and several people overheard. Since then no one has ever been brave enough to ask me to dance. I'm sure that is what she intended. I believe she's afraid if I meet any eligible gentlemen I might someday marry, and then she'd have to pay for a companion to replace me."

Melody crossed the room to embrace her sister, then sat beside her on the bed. "Well, perhaps some day a new gentleman will appear. Someone like Lord Dake, who won't be afraid of Aunt Augusta. Someone who'll snatch you away from her and carry you off."

To her surprise, Lily blushed rosily and fairly jumped up from the bed. "Any man who would snatch me up and carry me off from my gardian would hardly be likely to be a gentleman," she said tightly. "Only think of the disgrace! I would be quite ruined if any such thing happened, and no honourable man would ever make an offer for me after that. As you shall be, Melody, if anyone finds out what you've done."

"What are you talking about?"

"You know! Travelling alone with Lord Dake and Mr. Steele. No gentleman who knew about that would even consider making you his wife. You'd be ruined forever!"

"But we did nothing wrong! We were friends only—travelling companions. Where is the harm in that?"

"It doesn't matter what you did," Lily said. "It is appearances which count, after all."

"That is what Mr. Steele keeps saying," Melody admitted. "But I think he is just old-fashioned and disapproving."

"Mr. Steele is a very proper gentleman," Lily said. "You would have done better to listen to what he told you. And it is little wonder if he is disapproving. He and Lord Dake both must be scandalized by you. You're fortunate they didn't wash their hands of you."

Fortunately for what little sympathy remained between the two sisters, a scratching on the door signalled the arrival of the housekeeper with the news that Melody's room was ready. Melody swallowed back the retort she had been about to make and, gathering up Lucky, followed the housekeeper out of the room. Lily excused herself from accompanying them on the grounds that it was time for her to change her gown before seeing to Aunt Augusta. Melody was glad to be left alone. The return to constraint between them had depressed her spirits.

Later, by the simple expedient of leaving her door slightly ajar, Melody was able to hear her sister and aunt leaving for the assembly, Aunt Augusta's progress marked by the steady stream of commands which she addressed to Lily. Orders to fetch her black silk shawl, her smelling-salts, an extra lace handkerchief, her fan, her reticule, and her silver cane punctuated her stately descent of the stairs. Lily was kept running lightly to and fro, her murmuring voice providing a counterpoint to Aunt Augusta's sharper accents. Melody stood at her door listening for several minutes after they had gone, half expecting Lily to return on yet another errand whose urgency had only been discovered after Aunt Augusta had made her way to her waiting carriage. But no further sounds reached her from below, and after bidding Lucky to wait quietly for her, she slipped out onto the landing, closing the door softly behind her.

Melody knew now that she had made a serious mistake. The passing years had thrown a softening veil over her memory of Aunt Augusta's harsh edges. She had remem-

bered the old woman as sharp-tongued, but not ill-spirited
Either Aunt Augusta had changed or Melody's childhood
recollections were decidedly limited. Either way, her mem
ory—or her own desire to believe what she knew was not
true—had led her astray. She no longer imagined that she
could be happy staying with Aunt Augusta. Nor could she
imagine that Lily was comfortable here. She would like to
have done something to improve Lily's position. Lily was
wasted here, lonely and bullied, but she would have blos-
somed under Mr. Stanhope's tutelage. Lily was the sort of
girl Mr. Stanhope obviously had hoped Melody herself
would be: gentle, docile, easily led. She would have been
grateful for his care in selecting the proper husband for her,
and would have warmed to Mr. Stanhope's humourless,
conscientious nature as Melody herself never had. It would
be ideal if Melody could arrange for Lily to take her place
with Mr. Stanhope. Perhaps she could have her inheritance
transferred to her half-sister. The guardianship might even
follow the fortune, not the bloodlines. But that was something which would have to be deferred for later thought.
Melody was optimistic by nature, but even she could see that
arranging her own future was enough to engage all her in-
genuity for the moment.

If she had to plan strategy, though, she would need Lord
Dake. Lord Dake was a worthy ally to have in an emer-
gency. He was intelligent and daring, as little hampered by
convention as she and far less hampered by a strict adher-
ence to the truth. True, his ironical nature could at times
overcome his judgement, but Melody could easily make al-
lowances for that. And she had been impressed by his re-
sourcefulness once he had committed himself to her plan,
and even more impressed by the way he had handled Aunt
Augusta at dinner. He had a way of taking charge, not of-
fensively, as if he thought a person too foolish to take care

f herself, but gracefully, as if snobbish doctors and bully-
ng townsmen and hysterical sisters and dragonish aunts
were mere trivial impediments which he would remove as
simply and courteously as he would open a closed door for
her so that she might precede him through it. It was true that
he had not exactly swept Aunt Augusta out of her way at
dinner, but he had remained calm and self-assured, not at
all like poor Mr. Steele. And very likely he had said little
because he was planning how best to proceed.

Now that Aunt Augusta and Lily were gone, she must
contact Lord Dake so that they could lay their plans together. Even if he was as scandalized by her brazen behaviour as Lily believed him to be, Melody could not believe
that Lord Dake would abandon her now. And she was willing at last to do what Lord Dake had urged her to do all
along. She would go back to Mr. Stanhope's guardianship.
Perhaps Lord Dake would consent to escort her there. That
she could endure. But she could not endure the thought of
being dragged back to Mrs. Beehan's in disgrace by Aunt
Augusta.

Melody made her way downstairs cautiously. If she only
knew where Lord Dake was staying she might slip out of the
house herself and go to him. She was sure that she could
convince him to help her if only she could speak to him in
person. But it was not practical for her to roam the town at
night in search of him. She could see that quite clearly; she
was not as rash as some people seemed to believe. No, since
it would not be possible for her to go to him, she must arrange for him to come to her.

The sitting-room into which Lily had first ushered them
had a small ebony writing-desk in one corner. Melody re-
membered it particularly because she had had to call Lucky
away from it when he showed some signs of being too interested in it. She slipped into the room now, and made her

way to the desk. It was unlocked, and inside were paper, pe:
and ink, and sealing wax. She took up the pen, then pause:
for a long moment. She was finding it unexpectedly diffi
cult to compose her message. There were many things sh:
would have liked to say to Lord Dake, but it seemed impos
sible to express them in a note. She must make it clear to him
that she was neither childish nor wicked. She must make him
understand that she knew now that she had no choice but to
return to her guardian's care and wished only to be allowed
to do it with a bit of dignity. If only he would come, she
knew that she could explain it to him. But what could she
write that would ensure that he would come? Finally, she
wrote her message in one quick scrawl, afraid that she would
become paralyzed by indecision if she stopped any longer to
think.

"My lord," it said. "I must speak to you tonight. Aunt
Augusta and Lily have gone to an assembly, and I am quite
alone. Please do not fail to call upon me as soon as you receive my note. It is very important that we talk before Aunt
Augusta returns. I know that I owe you much already, but
the kindness you have shown me helps me dare to ask yet
another favour of you. And you yourself once urged me to
ask your advice whenever I should need it." She signed it
with a flourish, then scribbled a hasty postscript: "Please do
come—I have nowhere else to turn!"

She read it through. It did not please her. It was full of
pleas but presented no logical or compelling reason why
Lord Dake should respond. Fortunately, she believed completely in his kindness, and thought she might well trust
herself to it. With an air of resolution she folded the page
and sealed it firmly with the wax. She inscribed his name
upon it, then tugged at the bell-pull which hung nearby. By
the time the butler answered her summons, she had com-

posed herself and stood waiting for him with an air of great dignity which completely disguised her inner fears.

"I wish to have this message delivered to Lord Dake at once," she said.

"Certainly, miss," the butler responded civilly. "I shall have a boy deliver it to his hotel. Where is Lord Dake staying?"

"I am not sure," she said uncertainly, but recovered herself and hurried in. "But surely there cannot be so many hotels in a town this small. Have the boy enquire for Lord Dake at each until he locates him. Tell him to start with the best," she added shrewdly.

"Very well, miss," he responded, and taking the message from her, he stalked majestically from the room. Once he was gone Melody's calm deserted her. She had the irrational fear that the butler would throw away her message as soon as he was out of sight, or, even more frightening, that he would save it to show to Aunt Augusta when his mistress had returned. But she had done all that she could, and she resigned herself to await the outcome of her actions.

With the thought of Aunt Augusta's eventual return nagging at her, Melody felt as if the moments she passed in waiting were hours. When at last the door opened, she jumped up from her seat, in an agony of apprehension as to whether the newcomer would be Lord Dake or a vengeful Aunt Augusta, somehow summoned home from the assembly by her butler. In the event, it was neither. It was Mr. Steele who hurried into the room and greeted her with a harried frown.

"Miss Maitland," he said with a barely civil nod. Melody, who had become accustomed to hearing herself addressed by her first name by all of her companions on the flight to Yorkshire, was a little dismayed at this new formality.

"Good evening, Mr. Steele," she said politely. "What a surprise to see you again so soon."

"I apologize for intruding," Mr. Steele said, and this time Melody was left in no doubt of his disapproval. "But a boy came to the Royal Arms with a message for Lord Dake which he said came from you. I thought it must be something important for you to write to him so soon after our parting, so I came to tell you he was not available."

"Oh. I thought perhaps you had read the message and come in his place to see what you might do for me."

"Certainly not! The message was marked for Lord Dake's attention," Mr. Steele said a little huffily. "I do not open and read my cousin's mail, Miss Maitland. I'm afraid I am more conventional than you think."

"Yes, I am afraid you are, too," Melody said a little sadly. "But I did not mean to insult you. I thought perhaps you might feel it was acceptable for you to read my message, since we have all been comrades-in-arms, so to speak, for these past few days. It's brought us all closer than one would expect upon such a short acquaintance, don't you think?" she added wistfully.

"No, I don't," said Mr. Steele, who regarded the past few days not as a glorious adventure in which he and his companions had been comrades, but as a horrible nightmare in which they had been caught and from which he had only completely awakened with their arrival at Augusta Napier's home. He had viewed Aunt Augusta's plans for Melody's future with great relief. However much he might be terrified of Aunt Augusta's forceful personality, he was unshaken in his belief that she had reacted as any gentlewoman would to Melody's irresponsible escapade. Aunt Augusta, he was sure, would restore order, uphold convention, and set Melody's feet firmly on the path of righteousness. That is why the message for Lord Dake from Melody had upset Mr. Steele. He felt sorry still for Melody, but he was now completely in sympathy with those who deplored her headstrong and very unconventional behaviour. He had been sure that Melody under Aunt Augusta's roof was a tamed and chastened Melody, one who would have no choice but to acquiesce to the future which her aunt had outlined for her. The message had put an end to his fragile peace of mind. It represented the threat that Melody was not yet subdued, that her adventures, and his involvement in them, might not have reached their conclusion after all. The nightmare, he was very much afraid, might be about to begin again. Melody's next words confirmed his fears.

"I'm sorry that you were troubled to visit me, Mr. Steele," she said. "In my message I sent for Lord Dake to come to me, so that we might discuss what I am to do next."

"You know what you are to do next, Miss Maitland," Mr. Steele replied desperately. "Your aunt is taking you back to your school."

She looked at him in silence for a moment, as if deciding whether to confide further in him, then smiled a little sadly.

"I am very sorry that you do not like me any more," she said sadly. "Still, you have been very kind to me and I shall always be grateful. I wish you will ask your cousin to call upon me when he returns to the hotel."

"Please, Miss Maitland," the soft-hearted Mr. Steele said unhappily, "You mustn't think I have taken you in dislike. Just a child; you don't understand how badly you've behaved. There are standards of behaviour young ladies must observe. Gentlemen, too," he added fairly. "You've involved my cousin far too deeply in your escapades already. You must allow your aunt to guide you now."

"I involved *you,* Mr. Steele," Melody said quietly, "and that very inadvertently. It was you who then involved Lord Dake. We begged you to let us go on our way when you'd found us in your stables, and you refused to do so."

"Well, I wish to God I had listened to you now," Mr. Steele said, abruptly abandoning the awful formality which he had hoped might protect him from further entanglement in Melody's affairs. "You're quite right, I did involve Bredon. But the problem with Bredon is that whereas one can enlist his aid, one cannot control how he will go about giving it. Very strong-minded, my cousin. And very set on getting his own way."

"He is very determined," Melody admitted with a smile. "But he is also very generous, and I'm sure he would not fail to help me or anyone else who asked his assistance. If you will give him my message, that is," she added.

"Of course," Elliot said. "It is not my business to say who Bredon will or will not help. But I warn you, he may be quite late."

"Oh, dear. I hope he returns before Aunt Augusta comes home from the assembly," Melody said. "I did particularly want to speak to him tonight."

Mr. Steele shook his head regretfully. "I'm sorry," he said. "I assumed you'd know. Lord Dake has taken your aunt and your sister to the assembly, and he'll be bringing them back here later. So I'm afraid there's no possibility that he can see you before your aunt's return."

"Oh. I hadn't known. How provoking of him, when I wanted him particularly. Why would he do such a thing?"

"Because your aunt asked him to. She wanted to confer with him about the story they were concocting to account for your behaviour as respectably as possible."

"I see. I don't know why you couldn't have gone instead, since you're so interested in respectability, and then I could have spoken to Lord Dake."

"I'm very sorry to have inconvenienced you," Mr. Steele said a little coldly. "But as it happens, I was not invited. Your Aunt Augusta seems to have taken a dislike to me."

"She seems to have taken a dislike to everyone, hasn't she?" Melody asked candidly, her momentary vexation abandoned. "I'm sure Lord Dake cannot be enjoying himself at all. He'd probably much rather have remained behind, and then we could have planned."

"If you say so," Mr. Steele said dubiously. "I don't see why Bredon would rather be here hatching some harebrained scheme with you instead of escorting a diamond of the first water like your sister to the assembly, but no doubt you know better than me."

Melody ignored the irony in his voice. "Do you really think Lily is so beautiful?" she asked.

"Of course I do. Any man would. Your sister is a lovely young woman, and her manners are excellent."

"Not like mine," Melody could not help murmuring ruefully.

"Not in the least like yours," Mr. Steele replied with devastating candour.

"Oh."

Mr. Steele realized what he had said. "No, no," he said hastily. "I didn't mean to be so harsh. You're only a girl, after all. Perhaps you'll be more like her in a few years."

"I shouldn't think so," Melody said realistically. "I don't think we're much alike at all. Do you suppose Lord Dake also admires my sister?"

"I'm sure he does," Mr. Steele said. "She's the most beautiful young lady I've ever seen. Even more beautiful than Miss Otterleigh."

"Who is Miss Otterleigh?"

"My fiancée—or, she was to be. Now I don't know what she is. I mean, I hope she will still do me the honour of becoming my fiancée. But since I left London without extending her my regrets on the very day that we were to announce our engagement, I hardly know what to expect."

"Oh, no! Because of me, do you mean? Did you really abandon your fiancée in order to help me?"

"Yes, I did," said Mr. Steele, forgetting for the moment the relief he had felt at the necessity of doing so. "And after what has happened in the last few days, I can't think what Miss Otterleigh will say. Or my mother."

"I'm very sorry. I never meant to cause you any difficulties. Have I spoiled Lord Dake's plans, too?"

"Probably," Mr. Steele replied with offhand honesty. "My cousin is a very popular man. Bound to be many engagements he's missed while we've been gallivanting about the country with you."

"Oh, dear," Melody repeated in a chastened voice. "I'm so sorry. Do you think Lord Dake resents me as much as you do?"

"I never said I resented you," Mr. Steele protested. "I've just tried to point out what happens when you go racketing about the countryside involving total strangers in your schemes. I know you didn't mean any harm. You're just a green girl, after all."

"Just a troublesome brat!" Melody said with a wry attempt at a smile.

"Exactly!" Mr. Steele agreed, relieved to have made himself understood. "And I'm sure Bredon doesn't hold you to blame for anything. Probably doesn't even think about you much," he added thoughtfully. "Stands to reason. He's a man of the world. He might spare some thought for a young lady like your sister, but I'm sure he just thinks of you as a chit that he'll have off his hands in a few more days. He won't be feeling the slightest rancour against you. Not Bredon. He's a very fair man, after all.''

''Mr. Steele,'' Melody said miserably, ''do you think your cousin might fall in love with my sister?''

''Lord, I hope not,'' cried Elliot. ''Suppose they got buckled. That would make us relatives of a sort, wouldn't it? What a thought! But you're probably right,'' he added bitterly. ''It would be just the sort of thing that would happen to me. And you couldn't blame him, could you? Any man might fall in love with your sister.''

Mr. Steele appeared much struck by the thought. Melody watched him for a bit, then returned wearily to her seat.

''Thank you for coming, Mr. Steele,'' she said at last. ''You're right; if Lord Dake is escorting Aunt Augusta and Lily, he cannot be of any use to me. There's no need for you to give him my message after all. Please just throw it away.''

''Yes, of course!'' Elliot came back to himself suddenly. He bid Melody good-night, scarcely noticing how dejected she appeared, and let himself out with a feeling of relief. All the way back to the hotel he was congratulating himself on his escape from Melody's drama, but for some reason he found that he did not feel as happy as he had expected to have the adventure now safely behind him.

CHAPTER THIRTEEN

TOM SLIPPED into the stables behind Augusta Napier's house and cast a nervous eye about for his father. But Alf was nowhere to be seen, and Tom was at ease for the first time since he had decided to return to Miss Napier's household in order to see Melody.

He had been worried about Melody since arriving in Ilkley. His view of Melody's Aunt Augusta was more realistic than hers, and he had doubted from the beginning whether Melody could be happy living with her. True, the journey they had made and Melody's behaviour during it had shocked him a little, and had dimmed some of the lustre of Melody's charm for him. But he was loyal still, and the feeling that he had somehow failed her was like a bitter medicine in his mouth.

When Melody had persuaded him to take her back to Yorkshire with him he had been almost relieved to give up his short bid for independence. But the closer they came to Augusta Napier's estate, where his father was to be found, the greater had been his uncertainty as to the wisdom of that reunion. Alf Baxter was not a sympathetic or understanding father. Tom had often felt his father's belt across his back or the careless blows of his heavy hand across his ear, and he did not welcome the scene which he was sure awaited him when next he saw Alf.

they had arrived in Ilkley, Tom's nerve had de-
entirely, and he had been glad to slink off to be-

speak a room for Lord Dake and Mr. Steele at the Royal Arms, leaving those gentlemen alone to champion Melody as she braved the dragon's den. But his conscience was sensitive, and the message from Melody which Augusta Napier's junior footman had brought to the hotel for Lord Dake had chafed Tom's soul. Melody must be in trouble if she had called for Lord Dake again so soon after they had parted. Tom's pride smarted at the knowledge that it was to the baron, and not to him, that Melody turned. He told himself bitterly it was only to be expected, since his lordship, unlike Tom, had had the gumption to see Melody to the final stage of her destination. So he had swallowed his pride and carried the message up to the room Lord Dake and Mr. Steele shared, only to be informed by Mr. Steele that Lord Dake had escorted Miss Napier and Miss Lily Napier to the assembly and was likely to be gone for some time. And when Mr. Steele had decided he had best see what Melody wanted with Lord Dake, Tom had meekly agreed to remain behind. That was only right; Mr. Steele, too, had not turned tail and run from the encounter at Augusta Napier's household, and had, therefore, earned the right to defend her.

But Mr. Steele had returned from that meeting and had met Tom's anxious queries with the news that Melody no longer needed any assistance. That did not sound right to Tom, and Mr. Steele's preoccupied air did little to reassure him. So he had gathered up his courage and had come to Augusta Napier's house, determined to do his humble best to help Melody in whatever way she required. But he could not help but be relieved that a confrontation with his father was evidently not to be the first order of business.

Getting into the house presented no challenge to Tom. He knew that the servants in Miss Napier's household never went to bed until their mistress retired. Even the cook waited up, for Miss Napier often required hot milk or a light snack before she went to bed. So he scratched confidently upon the kitchen door, and Mrs. Plum admitted him as he knew she would. Tom was a favourite of Mrs. Plum, who had made a life's mission of her desire to fatten him up, and beyond scolding him for disappearing the way he had done and prophesying that his father would make him regret his actions the next time they met, Mrs. Plum made no protest when Tom entered her kitchen. She made him sit at the table while she cut him some bread and ham and poured him a cup of tea from her own teapot, but she listened to his story all the while he ate. Since Mrs. Plum had often heard Tom's rather exaggerated accounts of the closeness of his earlier friendship with the much-younger Miss Lily Napier and her sister Melody, she found nothing so strange in the latter young lady's choice of Tom as an escort. Nor did she show any inclination to disbelieve him when he claimed that Miss Melody had sent for him and wished to see him, merely recommending to him that he finish his nice cup of tea before he went up to her. When Tom drained his cup hastily, she made him promise that he would tell her a more complete version of his recent adventures at another time, and did not detain him further as he set off abovestairs. She was even able to direct him to the proper room, for there was little that went on in Augusta Napier's household that Mrs. Plum did not know.

Tom scratched quietly upon Melody's door. There was no answer, and he tried again, barely louder. Mrs. Plum held no terror for him, but the butler, Mr. Mapps, was another matter, and Tom preferred not to attract his attention if possible. But there was no answer, and when Tom knocked louder, he heard a series of unhappy whines from within that told him that Lucky, at least, was not asleep. Lucky began to make so much noise that Tom was sure Melody could not have slept through it, and he eased the door cautiously open.

"Melody! It's me, Tom," he whispered.

But there was no answer, and when he entered the room he soon discovered why. Lucky was there, and very glad to see his old friend. But of Melody there was no trace. None, that is, but the sealed note which he found propped up on her dressing-table. Tom himself had never learned to read, but he could interpret signs, and he was sure that the note was a bad omen. Melody had run away on her own before, and Tom was very much afraid that she had done so again. With no thought to his father, he sailed down the stairs and out the kitchen door to the stables, where his worst fears were confirmed. One of the mares was missing, and though the stable-boy he awakened had heard nothing and had not saddled for Melody, Tom was sure she had taken her. He stood for a moment running his hands through his hair in panic, then whirled and set off for the hotel where Mr. Steele and Lord Dake were staying.

Mr. Steele, who had gone to bed for the night, was slow to answer Tom's knocks upon his door. When he had done so, the sight of an obviously agitated Tom on his threshold did not appear to please him.

"Oh, Lord," he said with a groan. "It's you again. Do you know what time it is?"

"No, I don't," Tom gasped, but before he could explain the purpose of his visit, Mr. Steele had interrupted him again.

"No more do I," he said. "But I do know it's the middle of the night, and I was finally sleeping in the most comfortable bed I've found since I left London, and I was dreaming that I was home and all of this was behind me."

"But, Mr. Steele," Tom said. "You ain't home, and it's started up all over again, sir. Melody's run off again!"

"Damn the girl!" Mr. Steele cried, "I should have known she'd do something like this. She doesn't give up, not her. We've got to inform Bredon of this."

"But Lord Dake is still at the assembly with Melody's aunt, Mr. Steele. How can we let him know without her finding out?"

"We can't, obviously. But she'll have to know in any case. You're absolutely sure Melody is gone?" he added, hurriedly pulling on his clothes.

"Yes, sir. Her room's empty. She left a note on her dressing-table. And one of the mares is gone from stables."

"A note? What does it say?"

In answer Tom pulled the still-sealed note out of his pocket where he had stashed it and handed it over to Mr. Steele, who went to sit near the candle on the bedside table. Despite the fact that it was clearly addressed to his cousin, Mr. Steele showed no hesitation in ripping the note open and reading it. It was not very long, but its effect on Mr. Steele was profound.

"You're right," he said hollowly to Tom. "She's off again. Says she can't bear the thought of going back to Mrs. Beehan's with her aunt. Says she's thought it over and she's going back to London to her guardian's house. No need for him to trouble himself with her, she says, as she'll make the arrangements for her travel herself." He paused and grimaced at Tom. " 'Make the arrangements herself,' " he repeated bitterly. "Lord knows what kind of hubble-bubble she's made of things." He returned gloomily to the note. "Says she doesn't want to bother Bredon further, and that once she's back at her guardian's house, perhaps the whole matter will be forgotten. And she asks him to take care of her dog for her. Damn that dog," he added savagely.

"Do you suppose she means to ride all the way back to London?" Tom asked. "She's taken a horse."

"Don't ask me to suppose anything where that girl is concerned," Mr. Steele replied. "I can't imagine what she has in her head. But whatever she's planning to do, you can wager it's as ramshackle as her other schemes, and we'll have to come to the maggoty girl's rescue again. Do you know where the assembly that Miss Napier is attending is?"

"At the assembly hall—only place it could be."

"Fine. You go there and fetch Lord Dake. Show him the letter. In the meantime, I'll start out after Melody myself."

"No! I'm not going to fetch Lord Dake. I told you, Melody's aunt will find out. We've got to go after her now and bring her back before her aunt even knows she's gone again."

Mr. Steele did not share Tom's optimism, but he knew better than to argue with that tone of voice. He considered fetching Bredon himself, and leaving Tom to go on alone, but the idea of interrupting an assembly in a town where he knew no one in order to try to explain the situation to Bredon and, inevitably, to Melody's Aunt Augusta, did not appeal to him. Besides, he didn't trust Tom to persuade Melody that she must return. He'd have to go with him. Mr. Steele seized a piece of paper from the dresser and scribbled a note on it for Lord Dake. He left it on the bedside table, and left the candle burning so that his cousin would be sure to see it. Then he followed Tom out of the room and down to the stables, where they could have horses saddled for them.

Mr. Steele hoped Melody would not be too hard to find. Thanks to Tom's concern, her flight had been discovered almost immediately, and if she did not suffer some accident on the road at night or meet some villain who would do her harm, Mr. Steele was fairly sure that he and Tom would catch up with her. There was only one road leading south out of Ilkley, after all.

They might have missed her at that, had Tom not spotted the horse she'd taken in the lighted stable-yard of an inn outside of the town. Mr. Steele was dubious at first, but Tom insisted they stop. He was sure the neat bay mare tethered in the yard was from Augusta Napier's stables.

"I've looked after Miss Napier's stables for the last nine years," he insisted. "I know her horses as well as I know my own face. That's Bella there, all right, when she should be snug in her stall this time of night. What do you reckon Melody can be thinking of, Mr. Steele?"

Inside the inn Melody was asking herself the same question. Back in her room at Aunt Augusta's house her plan had seemed perfectly adequate, if not ideal. True, she had had to take the store of pin money which Lily, luckily, still kept in the flowered china box on her dresser. The box was a relic from their childhood. Melody had recognized it when she'd sat at Lily's dressing-table, and the sight of it had given her the impetus for her plan. Just as she'd suspected, Lily still used the box to hold her savings, and Melody had appropriated them, consoling herself with the knowledge that she had left behind her pearl set and a note for Lily, explaining that she would repay her sister by mail from London.

And she had had to borrow one of Aunt Augusta's horses to make her way to the inn. There was a more serious problem, for she had not dared to instruct the ostler to have the animal returned to Aunt Augusta for fear of giving rise to questions which she would have found awkward to answer without resorting to lies. Melody had been accused of theft once on this journey, and she did not wish to fall under suspicion again. But she'd had enough of Lily's money left after purchasing her ticket on the stage to pay to have the mare stabled till called for. Once her flight was discovered, Melody was sure that Lord Dake, at least, would be intelligent enough to search for her at the staging inn. She'd found out its location herself by the simple expedient of asking a passer-by on the street where was the nearest place one might arrange for passage to London, and had been pleased to find how close by the inn was. Lord Dake would do the same—although not, she hoped, until the next morning, when she and the stage would both be long gone—and would find Aunt Augusta's mare where she had left it. Melody was sure he would not forget to restore the beast to Aunt Augusta's stables; it was the sort of detail Lord Dake seemed never to forget.

It was the thought of Lord Dake—or, rather, of her promise to him—that had given Melody the greatest pause in planning her escape. But after some reflection she had decided that she was staying within the letter, if not the spirit, of their agreement. She had fulfilled her original promise once they'd arrived at her aunt's house. She had promised not to run away from him, but nothing had been said about her running away from Aunt Augusta.

But she had not arrived at the inn in good spirits, despite the relative ease of her escape so far. And once she had purchased her ticket on the stage and arranged for her horse to be stabled, she felt even more dejected. The public parlour at the inn was full of a large crowd of noisy people. They could not all be waiting for the stage, and Melody soon realized that the inn was a favorite of the locals as well as a posting inn. There were a few other women present, older women obviously travelling with their husbands, but she was the only single female there, and the youngest. And she was not very comfortable with the looks she was receiving from the others.

Melody would have denied charges of snobbery, but the fact was that she was beginning to feel that the sort of people one was likely to find waiting in a public parlour for a night stage were not the sort of people with whom one might look forward to travelling. And ever since the incident in the market-place at Grampton, she had been aware of the sort of looks a young girl alone could attract from strange men. She was beginning to understand the vague warnings she had received from Mr. Steele and Lord Dake and even from dear Lily about the dangers which awaited an unchaperoned and unprotected lady in public. There might even, she now realized, be some justification for the endless prosings of Mr. Stanhope and the mistresses at Mrs. Beehan's Academy about ladylike behaviour and observing of convention. Melody did not like to think that the world was such a harsh place that an inoffensive young lady could not make her way from one place to another without being exposed to grave danger. But just because she did not like to think it, she now saw, did not mean it was not so. Melody wondered whether she would have had the courage now to leave the safety of Mrs. Beehan's Academy as she had done so carelessly just one week earlier. Of course, as it happened, she had been perfectly safe once Fate, in the person of Mr. Steele, had brought her to the attention of Lord Dake. She thought of her journey to Yorkshire, those leisurely days riding alongside Lord Dake in the carriage, the pleasant conversations they had had along the way. Melody could not help but compare those days with the prospect of her solitary journey back to London on the public stage, and found herself blinking back sudden tears.

It was the tears that accounted for her failure to see Mr. Steele and Tom when they entered the room. But they saw her immediately, and started towards the corner where she sat. Before they could reach her, however, their progress was impeded by a vast man with a thick black beard and a bald head who grabbed Tom by the shoulder and spun him round to face him.

"You, boy, what are you doing here, then?" he demanded truculently.

Mr. Steele's mouth fell open in surprise. He looked to Tom for an explanation, but saw nothing but confused terror on the boy's face.

"Da!" Tom cried out in dismay. "I didn't see you."

"No, I'll wager you didn't, or you'd have turned tail and run out of here for sure, wouldn't you, boy? What's the idea of your running away like you done? And why have you come back now, you young fool? Walking into an inn big as you please. Who's this you're with?"

"This is Mr. Steele. He's a friend of mine."

"A friend of yours? Looks a might high in the instep for that, don't he? Or do you fancy yourself one of the Quality now, boy? What have you been getting up to since you left us?"

"Nothing, I promise. I met up with Miss Melody in London, is all. You know, Da, Miss Lily's sister. She wanted to come back here to visit her auntie, and I said I'd bring her. That's all, honest."

The bearded giant roared and shook his head. "That's all! Sounds like a good deal too much to me. Mischief, boy, that's what you're up to. You got no call to go mixing with your betters that way. I told you so when you were a little 'un and you'd play with master's daughters, and I'm telling you so again now. You come back away from here; we're going home."

Tom squirmed wildly but unproductively in his father's grasp. "But I can't go now. I've got to help take Miss Melody home. Mr. Steele and I came to do it. Miss Melody's set to run away again unless we stop her."

"Stop her! Kidnapping her, is what it sounds like. This high-born friend of yours ain't no gentleman at all, you mark my words, and he's talked you into doing his evil work for him."

"No, here, I say," Mr. Steele protested indignantly. "I haven't talked Tom into anything. In fact, I distinctly asked him to fetch my cousin while I came for Miss Maitland, but he insisted on accompanying me."

"Oh, aye, put a spoke in your plans, I wager. Would have preferred going after the young lady on your own, then, wouldn't you?"

Mr. Steele, who knew a hopelessly belligerent drunkard when he saw one, made as if to slip away, but Alf Baxter's huge, hamlike fist descended upon his shoulder and fastened inexorably upon his coat.

"Where do you think you're going, then? Off to try to kidnap the young lady? Well, you're too late, my fancy gentleman, she's gone now."

"Gone!" Mr. Steele twisted to look at the corner where Melody had sat only moments before and saw that Alf Baxter was right. The bench upon which she'd sat was empty, and Melody was nowhere to be seen. He turned back to his tormentor in fury. "Damn it, man, you've let her get away." Mr. Steele pulled free and set off towards the corner where he'd last seen Melody. Alf Baxter let him go, but he flung an accusing hand at his retreating back.

"Villain!" he bellowed. "That man's a villain. He's abducting a young lady, and doing his best to corrupt my innocent boy into helping him. He's a villain, I say, and if I didn't believe in minding my own business I'd whip him out of this inn myself."

"Da, no!" Tom twisted helplessly in his father's grasp. "Mr. Steele isn't abducting Melody; he's trying to help her."

But his voice was lost in the general hubbub that the accusation had caused, and before he could try again his father had dragged him relentlessly from the inn and to the gig that would carry them both back to Miss Napier's stables.

CHAPTER FOURTEEN

MELODY'S THOUGHTS upon Lord Dake were interrupted by the sudden shouts in the public room. She looked up curiously, and found that the loud individual was a huge, bearded man, and that he was holding Tom by the shoulder as he shouted. Dim memories from long ago came to her; she could see the same man holding a much younger Tom by the arm and shouting at him to stop wasting his time playing with the young misses and get back to work. She had come to Tom's rescue on that occasion long ago, and her first impulse now was to do the same. But as she rose to do so she saw that the willowy gentleman near the centre of the commotion was Mr. Steele.

Something very like panic seemed to rise in Melody's throat, and she whirled and ran from the room. The narrow corridor leading down to the kitchen was deserted, and Melody ran lightly down it and through the kitchen and to the courtyard beyond. She did not know where she was going. She simply knew that she could not let Mr. Steele and Tom take her back to Aunt Augusta's house. Aunt Augusta would be furious, and Lord Dake would have been exasperated by yet another of the childish episodes which had led him to think of her as a troublesome brat. True, he did not *act* as if he thought of her that way. After she had given her promise not to run away again he had actually seemed to enjoy the time spent travelling with her, but no doubt that was attributable to his kindness and courtesy.

Lily insisted that Lord Dake must be scandalized by her, and Mr. Steele, who was his cousin and knew him well, had made it clear that Lord Dake saw her merely as an annoying responsibility. Melody could not bear to exasperate him further.

Melody had slipped from the room before Alf Baxter accused Mr. Steele of attempting to abduct her. No doubt if she had heard the accusations she would have tarried to refute them. But by the time Baxter's accusations had been made, Melody was on her way out of the inn. Mr. Steele was not so fortunate. The group of people who had gathered round to listen to Alf Baxter had begun to murmur loudly against him even before Alf had dragged Tom away. Once father and son had left, however, Mr. Steele found that the rest of the crowd was not inclined to let the matter rest. The comments were getting uglier by the minute, and several hands actually tugged at Mr. Steele's jacket as he pushed his way through them and hurried out the passageway.

There was no sign of Melody in the dimly lit passage, but in the kitchen Mr. Steele found her trail. A kitchen maid had seen the young lady slip out into the courtyard. Once in the courtyard he could see no sign of the girl, but the thought of the angry crowd he had left behind him sent him out in the direction he thought Melody must have taken. The courtyard opened up onto the road, and in the distance Mr. Steele thought he could see a figure hurrying away.

"Melody!" he shouted, and the figure stopped, then turned and ran off the road and onto the moors. Cursing, Mr. Steele followed. It was dark, and he stumbled over the uneven surface of the ground as he ran. Melody ran on ahead of him; she seemed to have less trouble seeing in the moonlight than he did. The pursuit seemed to go on for hours, when finally Mr. Steele ran his quarry to the ground.

He found her slumped against a crag of rock, almost sobbing from exhaustion.

"Why are you running away from me?" he gasped as he came upon her. "Have you gone mad?"

"Why won't you leave me alone?" she cried passionately, turning upon him as he came up. "Everything was going to be all right. I had my ticket for the stage, and I was on my way back to London. Now you've made me miss it! Why must you keep interfering with my plans?"

"Interfering!" Mr. Steele said hotly. "I like that! You were happy enough to have me interfere when you wanted a ride to Yorkshire. And when you wanted that damned dog rescued. And I didn't hear you complaining about interference in Grampton when we kept that crowd of yokels from hauling you up before the magistrate as a common thief. And if I am interfering now, you've got no one to blame but yourself; you were running away again, and you promised that you would not."

"I promised not to run away until I got to Aunt Augusta's house, and I kept my word," Melody protested. "Besides, I was not running away this time. I was going home to Mr. Stanhope, just as you have always wanted me to do."

"No one wanted you to go away on your own; you know that," Mr. Steele said with as much patience as he could muster. "Now please let me take you back to your aunt's house, Miss Maitland; you've caused enough trouble for one night."

"You are the one who has caused the trouble," Melody said. "I'd be safely on the stage and on my way back by now if you hadn't come after me."

"Yes, of course, I might have known it would be my fault," Mr. Steele said bitterly. "No doubt I did it all for my own pleasure, too. Nothing could please me more than to be dragged from my bed with the news that you've run off again, to be forced out into the night to look for you, and to end up at an inn with a crowd of dirty thugs who've been told that I'm a villain bent on abducting innocent young women.''

"Oh, no!" To Mr. Steele's extreme disapproval, Melody could not quite choke back a little laugh. "Is that what happened, Mr. Steele?"

"That is exactly what happened. Tom's father seems to have turned up. From the way he behaved I'd wager he'd spent the evening drinking himself into an ugly mood, and he got it into his head that I had led Tom astray and that I was trying to force Tom to assist me in abducting you. As if I would!"

"Oh, no, of course you would not, Mr. Steele. How terrible for you. I am truly sorry."

"Yes, you think it's very funny, don't you?"

"No, I promise you I do not. Please forgive me for laughing just now; but you sounded so disgruntled, and I could not help myself."

"Disgruntled! I should think I sounded disgruntled. And so would you if you found yourself with a group of roughs all demanding to know what you were doing chasing an innocent girl through the night."

"Poor Mr. Steele! I promise you, I would not have had this happen for the world. I would never have left the inn if I had known what was taking place. Let us go back there together now, and I shall explain to everyone that you have not made the slightest attempt to abduct me."

Mr. Steele, who had been taking his bearings during Melody's speech, was far from mollified. "Excellent," he said briefly. "Do by all means let us go back to the inn, and if you tell your story in time I may even escape from that mob with my life. But there's just one difficulty, Miss Maitland. Have you the faintest notion where the inn is?"

"Oh, don't be silly," Melody said stoutly. "We cannot have travelled so far. The lights will be visible, no doubt."

But when she had looked around her, she had to concede Mr. Steele's point. At her urging Mr. Steele scrambled up atop the boulder by which they stood, but it was no use. There were no lights visible. There was nothing, in fact, to indicate where the inn stood.

"How can we have lost it so quickly?" Melody asked uneasily.

"Did it seem so quickly to you?" Mr. Steele asked. "To me it seemed as if we had been running for hours. But you may be right. It may be quite close by—no doubt you failed to notice that the inn stood in a hollow. We would have to be almost upon it before we could see the lights."

"But it is right on the road. Once we find the road, it will take us straight back."

"I see even less chance of our finding the road in this darkness," Mr. Steele pointed out with a sweeping gesture at the open moor in which they stood.

"Can we not follow our own trail back to the inn?" Melody asked.

"Perhaps we could, if I were some sort of a Red Indian," Mr. Steele retorted. "But not until daylight, certainly. You've led me up and down so much I've no notion which way we came. Do you?"

Melody was sure that she did, but a look around left her confused. The moor was very wild, and everything looked the same to her, especially in the moonlight. She turned back to Mr. Steele in dismay.

"Then what are we to do? We cannot spend the night out here."

"I don't know, Miss Maitland," Mr. Steele replied. "You are the one with all the plans, after all. My part in this from the beginning has been limited to playing cat's-paw to you.

No doubt this is what I deserve for my stupidity. Bredon will tell me so, you may be sure."

"Lord Dake!" Melody clasped her hands to her face and looked up at Mr. Steele piteously. "Oh, what will he think when he finds out what I've done this time?"

"He'll think you are the most troublesome brat he's ever known in his life and that I am the biggest idiot," Mr. Steele said savagely. "And he'll damn well be right."

"But Mr. Steele, if we spend the night out here alone together, I'll be ruined, won't I?"

"Damn the girl! A fine time you pick to come to that realization. Bredon and I've been trying to get you to understand that while you led us over half of England, and now that we're out here and have no choice but to spend the night here, you finally begin to worry about your reputation."

"Well, I thought I did not have to worry about it, not with Lord Dake and you, as you are both such kind gentlemen. But Lily tells me I am badly compromised already. She said the only redeeming fact was that I had never been alone with either of you. And now here we are—alone together."

"I'm very sorry, Miss Maitland," Mr. Steele said more patiently. "Please don't take on; nothing dreadful will happen. We'll find our way back tomorrow and put the whole thing in Bredon's hands. He'll know what to do."

"I don't want to put it into Lord Dake's hands! It's not fair that he should have to be bothered with me again," Melody protested.

"Listen to the girl!" Mr. Steele implored the silent night. "Now she doesn't want Bredon to be bothered with her affairs. That's not what you said before, Miss Maitland. You sent for Bredon only this evening, and if it wasn't to involve him further in your affairs I don't know for what it could have been."

"That was different," Melody wailed. "That's when I thought we were friends—allies. But you tell me that Lord Dake doesn't regard me as a friend at all. You say he regards me as a troublesome chit, and that I've put him to a good deal of inconvenience and have disrupted his life already. Don't you see how that makes everything different? I can't keep asking him to rescue me if he doesn't want to! And if you don't stop calling me Miss Maitland in that disapproving tone of voice, I shall scream," she added. "You used to call me Melody."

"That's because I used not to know any other name to call you by," Mr. Steele replied. "And I can't help but sound disapproving, when I think of the trouble you have got us both into. I don't know how I am ever to explain to your sister what happened. I promised her myself that you would come to no harm, and look what you've done now. She'll never forgive me for this. No one could. And I don't even dare to think about what your aunt will say. All I can do is hope that Bredon isn't so disgusted with us both that he washes his hands of us."

"Do you think Lord Dake will wish he could wash his hands of me?" Melody asked wistfully.

"Yes, of course. Bound to."

"He didn't seem to find me tiresome before. He seemed to think I was quite amusing at times, and when we had those conversations in the chaise and you and Tom said my ideas were disgraceful for a young girl, Lord Dake said that he thought I showed a refreshingly sensible mind."

"Lord, that's just Bredon. I've told you, he likes to shock people a little himself at times. But you needn't think that will excuse your behaviour in his eyes. There's a great difference between a man like Bredon saying outrageous things from time to time and a young girl acting like a hoyden.

Bredon won't think there's anything refreshingly sensible about this escapade, believe me.''

Melody did believe him, so much so that a great feeling of dejection descended upon her. She said no more, and allowed Mr. Steele to persuade her that it was useless for them to wander all over the countryside in the dark. They settled down in the shelter of the large boulder, sitting side by side in silence. Mr. Steele gave Melody his coat. She tried to decline it, but he urged her so strongly that she let him tuck it round her.

They had a long and sleepless night's wait. Mr. Steele consoled himself with the knowledge that dawn would come early on the open moors, so that they might with luck make their way back to the inn before its inhabitants roused themselves. He hoped that most of the occupants of the public parlour who had overhead Alf Baxter's accusations had boarded the night stage and would be long gone before he and Melody appeared there again.

Melody, however, could find no such consolation. She spent a lonely, uncomfortable night contemplating the reaction of her family and of Lord Dake to what she had done. Lord Dake would hold her in complete aversion. He would probably even refuse to take her back to Mr. Stanhope's residence. She would have to face the ordeal of the reunion with Mr. Stanhope without Lord Dake to back her up. In fact, she would have to face the rest of her life without Lord Dake, and that thought brought tears to her eyes. No doubt she would never marry anyone; even the suitable men that Mr. Stanhope had in mind for her would shrink from marriage to a young lady who had ruined herself so completely. And Mr. Steele would never marry her—not that she wanted him to. He had a fiancée waiting for him back in London. No, she was doomed to a life of loneliness and disgrace, she was sure of it.

She tried to think what she could do next, but it was difficult to think about the future now. First, of course, she
must go with Mr. Steele to the inn in order to clear his name.
There would be a good deal of fuss after that, much unpleasantness. Wistfully, Melody considered several means
by which she might hope to avoid the accounting which she
knew was coming. She thought she might go right away as
soon as she'd explained about poor Mr. Steele, somewhere
no one would know her. She thought she might have a future on the stage—she'd been much admired in the last
pageant at Mrs. Beehan's—or as a governess or English
mistress in some French household. Or she might even become a serving girl. They seemed to have more freedom in
their lives than heiresses, and while Melody did not believe
she would be happy as a servant, she thought it did not
matter, as she fully expected never to be happy again. But
in the end she admitted what she had already known. Such
day-dreams of escape could only be day-dreams. She could
not hope to escape reality. She would go back to the inn with
Mr. Steele, and she would let him take her to Aunt Augusta's house. Aunt Augusta would be livid and would lock her
away in her room until she could see her safely back at Mrs.
Beehan's—if, indeed, that very proper lady would agree to
take back a pupil who had so thoroughly disgraced herself.
Lily would be shocked and would cry at her wickedness.

And Lord Dake would return to London and be free of
her forever. Perhaps he'd fall in love with Lily, who, Mr.
Steele seemed to think, was irresistible. Perhaps he'd already done so, tonight at the assembly. That would be good
for Lily; if she wed Lord Dake she wouldn't have to be
lonely and unhappy with Aunt Augusta any longer. He'd be
the most wonderful husband imaginable, and Lily would
finally have a chance to bloom. With such consoling
thoughts, Melody passed the dark hours till dawn.

CHAPTER FIFTEEN

LORD DAKE was finding it very hard to hold on to his patience. It had been a trying evening for him. Watching Melody's trepidation as they had approached Aunt Augusta's house had made him feel that he was about to hand her over to a terrible fate from which he was helpless to rescue her. Keeping a guard on his tongue during supper, while Augusta Napier bullied Melody, had been more difficult still. The glance Melody had thrown him as she was being led upstairs had wrung his heart, and thinking of her crying alone in her room, as he supposed her to be, was making Lord Dake, a very civilized man as a rule, think longingly of the days when a man might fling a damsel in distress up on his saddle and ride off with her to safety. Such a thing was not possible, not in this day and age, but Lord Dake thought it must have been very satisfying, far more satisfying than meekly escorting Melody's chief tormentor and her little mouse of a sister to a stodgy assembly hall in a backward Northern town for a torturous evening of stifling conventionality and decorum.

But Lord Dake was a realist, and if he could not do what he wanted to help Melody, he must do what he could. So after hiring the closest thing in Ilkley to an elegant carriage and returning to the Royal Arms to dress—and giving silent thanks to the distant Parker who had had the foresight to pack evening wear for his master's trip—Lord Dake arrived promptly at half past ten o'clock at Augusta Napier's home and took Miss Napier and Miss Lily Napier up with him. Miss Napier refused to discuss Melody's situation on the way to the assembly, and as Lily was evidently too timid to speak without her aunt's express permission, the drive afforded Lord Dake with the opportunity for much silent, and largely fruitless, reflection. Once inside, there was little opportunity to talk, as a great many people, all of whom Lord Dake sincerely wished at the devil, approached to pay their respects to Miss Napier, who seemed to be held in a great deal of awe, and to meet the newcomer to Ilkley. Lord Dake shook hands with the gentlemen and bowed to the ladies and exchanged polite, smiling greetings while he fumed inside with impatience for the privacy to discuss Melody with her Aunt Augusta. But after a while he came to feel a grudging sort of admiration for Miss Napier's tactics. He was being introduced as the son of Augusta Napier's old school chum, unfortunately long since departed, and Lord Dake would have been very surprised if by the next day there was anyone in Ilkley who did not know that he was an old friend of Miss Napier's family and, therefore, a natural choice as escort for her schoolgirl niece. He was beginning to realize that Augusta Napier could be a valuable ally, despite her sharp tongue and autocratic manner.

There had evidently been a strict if unexpressed observance of precedent among those who approached to pay their respects to Augusta Napier. The dowager ladies had been the first to arrive, followed by several elderly and prosperous-looking gentlemen. After that had come a smaller group of middle-aged ladies and gentlemen, and only when all of these individuals had exchanged their leisurely remarks and drifted away did the few younger people approach, the young ladies escorted, generally, by their mamas, to be introduced to Lord Dake. He gave them all his charming smile and bowed politely over their hands, but he refrained from doing what he knew was expected of him and asking any of the young ladies to dance. He did not intend to be separated from Augusta Napier's side till they had had their discussion, and though several of the young ladies lingered hopefully for some time, eventually they all gave up. In the end, however, Lord Dake was thwarted not by social obligation but by his iron-willed companion. Several young gentlemen had joined the group, attracted, he was sure, by the presence of the beautiful Miss Lily Napier. Evidently Augusta Napier shared his opinion, and when one young gentleman, a ginger-haired youth who'd been introduced as Mr. Corbley, dared to ask Lily to dance, she raised her cane as a barrier between him and her niece.

"Lily's promised this dance to Lord Dake," Augusta Napier snapped, and his lordship was left with no choice but to offer Melody's sister his arm and lead her onto the floor. He was, no doubt, the envy of most of the young gentlemen present, for Miss Lily Napier was by far the loveliest woman in her room. She wore a gown of ivory satin, simply cut and far more modest than those most of the young ladies wore, almost dowdy compared to the daring fashions in London. But it suited her, setting off her dainty figure and creamy white skin to perfection. Delicate mitts of ivory lace covered her little hands, and the mother-of-pearl buttons at her wrists matched the fan she carried. A white silk rose was tucked into her soft blond curls, and her cheeks, whether because of her excitement at being at a ball or her embarrassment at being virtually propelled into Lord Dake's arms, were becomingly pink. She danced well, light and graceful as he led her through the steps, but Lord Dake could scarcely wait till the dance ended and he could take her back to her aunt's side. Apart from his impatience to talk to Augusta Napier, he had little interest in a milk-and-water miss so timid she answered his attempts at conversation with a few almost inaudible words and kept her lovely blue eyes fixed studiously at the level of his cravat. But Lord Dake felt some sympathy for her shyness, especially as he realized his own earlier irony had helped to make her so uncomfortable with him, and he exerted himself to set her at her ease.

"You must have been very surprised to see Melody turn up at your aunt's house this morning, Miss Napier," he said with a charming smile. "Had it been a long time since you'd seen her last?"

"Too long." She dared a glance up at him. "Aunt Augusta does not let me travel at all, you see, and Mr. Stanhope has only brought Melody to visit us twice in the years since her parents died. I believe he thinks of a trip to Yorkshire as a hardship, though apparently he is very fond of travel on the Continent. At any rate, I was very glad to see Melody again, even though I cannot approve of what she did. And I am very grateful to you and Mr. Steele for bringing her here safely."

"It was actually my cousin who agreed to escort Melody here," Lord Dake pointed out. "I'm afraid I refused to help at first, and only came along at the last moment."

"Mr. Steele is a very kind man." Lily's eyes sought his cravat again. "And a very fine gentleman. I think he has lovely manners, don't you?"

"I can't say that I've ever thought about it," Lord Dake said with a little laugh. "But Elliot is indeed a kind man. I have always thought so."

She shot him another glance then, as if she suspected he was making fun of her, but what she saw reassured her, and she even ventured a timid smile.

"I hope you will forgive me for making so personal a statement, Miss Napier," Lord Dake said after a few moments of silence, "but I must say that you and your sister do not resemble each other in the least."

"Oh, no." Lily's smile was more confident now. "We have never done. I took after our mother, but Melody has her father's colouring. And his character as well. My stepfather was a wonderful man, good-natured and generous, and quick to laughter. He loved our mother very much, and they were so close that we saw rather little of them ourselves, but we both adored him. And he was always as kind to me as if I'd been his own daughter. But Melody was his pride and joy. She's always had such spirit, and the mischief she could get into! She was younger than I, of course, but it seldom seemed that way. Hers was the stronger nature, even then, and she was the leader where we were concerned. There was nothing Melody would not do, but I have always been rather easily frightened. You must think I cut a sorry figure compared to her."

"Not at all," said Lord Dake, who did indeed think that very thing. "You are lovely, if I may say so, and very prettily behaved. And as for comparison with your sister, I'm sure most people would consider you a far better example of what a lady of Quality should be. I know Mr. Steele, for instance, is quite shocked by the scrapes Melody gets into."

Lily blushed at the reintroduction of Mr. Steele into the conversation. "Melody's scrapes are generally a result of her concern for others, though," she said after a moment. "I remember once there were doves nesting in the rafters of the stables, and she took it into her head that the babies were in danger of falling from their nests before they could fly. Something one of the stable-boys said gave her the idea, I believe. But Melody couldn't persuade anyone else that the baby birds were in danger, so in the end she climbed up into the rafters herself to bring the nests down where they'd be safe. I discovered her crawling along the rafters towards them and screamed so loudly she lost her balance and tumbled down. Luckily she fell into a pile of straw and was quite unhurt. Our mother wanted to punish her, being afraid Melody would try it again and hurt herself, but her father just laughed and said she'd meant well. And he explained to her how the parent birds would abandon their babies if she tried to interfere again.''

It was the longest speech he had ever heard her make, and Lord Dake suspected that Lily was starved for the chance to talk about her family and the long-lost happiness of her youth. He smiled down at her, feeling that he had judged Melody's sister too harshly. "What about *your* father?" he asked gently. "Do you remember him?"

"Not really. I have a few vague memories, but I think mostly they are more memories of what I've heard about him than what I knew myself. He was rather like his sister, from what I've heard."

Involuntarily Lord Dake's gaze went to Augusta Napier, then he smiled reassuringly down at Lily. "But you take after your mother," he reminded her, and she blushed and gave him a grateful smile in return. But she lapsed almost immediately into pensive silence.

"I beg your pardon, Miss Napier," Lord Dake said gently after a few minutes. "I know this is none of my affair, but it seems to me that you are not very happy here with your Aunt Augusta."

She looked up at him in surprise, and her gentle blue eyes were troubled. "Oh, no," she said simply. "I'm not happy here at all. Aunt Augusta doesn't want me to meet anyone who might be amiable or kind. She complains about me all the time, but she doesn't want to take the chance that I might marry and leave her. I shall be stuck here with her until I'm far too old to think of marriage."

"But surely you are of age, Miss Napier," he protested gently. "Can she really keep you locked away from everyone forever? There must be some way you could meet young people, could get away even just occasionally and enjoy yourself."

Lily looked up at him, plainly puzzled. "But how?" she said simply. "There's nothing I can do."

Melody would think of something, he thought, but he did not say it. Instead he smiled at her reassuringly and chatted about inconsequential matters till the dance came to an end. When he had thanked her for the dance and taken her back to her aunt, Lord Dake discovered how little escaped the elderly woman's shrewd eye. Augusta sent Lily off to the cloakroom to fetch her shawl, then turned to Lord Dake. It was the first time all evening the two of them had been alone.

"Best make up your mind, young man," Augusta Napier said. "I thought it was the other one you were after."

Anger lit up Lord Dake's eyes, but he kept a tight rein on it. "Your nieces are both quite lovely young women," he said calmly.

"Fools, both of them," the old woman said. "But gently bred girls, and I won't have them trifled with. You'll have to chose one and leave the other alone."

"I'm afraid you are labouring under a misconception, Miss Napier. I assure you that I have never offered either of your nieces any insult, and never shall."

"Oh, I've no doubt you've behaved well," Aunt Augusta said disparagingly. "But you've made that chit Melody fall head over heels in love with you, and just now I saw Lily smiling at you as if you were her knight in shining armour. I don't know what you said to the girl, but I can't think when I've seen her light up like that. You're a dangerous man, my lord."

"Neither Lily nor Melody is in the slightest danger from me," he said stiffly. "Lily was merely smiling at some rather pleasant memories which our conversation evoked, and as for Melody, you are quite mistaken. She has not fallen 'head over heels' in love with me. In fact, if she is fond of me at all it is as a child might be fond of an older brother or an uncle."

"Ha!" Aunt Augusta's scornful outburst of laughter caused several people nearby to look towards them, but she glared back and the heads swiftly turned away. "You're a fool, my lord," she said more softly. "It's not a brother Melody thinks of when she thinks of you, nor yet an uncle. The girl's in love with you—you've only got to look at her to see it."

"She is too young," Lord Dake protested despite the hope that Miss Napier's words had engendered. "Still scarcely a woman."

"Woman enough to know what she wants. And not so young as all that. Plenty of girls are married at her age. Your mother, for instance, married your father when she was younger than Melody is now."

"Indeed." Lord Dake was silent, and Aunt Augusta turned from him to Lily, who was hurrying to join them with the shawl she'd been sent for.

"Give me that," Aunt Augusta commanded when Lily would have draped it over her shoulders for her. "You can never get it to lie as it should. What took you so long, girl? I might have frozen to death in this draught."

Lily murmured an apology and subsided into her characteristic silence. A short time later Augusta Napier informed Lord Dake that she was ready for him to escort them back home. She refused to let him hand her down out of the carriage, sending Lily to the door to fetch Mapps for the delicate operation, but once she'd alighted, she slapped the butler's supporting hand away and ordered him back into the house.

"I'll expect you promptly at eight o'clock tomorrow morning, young man," she told Lord Dake as soon as he'd gone. "Lily can pack for me as soon as she rises, and we'll be ready to leave after breakfast. Best get the girl back to where she belongs before she's up to any more mischief."

"Shall you both accompany us then, Miss Napier?" Lord Dake asked.

"Certainly. I'm not about to let you and your pea-brained cousin escort the girl back on your own. She's too much for you to handle, from what I've heard, and she'll charm you into doing whatever she wants. Besides, I want to give that Beehan creature a piece of my mind. And Lily will come as well, so she can keep me company on the return." She turned then and went in, the door swinging closed behind her and Lily, cutting off the last of the complaints she was addressing to her niece.

Lord Dake dismissed the carriage and walked the short distance to the Royal Arms. The candle had burnt down in his room and it was dark, but he did not light another. He undressed in the darkness and slipped quietly into bed. He did not wish to wake Mr. Steele, whom he assumed was asleep in the room's other bed. Lord Dake was fond of his cousin, and he had his own reasons for being grateful to him for involving him in Melody's life. But he found soothing Elliot's jitters wearying, and he had already had a tiring evening. Dealing with Aunt Augusta had taken a great deal of effort. He had been well rewarded, however, and was on the whole content with the evening's results.

HIS CONTENTMENT was to vanish rather quickly the next morning. He was slightly disconcerted to discover that Elliot was not in his bed. It had obviously been slept in, how-

ever, so it appeared that Elliot had for some reason risen
unaccountably early and taken himself off. Lord Dake did
not find the note which Elliot had left on the bedside table
for him; he had tossed his clothing carelessly in the chair
beside it when he undressed in the dark, and the movement
of air had sent the note sailing unnoticed to the floor under
the bed. Lord Dake was not unduly concerned about his
cousin's absence—no doubt he was in the stables inspecting
the accommodations for the horses—and left the inn without searching for him in order to call upon Aunt Augusta as
they had arranged the night before.

Lord Dake arrived before the time they had agreed upon,
but the butler who showed him in seemed to be expecting
him. Miss Napier had not risen yet, he was informed loft-
ily, but her niece would no doubt see him. Lord Dake, who
had come early in hopes of seeing Melody alone for a few
minutes, nodded and waited docilely in the room which the
butler indicated. He was joined a short time later by Lily.

"Lord Dake! Thank God you're here."

He rose to greet her, looking curiously down into her distressed face. He found her welcome a little bewildering,
since Lily had known perfectly well that he was to call this
morning. But he did not let his bewilderment show, merely
bowing politely over the hands which Lily had stretched out
imploringly to him.

"Miss Napier. I am pleased to see you. I understand your
aunt has not arisen yet, but I wonder if I might have a word
with your sister."

"No!"

Lord Dake was taken aback. He had not expected his request to be met with such a cry of outrage. He raised one
eyebrow enquiringly, and Miss Napier blushed.

"Oh, I do beg your pardon. I did not mean to be rude. It's just that you cannot see Melody because she is not here. The wicked girl has run away again!"

Lord Dake's eyes narrowed. "When did you discover this, Miss Napier?" he asked.

"Only just now! When Mapps told me you had arrived. I had already risen and dressed, but I had not done my hair. I went to my dressing-table to do so, and it was then that I saw the note she'd left for me. She'd tucked it under my jewellery box, and I hadn't noticed it last night when I sat at the table. I lit only one candle, you see, because Aunt Augusta doesn't believe in extravagance, and the room was quite dim. But this morning I could see it clearly."

"I see. May I read the note, Miss Napier?"

She produced it from her pocket and handed it wordlessly to Lord Dake. She searched his face closely as he read it, and saw his expression grow steadily more grim.

"She has borrowed some money from you, I collect. Would you happen to know how much?"

"Not really," Lily said apologetically. "It was probably quite a lot, though. The allowance from my estate is modest, but I have no real use for money here. Aunt Augusta does not encourage me to buy fripperies, so I'm afraid I've got into the habit of stashing my pin money in the jar on my dresser. I used to do the same as a child; that's why Melody knew where to find it, you see. She shouldn't have helped herself, of course, but she does mean to return the money in time. She's very honest, Lord Dake, whatever her other faults."

"I'm sure she is. It is not the fact that she has taken your money without permission which bothers me. It is simply that now she probably has enough money to buy a ticket for the stage. And that is what she has done, you may depend upon it."

"What are we to do?"

"*You* shall do nothing," Lord Dake said firmly. "I shall find her and bring her back. Where is the nearest posting station?"

"Posting station?"

"For the stage," Lord Dake said, unable to avoid comparing Lily unfavourably yet again to her quick-witted sister.

"Oh. That would be the Lion and the Lamb; it's on the outskirts of town. But surely if Melody is travelling by stage she'll be gone by now?"

"It depends upon when the stage leaves," Lord Dake explained patiently. "And in any event I'll have to go there to see whether anyone remembers her buying a ticket. If she has gone already I'll follow the coach. Don't worry, Miss Napier. I promise you I shall catch up with Melody in short time. The stage is not the fastest way to travel, after all; they'll be stopping every ten miles or so to change horses. I'll bring her back before you know it."

"No, wait!" Lord Dake had started towards the door, but Lily's cry made him turn around again. "I shall go with you."

"You'll slow me down," he protested. "The best thing would be for you to stay here till I return."

Lily's face assumed a mulish expression most unlike her normally meek countenance. For the first time Lord Dake could see that she and Melody were truly sisters. "It may be the best thing for you," she said firmly. "But not for me. Aunt Augusta will be rising soon. I am not going to be here to answer questions when she wakes. I'm going with you."

"Very well," Lord Dake said brusquely. "But I'm leaving immediately."

Lily nodded in agreement and took his arm, almost dragging him towards the door. Lord Dake led her outside and tossed her up into his chaise, ignoring the startled look that the butler gave him as they passed him in the hallway. Lily sat beside him, rigid with tension, and directed him to the inn. They swept inside, and almost immediately were greeted by Mr. Steele's familiar tones from within the public parlour.

"Alf Baxter was obviously drunker than a dog last night," Mr. Steele was saying, "and had no idea what he was talking about. This young lady and I are travelling together. I have not abducted her, nor am I asking your approval of our arrangements. I have simply asked you to serve us some tea while we are waiting for our horses to be readied."

Lord Dake pulled up so abruptly that Lily ran into him. She clung to him for support, though it was hard to say whether her pallor and weakness owed more to relief or to the obvious horror she felt at the words she had overheard. She started to speak, but Lord Dake held up one hand, silencing her. A smile was playing on his lips, and Lily looked up at him as if he were demented.

"Don't be ridiculous!" came the voice Lord Dake had been waiting to hear. "I've told you that Mr. Steele is not abducting me, no matter what Alf Baxter said. Don't you think I would know if I were being abducted?"

"Ah, Elliot," Lord Dake said sweetly as he entered the room, Lily silent and pale behind him. "Are you finding that it is not as easy as you had expected to kidnap young ladies nowadays?"

"Lord Dake!"

"Hello, Melody," his lordship said suavely. "Is this villain giving you problems?"

"No, of course he is not! Lord Dake, your jests do you no honour. Poor Mr. Steele has had a terrible night, and it isn't fair of you to tease him."

"He does look as if he's had a terrible night," Lord Dake agreed amiably. "Is that mud all over your shoes, Elliot, or something even less pleasant?"

"Mr. Steele!" cried Lily, who had been standing almost hidden behind Lord Dake. "What are you doing here?"

"Miss Napier!" Mr. Steele stared at her in open-mouthed dismay.

"Hello, Lily," Melody said composedly. "Mr. Steele came after me, and he's brought me back to the inn. He was very kind to me again. It wasn't his fault that we spent the night alone together."

"Melody!" Lily's wail of dismay filled the whole room. Lord Dake moved to take her arm.

"I believe that we could best continue our conversation in private," he said. "You, there! Is there a private parlour? Please conduct us to it and have breakfast served to us."

The innkeeper, who had been locked in an argument with Melody and Mr. Steele, turned his sullen face towards Lord Dake.

"This is an honest house," he said. "We don't serve the likes of you here."

Lord Dake narrowed his eyes, and the landlord faltered to a halt. Melody took the opportunity to break in. "This is Lord Dake, and he is a very important and honourable man," she said. "And I told you that Mr. Steele is a gentleman, too. He was not abducting me. Lord Dake, I don't know why this person is being so unreasonable. I have told him that Mr. Steele is not abducting me. And we have already asked for a private parlour, but he refused to let us have one. If Mr. Steele were abducting me, then surely I would be an innocent victim, so I don't know why he won't let me have a private parlour as I've asked. And if Mr. Steele is *not* abducting me, then why should we not have the parlour?"

Lord Dake did not bother to enlighten her as to the reasons for the landlord's antagonism. He merely repeated his request to that individual in a soft, courteous voice that went badly with the look in his eyes, and they soon found themselves being guided to a private parlour with the promise of breakfast to come. There was an awkward silence while they waited; only Lord Dake seemed not to feel any discomfort. Once the serving maid had brought their food, he ushered them all to the table and urged them to eat.

"I cannot eat," Lily protested unhappily. "How could I think of food at a time like this?"

"It is morning," Lord Dake pointed out. "It seems an ideal time for breakfast to me. Have some tea, Miss Napier. It will help soothe your nerves."

"It will take more than tea to soothe my nerves," Lily cried dramatically. "My sister has ruined herself utterly. Tea cannot solve that. Mr. Steele, you must do something! If you and Melody really spent the night together, you must marry her. Otherwise she shall be ruined for life."

"Don't be ridiculous," Melody cried. "Mr. Steele cannot marry me. He doesn't want to. Do you, Mr. Steele?"

"No," Mr. Steele said distinctly.

"Elliot, you astonish me," Lord Dake said, as he poured tea for Melody. "Such a lack of chivalry. And if you did not want to marry Melody, then why, pray, did you spend the night with her?"

"Because we got lost on the moor, that's why!" Mr. Steele retorted. "She ran away again, and Tom and I followed her here. But before we could bring her back, Tom's father appeared and hauled him off, after accusing me of being intent on the worst type of villainy."

"Ah, that explains the abduction theory. Thank you; I was wondering. And having been accused of harbouring such disgraceful motives, you resolved to fulfill the expectations of your accusers, is that it?"

Mr. Steele choked on his tea, speechless with indignation. Melody came to his rescue.

"I ran out of the inn when I saw Mr. Steele," she explained sternly. "Mr. Steele followed me, and when I saw him approaching, I ran off the road into the moor."

"Yes, you would, naturally," Lord Dake murmured.

Something in his tone made Melody look up at him in sudden hope. "Mr. Steele followed me out onto the moor," she went on, watching him narrowly all the time. "And we both got lost. We had to wait till dawn before we could find our way back here."

"Ah. That explains Elliot's disreputable appearance, I suppose. Though you seem to have weathered a night on the moors without suffering the same ravages."

A tentative smile lit Melody's face. She picked up her tea and sipped at it. "At any rate, Mr. Steele was a perfect gentleman, and there is no need at all for him to marry me," she concluded staidly.

"Don't you see," Lily said. "It doesn't matter what actually happened. It is the appearance of wrongdoing which we must prevent. If Mr. Steele won't marry you, you'll be ruined."

"Well, he's not going to marry me. I don't want him to."

"No, nor do I," Mr. Steele agreed with uncharacteristic firmness. "I won't marry her, not when it's you whom I love, Miss Napier."

"Mr. Steele!" Lily's voice was awed. "Oh, Mr. Steele. You do me such an honour. But you must not. We must sacrifice our love for Melody's sake!"

"I don't want you to sacrifice yourselves," Melody pointed out. "I didn't realize that you had won Mr. Steele's heart, Lily, but I should have. And I think it's just wonderful. You'll deal beautifully with each other."

"Oh, Melody, it's so sweet of you to say so, but it cannot be," Lily said tragically. "You don't understand how censorious the world is. You must marry Mr. Steele."

"I don't like to interrupt," Lord Dake said apologetically, looking up from his plate, "but I'm afraid I must. Melody must not marry Elliot. In fact, she cannot, because she is going to marry me. That is, if she'll have me."

"Have you?" Melody echoed faintly.

"Yes, my love. If you'll have me, I want you to be my wife. I have wanted nothing more almost since I met you, but I was sure that you would think me one of those unsuitable suitors you ran away to escape."

"Unsuitable? How can you say that! You're the most wonderful man I've ever known. But you don't want to marry me. You're only saying that because you feel responsible for me. Mr. Steele explained that you regard me as nothing more than a troublesome brat. But I shan't be troublesome any more, Lord Dake, I promise. You are not obliged to marry me."

"If I were not so indebted to Elliot for bringing us together, my love, I would be seriously angry with him for saying any such thing. But you mustn't refine at what Elliot says. He is not as intelligent as he appears. I do not regard you as a troublesome brat. I have been in love with you almost from the day we met, but I was sure that you regarded me only as a prosy marplot, a sort of annoying uncle you couldn't quite escape from. It was not until last night, and some of the things that your Aunt Augusta said to me then, that I realized I might be wrong. Aunt Augusta seemed to feel that you were in love with me. It seemed improbable, but she was very sure of herself. Could she possibly be right?''

"Oh, yes, Bredon. She is right, indeed. But do you truly love me?''

Lord Dake put down his teacup carefully, and took her as carefully into his arms. He kissed her gently, then more passionately.

Lily watched them in shocked silence. "Melody!" she cried at last. "What are you doing?''

Lord Dake put Melody gently from him, and turned to her sister. "I apologize, Miss Napier. But Melody and I are now engaged. You must permit me to celebrate.''

"But Lord Dake. Are you sure that you wish to marry Melody? I'm very happy for you both if you do, but she's just out of the schoolroom, and has so much to learn about how to be a proper lady.''

"Well, I like that,'' Mr. Steele interrupted indignantly. "You were willing enough to have *me* marry her! And if Bredon loves the girl, then that's all there is to be said about it. Especially as she apparently loves him, too. Seems all very suitable to me. Besides, Bredon might as well marry her. He's obviously going to be entangled in her affairs from now on anyway.''

"Mr. Steele, do you think it is wise?''

"Yes, I do, Miss Napier,'' Mr. Steele said firmly. "It's always best to let Bredon handle things; he knows best, you'll see.''

"Well said, Elliot,'' Lord Dake said. "I almost forgive you for your former stupidity.''

"Yes, but, Bredon, what *are* we going to do about the scandal?''

"What scandal? I see no reason for scandal.''

"After what happened here last night?''

"No one knows what happened except for you and Melody, and you're not going to tell anyone, are you? I believe the innkeeper can be made to forget anything he might have overheard for a suitable sum. As far as anyone else will know, Melody and I met in London and became engaged. I think Mr. Stanhope must have invited me to dine with you at Christmas, don't you, Melody? Would he consider me suitable enough for you?"

She gave a happy gurgle of laughter. "He'd consider you far more suitable than those other men, my lord," she said. "And so would I."

"I am extremely gratified to hear it. I would be even more gratified if you would return to calling me Bredon, as you did just a moment ago."

"Bredon, then," she said shyly. "Mr. Stanhope would consider you very suitable, I'm sure."

"Well, then, that's settled. We met at Mr. Stanhope's residence last Christmas and became unofficially engaged; the formal announcement to wait until after you came out in the spring. Then when word came from your Aunt Augusta that she was very ill and that she wanted to see you, and as your guardian was unavailable on the Continent, naturally I and my cousin came to escort you to visit her."

"But word didn't come that Aunt Augusta was ill," Melody objected.

"I'm sure that Mrs. Beehan will say that it did, if anyone should be so rude as to ask."

"But that would not be truthful," Melody objected with a twinkle in her eye.

"I can see that you will have a heavy responsibility in reforming me," Lord Dake said blandly. "I hope it is not one you will shrink from."

"No, my lord," she said demurely. "It is one I look forward to."

"Yes, but, Bredon, do you think it will work?" Mr. Steele persisted. "What about the fuss that Tom's father raised here last night."

"The confused belligerence of a drunken stable-hand. I hardly think it will stand against our story, especially when Melody and I are married out of Miss Napier's home, with her guardian in attendence, and with signs of harmony between us all. Aunt Augusta will become part of the family now," he continued musingly. "That alone ought to convince you that I love you, Melody. No man would marry into Aunt Augusta's family unless he were head over heels in love."

CHAPTER SIXTEEN

AUGUSTA NAPIER'S RAGE, when the little party had returned to her house, more than justified Lily's reluctance to be left to explain matters to her when she awoke. Evidently it was the butler, Mapps, to whom the task had fallen, and though Lord Dake had not previously found that individual to be particularly sympathetic, he could spare him a bit of pity at the thought of what that interview must have been like. Mr. Steele took one look at Miss Napier's face and had to restrain a most violent impulse to flee. Only the close presence of Lily, and the thought that he could not leave her to face her aunt's anger alone, sustained him. Even Melody's courage seemed to fail her; she crept closer to Lord Dake as her aunt began to heap abuse upon her. But when Lord Dake smiled calmly down at her, her spirits began to rise. When he took her hand and placed in gently in the crook of his arm, she was revived to the extent that she clung to him more for pleasure than for borrowed courage. Melody found suddenly that it no longer seemed to matter what Aunt Augusta said. The news, delivered in a cool voice by Lord Dake, that Melody had done him the honour of accepting his hand in marriage, did not seem to improve her aunt's mood.

"Oh, so that's the way things sit, is it?" she said harshly. "Well, I can't say I'm surprised. I saw the way you looked at him last night, missy, and in my day no young lady would look at a man that way. But I suppose he likes it."

"I love Lord Dake, Aunt Augusta," Melody said. "And he loves me, too."

"Of course he does. He's as big a fool as you. In my day we didn't dare to love each other until we were told by our elders that it was all right to do so. A young lady of Quality would rather have died than to be seen making sheep's eyes at a man the way you were doing last night. But then young people nowadays have no standards. I suppose we ought to be grateful he's offered for you. Mr. Stanhope obviously can't handle you, and that Beehan creature is worse than useless. You want the handling of a strict husband, missy. The pity is he's so besotted he'll fail to give it to you, if I know anything about it. Still, it's the best solution to a bad situation, I suppose. But what about permission? Have you asked Melody's guardian about this, young man?"

"I regret that I have not," Lord Dake replied, "But I am about to do so. I would like to leave Melody here with you while I find him."

"Oh, you would, would you? And I suppose what *I* would like doesn't matter."

"On the contrary. If you would prefer, I shall take Melody back to London with me and leave her with my Aunt Clarice while I track the elusive Mr. Stanhope. I had merely thought you might wish to see Melody married from your house. It would put an end to any gossip that ours is a runaway romance."

"Threatening me, are you?"

"Not at all," Lord Dake said gently. "I am merely pointing out that you yourself would no doubt prefer not to have our match give rise to idle gossip, and that the best way to ensure that lies within your power. It was you who laid the foundation last night, after all, introducing me to your friends."

"Oh, yes, you've got quite a way with words, haven't you, you young pup. Just because I have the sense to realize you're the only hope for getting the girl married off respectably doesn't mean I sanction her running away again like a little fool, or the two of you making your plans without consulting anyone else. If we'd taken her to Mrs. Beehan's as I wished, you could have discussed the matter with Mr. Stanhope at your leisure, instead of racketing all over the Continent looking for him. And then you could have carried out a decent courtship, all proper and unlikely to give rise to any rumours. But no, you can't be satisfied with anything but your own ramshackle plans, and I'm to keep the girl here with me. I suppose you'll want me to pay for a big wedding, too."

"Naturally not. Neither Melody nor I is in any way dependent upon you financially, Miss Napier. Simply present me with the bills, and I shall see to them."

"Oh, no you won't! I'm not the miser everyone says I am. I'll pay for Melody's wedding, and a fine wedding it'll be, too. You'll see that we can do things as well here as in London. And wait till Maria Leyton and all her high-in-the-instep friends see that my niece has married into the nobility. She'll be jealous as a cat."

"But, as you have pointed out, Melody is not actually your niece," Lord Dake said.

"Ha! She's always called me Aunt Augusta, hasn't she? She's my niece all right, if I say she is. She's a foolish, brazen chit, and she's done her best to bring disgrace upon us all, but you'll have it your own way, that I can see, and if you want to marry her, I'll not try to talk you out of it. The chit can stay with me till the wedding. But don't expect me to watch over her for you; she's your responsibility."

"Thank you. She is a responsibility I very much desire. It's very kind of you to keep her."

"You won't butter me up that way, young man," Aunt Augusta snapped, but it was obvious that her heart was no longer in her protest. The events of the morning appeared to have tired her out. She was much weaker than she'd seemed the night before, and soon allowed Lily to take her upstairs for a rest. Mr. Steele waited till he thought the dragon must be safely gone, then left the newly engaged couple alone, showing, Lord Dake thought, unusual tact. When he returned Lily was with him, looking very sad.

"Are you worried about her?" Lord Dake asked. "She seems extremely tired."

"No, she'll be all right," Lily said. "She's stronger than you might think. She has worn herself out with worry and anger. Once she has had a nap, though, she'll be in fine fettle."

"Then what is troubling you?" Melody asked, disturbed that everyone should not be as happy as she.

"Nothing. I'm very happy for you and for Lord Dake."

"And for you and Elliot?" Melody prompted.

Lily turned away, tears starting up in her eyes.

"Oh, Lily, what's the matter?" Melody cried. "Mr. Steele loves you, I know he does. And I think you must love him, too."

"You don't understand," Mr. Steele said in a strangled voice. "I have told Miss Napier about my fiancée. We both agree that I cannot honourably ask Miss Napier to marry me, when Miss Otterleigh believes that we are engaged. In fairness to her, we must deny ourselves."

"I should not worry if I were you, Elliot," Lord Dake pointed out. "I doubt very much that Miss Otterleigh would consent to marry you now even if you asked her again. She is unlikely to forgive your failure to appear at your own engagement party, and I doubt she will be pleased when she hears how you have been spending the past few days."

"Will she throw me over, do you think, Bredon?" Mr. Steele asked with a glimmer of hope.

"She's sure to, I'd say. Miss Otterleigh wants the type of man she thought you were, Elliot. I don't believe the new, independent Elliot would suit her at all."

"Well, she wouldn't suit me, either," Mr. Steele admitted. "Not even if I were not in love with Miss Napier. But do you really think Miss Otterleigh would release me from my pledge to her?"

"Yes, I do. Come back to Town with me, and explain to her what you have been up to, Elliot, and I believe your worries will be over. And if by chance she still wants to marry you, you must explain to her that you have decided you will not maintain your Town house, because you want to live in the country and devote yourself to your stables. If she hasn't thrown you over already, she'll be sure to then."

"Miss Otterleigh would never agree to that," Mr. Steele gasped. "She hates the country. She's already told me that we shall live in Town year-round."

"Precisely why you must make it clear that you shall live in the country," Lord Dake said.

For a moment Mr. Steele looked doubtful; then he laughed and pumped Lord Dake's hand heartily. "You're right, Bredon. I should have known you'd come up with a solution to my problems. You always do! Miss Napier, I believe that if I accompany Bredon to Town I may be able to return and make you an offer very soon. That is if you would be willing to entertain an offer from me?"

"Oh, Mr. Steele. I hope you are right. If Miss Otterleigh releases you and if Aunt Augusta agrees, I would very much like to entertain an offer from you," Lily said with a very pretty blush at her own boldness. Mr. Steele kissed her hand, then straightened as a new thought seemed to occur to him.

"Shall I have to ask your Aunt Augusta for permission?" he demanded.

"She is the head of my family," Lily said. "You must ask her permission, Mr. Steele."

"Will you come back with me after Miss Otterleigh has thrown me over, Bredon?" Elliot asked. "To help me ask Aunt Augusta's permission?"

"Certainly not," his cousin replied firmly. "That is your own business, after all, Elliot. I cannot do it for you."

"No, of course not, Bredon. Wouldn't expect you to, of course. But if you could just come back with me and lend me your moral support, so to speak. She won't kick up a fuss if you're with me; she likes you, I can tell."

"I'm sorry, Elliot. I believe you must handle this yourself."

"Bredon, how can you be so unkind?" Melody interrupted. "After all Mr. Steele has done to help us both! Say you'll come back with him and face Aunt Augusta. It's the least you can do."

"I see you are going to be a managing wife, my love," Lord Dake said with mock resignation. "Very well; if it will please you, I shall return as soon as I have obtained your guardian's permission for our match, and I shall lend Elliot all the support he needs to face Aunt Augusta."

Melody raised her face to him adoringly, and laid her hand upon his arm. "So kind," she murmured happily, and Lord Dake bent over her.

"Foolish child," he said. "I have told you before, I am not as kind as you think. I have my own reason for wanting to return to Yorkshire as soon as possible, after all." He kissed her then, and Melody sighed with contentment. But Mr. Steele's hand, clapped on his cousin's shoulder, interrupted them.

"That's wonderful, Bredon," he said happily. "I knew I could rely on you. And do you know, I believe I *will* live in the country year-round, too. Let mama and my sisters have the Town house; they're always complaining about being stuck out in the country. If that's all right with you, Miss Napier," he added anxiously.

"It's not for me to say yet," Lily protested. "But if Miss Otterleigh does release you, I think it would be wonderful to live in the country. Although I should like to visit London occasionally," she added.

"Yes, of course. Visit whenever you like. And if we don't care to stay at the Town house with mama and my sisters, I daresay Bredon will let us stay with him. Good! That's settled, then. Believe I'll take Tom along with me, too. He knows more about horses than anyone I've ever met. Harkness is getting on, you know. Need to be grooming someone to take his place eventually."

"But what shall we do with Aunt Augusta?" Lily asked. "She's growing too old to stay alone."

A look of pure panic came over Mr. Steele's features. Then he smiled and shook his head. "Don't concern yourself about that," he said simply. "Bredon will know what to do. He always does. That's what I've always said, and he's never failed me yet!"

Following the success of WITH THIS RING, Harlequin cordially invites you to enjoy the romance of the wedding season with

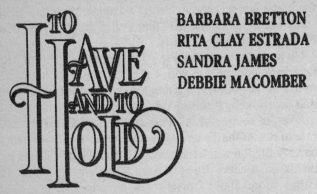

BARBARA BRETTON
RITA CLAY ESTRADA
SANDRA JAMES
DEBBIE MACOMBER

A collection of romantic stories that celebrate the joy, excitement, and mishaps of planning that special day by these four award-winning Harlequin authors.

Available in April at your favorite Harlequin retail outlets.

Take 4 bestselling love stories FREE
Plus get a FREE surprise gift!

presents
MARCH MADNESS!

Come March, we're lining up four wonderful stories by four dazzling newcomers—and we guarantee you won't be disappointed! From the stark beauty of Medieval Wales to marauding *bandidos* in Chihuahua, Mexico, return to the days of enchantment and high adventure with characters who will touch your heart.

LOOK FOR
    STEAL THE STARS (HH #115) by *Miranda Jarrett*
    THE BANDIT'S BRIDE (HH #116) by *Ana Seymour*
    ARABESQUE (HH #117) by *Kit Gardner*
    A WARRIOR'S HEART (HH #118) by *Margaret Moore*

So rev up for spring with a bit of March Madness...only from
Harlequin Historicals!

MM92